They were almost too late. Two medallion-wearing robed figures were about to thrust daggers into the chest and groin of their victim.

A ritual designed to summon a demon of the Fallen angel Moloch, Bianca thought. *Joe told me about this.*

"Stop! Police!" Bianca shouted.

The knives continued to descend. If they drew blood, it would be all over.

"Do it," Bianca said and fired, with Serrano and Tavon discharging at almost the same time.

The two hooded figures dropped to the ground, their daggers falling from their hands. The victim was not cut, but a bullet from Bianca's pistol went through the hand of one of the priests before striking her chest. A single drop of blood fell on the altar.

There was a cloud of smoke and the roar of rushing air. From the cloud there emerged a very naked, very male, horned demon, at least seven and a half feet tall with a layer of red scales.

In each hand he held a priest, both of them suspended by the medallions that were now around their necks.

"Who summons Zeng, Demon of Moloch?"

The question was rhetorical as Zeng was staring at Bianca when he asked it.

"I did. I'm Bianca Jones. I think your boss has heard of me."

PADWOLF PUBLISHING BOOKS BY JOHN L. FRENCH

Bianca Jones
Here Be Monsters
Monsters Among Us
The Last Monster
Shadows & Brimstone a Mystic Investigators™ omnibus (Bullets & Brimstone/From The Shdaows) (with Patrick Thomas)
Rites Of Passage: a DMA casefile of Agent Karver and Bianca Jones (with Patrick Thomas)

The Magic Of Simon Tombs

The Matthew Grace Casefiles
Past Sins
Mortal Sins

Agents of the Abyss
Frankenstein: Monsters of the Abyss (with Patrick Thomas)
Detectives of the Abyss (with Patrick Thomas)

The Devil of Harbor City
The Grey Monk: Souls on Fire
The Nightmare Strikes
Bad Cop No Donut (editor)
Mermaids 13 (editor)
Camelot 13 (editor with Patrick Thomas)

OTHER BOOKS BY JOHN L. FRENCH

Bianca Jones: Blood Is the Life
The Last Redhead
When The Moon Shines
Chessie At Bay
The Assassins' Ball (with Patrick Thomas)
The Santa Heist (with Patrick Thomas)
Devilish and Divine (editor with Danielle Ackley-McPhail)
To Hell in a Fast Car (editor)
With Great Power (editor with Greg Schauer)

THE LAST MONSTER

A Bianca Jones Collection

John L. French

PADWOLF PUBLISHING INC.
WWW.PADWOLF.COM
www.facebook.com/Padwolf

THE LAST MONSTER
a Bianca Jones Collection
© 2022 John L. French

cover © Daniel R. Horne

Lai Wan, the London Agency, Marv Richards, and Challenge of the Unknown are © C. J. Henderson.

Herne the Hunter (as presented in this book), Barton Karver, Mandi Cobb, the Department of Mystic Affairs and all related characters are © and TM by Patrick Thomas and used with permission.

Publishing History and Notes
"Tag Team Match with Hell" © Patrick Thomas, C. J. Henderson, and John L. French. It was originally published in a slightly different version in Patrick Thomas's DEAD TO RIGHTS, Padwolf Publishing 2010.
"A Gift Freely Given" was originally published in a slightly different version in THE SANTA HEIST by John L. French and Patrick Thomas, Bold Venture Press, 2019.
"Beast in Show" was originally published in a slightly different version Space and Time Magazine #133, Spring Summer 2019. All other stories are original with this book.
Except where noted, all stories are © John L. French

ISBN 13- 978-1-890096-96-0, 10-1-890096-96-2
First Printing.

To my fellow Wild Cats—Ron Hanna and Ver Curtiss
Ron for publishing my first novel
and Ver for first showing the world what Bianca looked like.
Thanks, guys.

TABLE OF CONTENTS

WITHIN A FOREST DARK
9

BEAST IN SHOW
11

WEIGHT OF A FEATHER
28

BETTER TO REIGN
42

TAG TEAM MATCH WITH HELL
43

THE THRILL OF THE CHASE
62

THE WILD HUNT
81

SEX AND DAMNATION
108

A GIFT FREELY GIVEN
131

TO REBEHOLD THE STARS
148

INTO THE DARKNESS
182

CODA
195

WITHIN A FOREST DARK

Midway upon the journey of our life
I found myself within a forest dark, For the straightforward pathway
had been lost
Dante Alighieri, Inferno, Canto I.

Lucifer Morningstar, Fallen Angel and Lord of Hell, stood at the top of the highest tower in the City of Dys and looked over his kingdom. It was immense, larger than any mortal mind could imagine, yet he could see it all. From the gates to the center, from the Plains of the Uncommitted to the Circle of Treachery, he saw it all.

It has grown, Lucifer thought. But that is the nature of Hell, that all who, by their actions or inactions, choose it are welcome while only a comparative few are permitted to leave. And so it grows.

Would they still sin, he wondered, not for the first time, *would they still reject the One if they knew this was the consequence of their choice.* He suspected they would, that if he could somehow transport Dys to the human world that there would be those who would demand passage through the Gates despite the warning written over them.

And what of those within the Gates? Do they learn nothing from their suffering? Our suffering, he corrected, for as the Lord of Hell he felt every torture as it was inflicted. *Their sins led them here. Do they not regret having committed them?*

Some did, he knew. He sensed it when regret turned to reflection and so on to repentance. When in their minds and ultimately their souls they realize that the warning over the Gates was just the first of many lies and the spark of Hope is rekindled. And when they finally say *The Words*, he feels their departure as they ascend.

"So why don't you?"

Like Paul of Tarsus's demon, the one that saint described as a "thorn in his flesh," a voice within his head plagued him. It was not the Voice, not the Word that had been made Flesh. No, this voice was a new torture, but not one inflicted by He who had cast him down. It was the voice of a small mortal who had dared to challenge him both on the mortal plain and before the Gates of Hell itself. It was the voice of one who had beaten him three times and by doing so had placed those whom she protected out of his direct reach. It was the voice of one who had stolen souls from him, souls that should have been his, souls that *were* his. And it was the voice of one who would dare to tempt him with forgiveness and salvation.

"Say the Words, Morningstar. Mean the Words and I'll grant you absolution myself," she had told him when they last met.

And as Lucifer Morningstar looked past his city and the wasteland that surrounded it, as he cast his gaze toward the mortal plain and the small spot of Earth known as Baltimore, he said to the small voice that plagued him, "I think not, Miss Jones, for I am not yet sorry for all that I have done."

BEAST IN SHOW

Nighttime. Running free. Unnoticed in a city with too many strays. Downtown, too many lights, too many tourists. Run to the darkness. Look for the prey that's alone.

*

"You're going where?"

That Lieutenant Tavon Greggs was going on a much needed vacation was not in itself unusual. It was where that surprised Bianca Jones.

Greggs sighed. He had expected this reaction. It was the reaction that he received from everyone. Why was it so surprising? Because he was the leader of one of the police department's Quick Response Teams?

Before answering, Greggs looked around Bianca's new office. It was larger than the one she'd had at the Police Headquarters building. There was room to spread out, room to hold meetings without having to take over a conference room. Greggs saw that Bianca had hung some personal items on the walls—a photo of her academy class, her commission as a police officer, letters of promotion to detective and sergeant, her much-delayed diploma from the Department of Mystic Affairs Academy.

"Where are you going to hang the new one, *Lieutenant* Jones?" Greggs asked with a grin.

"As soon as the city's print shop sends me the official certificate of promotion. There's an open spot next to Tromluí over there."

Greggs's eyes followed her pointing finger and rested on a long fighting knife from the fabled kingdom of Eire, a legacy from a long ago crime fighter who called himself The Nightmare.

"So that's the magic sword you used to kill the Bright One?"

"Just a sword now, Tavon. I think I used up all its magic. Just like this house."

"I hope you're right about the house, Bianca."

The building housing the new offices of The Extranormal Investigative Unit, better known to the members of the BPD as The Freak Show, was formerly haunted, prone to disappear and reappear at random. Bianca had banished the curse that had afflicted it when she sent the would-be messiah Apollonius to Hell.

Bianca allowed a smile to cross her face as Tavon repeated his destination. "A dog show. The Alcazar Kennel Club is one of the oldest in the country. They hold their annual show in a different city each year. This year it's at the Arena. I'm going. Anyway, I just stopped in to let you know in case anything—strange—came up you'd know to call my sergeant."

"Strange" was putting things mildly. The Freak Show was in charge of investigating anything supernatural, extra normal, or just plain weird that occurred in Baltimore City. To do this, Bianca had put together a special team of people within and without the BPD on whose talents she could call upon at need. Tavon was her heavy weapons man, his QRT people having sufficient firepower to bring down anything short of a twenty-foot tall gorilla or a giant lizard. And they were looking to upgrade just in case.

Greggs looked at Bianca as if daring her to laugh about the dog show. Although she did permit herself another smile, all she said was, "Everyone has to have a hobby. Joe has his books. Tammy her fashions. Beth collects those funny-looking dolls, what are they called?"

"Trolls."

Bianca shivered. "Yeah, Trolls. Ugly things. Hope we never meet a real one. It's just that I never pictured you …"

"Liking dogs? I was in the K9 Unit for six years."

"I was going to say liking any kind of sport that you couldn't bet on."

It was Tavon's turn to smile. "I've got twenty bucks on a Canaan Hound to win Best in Show. Odds are fifty-to-one against. There's also a new breed being introduced this year, something called a Border Speagle, whatever the hell that is."

"Sounds like something we fight against."

"Doesn't it? Anyway, I put money on its cold, wet nose to get to the final round. Being new it just might."

"How do you think a Barghest would do, Tavon?" A barghest was a hell hound of Fairie. One had almost killed Bianca.

"It would win."

"You think?"

"Of course, after it ate all the other dogs." Tavon looked at his watch. "Gotta go. My leave starts in thirty minutes."

"Have fun. Don't get fleas or distemper."

"You have enough temper for everyone."

"Ha, ha. Go."

Tavon was almost out of Bianca's office when he turned.

"You said everyone has a hobby. What's yours?"

All trace of her previous good humor left Bianca's face. "Monsters. What they are. What they do. How to kill them."

*

Garage underground. Like a cave, a den. The smell from cars masks the prey. Must listen, look, go by sight and sound. Wait in the shadows for ones alone.

Those two, fat and slow. No one else around. Strike quickly, kill both. Feast.

*

The crime scene was bad. Two dead, one with his throat torn out, the other looking like parts of him had been devoured. Add to that the lingering fumes of recently departed cars and the angry shouts of drivers who had been told that the Skipjack Downunder Garage was now a crime scene and no further vehicles would be permitted to leave.

That, thought Homicide Detective Bethany Steele, *is patrol's problem. Ours is solving the murders. If they are murders.*

It was looking less and less like they were. The crime scene people had found large, bloody paw prints going down the ramp. The Medical Examiner's investigators were discussing what kind of animal could have done this. Given the violence done to the bodies, it had to be a big one.

"I'd almost rather it be a lunatic killer," said McLarney, Steele's partner for the night. She looked at him in surprise.

"People can deal with murder, no matter how vicious," he explained. "Hell, this is Baltimore, they should be used to it by now. Mad dog killers are one thing. Mad dogs that eat people are another. This city's gonna be in a panic."

A bad feeling started in the back of Steele's mind. It wasn't the work that still had to be done even if the killer wasn't human—call the zoo, contact Animal Control, notify everyone from the Mayor down. No, it was something more primal. Something that struck from the dark and faded back into it. Something large and fierce. Something that hunted humans.

"Please, God, no," Steele prayed silently even as McLarney asked the ME field investigator,

"Well, what's the verdict?"

"Your killer's definitely not human. It took sharp teeth and claws to do this damage. From the marks, it's probably canine, a wolf or something. Whatever it is, it's a monster."

There was that word. "Monster." The city had seen too many of them, creatures of nightmare that saw humans as playthings or cattle, or simply annoyances that had to be crushed like bugs.

Steele had turned when McLarney asked his question. When the answer came she felt all eyes focused on her. A word formed in her mind, a word to define the type of monster that could do this. She forced it back, refusing to say the word even to herself. But she knew, knew that her first call would not be to the zoo, or to Animal Control, or even to the mayor. Steele knew that her first call would be to Bianca Jones.

She sighed, then turned back to the bodies and those around them.

"We're taking this." A quick glare at McLarney halted any objections from her partner. To the ME team, she said, "When you get these two to the morgue, make a note to have Dominic work on their bodies. Any fluids that he thinks may not be theirs get swabbed and sent to the Crime Lab as soon as possible. Their clothing goes there quicker than that. And tell Dominic to call in a forensic zoologist. I want to know exactly what we're hunting."

Bethany Steele thought she already knew and prayed that she was wrong.

*

Back at the Hotel Mount Royal, he sleeps in his weaker form, remembering the freedom of the night's hunt, the crunch of bone, and the satisfying taste of blood and flesh. Soon it will be time to awake and tend the beasts. And not for the first time does he wonder, what if one of them should…?

*

"Hello, Big Brother."

Looking up from the body on which he was working, Dominic Jones smiled and said in reply, "Good morning, Little Sister. I presume it is this tin man who brings you down today."

"Tin Man?" At first, Bianca Jones was puzzled, then she approached. Looking into the chest cavity, she saw the empty hole where a heart should be. "You ME's have a strange sense of humor."

"Doing this job, we need one."

The two made a strange pair, he was tall and dark, she was small and pale. His people came from the warm islands of the Caribbean, hers from the cold ones in the North Atlantic. One day, based on their shared name and their mutual involvement in the weird and bizarre, Dominic decided that they should be siblings. Bianca, who had always wanted a big brother, quickly agreed.

"So what can you tell me about these two?"

"That one," Dominic pointed to a neighboring table, "death from exsanguination, he bled out through the wound on his neck. This one," the ME indicated the body in front of him, "died of consumption."

"Consumption?" Bianca was always willing to play the straight man for her "brother."

"Yes, consumption done ate him."

The detective groaned. "That was bad even for you, Dominic. What's the official word?"

"Pending. We have not yet decided if 'sudden cardiectomy' is a proper cause of death or not."

"What did the zoologist say?"

Dominic shrugged. "What we already know. Something large with sharp teeth."

*

"Something large with sharp teeth." That opinion did not help Bianca. Homicide had already written the deaths off as "animal attacks" and had alerted the proper city and state agencies. Bianca would like to have done that as well, but she couldn't take the chance. She'd wait for the lab to send her the DNA results from the swabbings and clothing.

*

He would soon know. While exercising a Yorkshire terrier a larger dog had barked and startled it. The little bitch then panicked and snapped at his ankle, drawing blood. It happens. As long as the beasts don't bite a judge no one cares. Well, this time they might.

*

It was evening, the time of day when light gives way to darkness, when wild things both human and otherwise try to claim the city for their own. Bianca Jones tried to listen as her husband Joe told her of his day at the bookstore, something about a signed Raymond Chandler. Worried about the new menace on the street, wondering if it's animal, human, or something worse than either, she barely heard him.

Bethany Steele tried to sleep but couldn't. The fairies that usually haunted her dreams had been replaced by shadows quick, dark, and deadly. Finally, she gave up and went in to start her shift early.

Criminalist Tammy Dolan worked late, studying DNA results and entering them into the national database. She had had a date but canceled it. This was more important.

Tavon Greggs hurried through yet another fast-food meal, not wanting to miss the German Shepherd best of breed judging.

A mostly ignored man waited for the evening to pass, for the night to come in fully. Then he would hunt again.

*

The alleys this time, the dark places between buildings. Ignore the humans already there. They smell of decay and disease, their blood tainted and their flesh sour. Keep moving, look for the ones who make the wrong turn or take the shortest route. Search for the stranger who knows not the ways of the city. Hunt the strong ones who prey on the weak. I am stronger.

*

She was lost. There was supposed to be an Irish bar somewhere south of the Reginald F. Lewis Museum. So far she hadn't found it and she was getting hungry and thirsty. She'd try one more street then maybe head for Little Italy and wine and pasta.

He came up behind her fast and sudden.

"Don't move, bitch. Don't scream. Don't fight or struggle and you won't get too hurt."

A knife was pressed against her, digging in, drawing blood. She could feel it trickling down her side. "No!" her mind shouted as he forced her into an alley and she realized what was happening, what was going to happen. A part of her wanted to fight back, to scream for help, to break away and run. She tensed and the knife dug in deeper. Bleeding even more, another part of her decided that she wanted to live. As her attacker threw her down to the alley floor and groped under her clothes she decided that she'd do whatever he wanted.

Then came the growling.

*

Smells of fear, lust, anger. Take down the male, rip off his limb. Feed on the other. Strike now.

Pain! It hurts! Flee, feed tomorrow.

*

The body of the victim, most of him, lay in a rotting pile of garbage, what little blood he had left trickling from where his upper thigh should be. The thigh and the rest of his leg were a few feet south. Another savage attack that had left the victim mutilated and bleeding out.

"You say that this time it's a confirmed animal attack?" Steele asked the primary officer. "How do you know?"

"There's a surviving witness. That's how we found out about this. She ran out on to President Street. Almost got hit by a cab. Cabbie said she was screaming something about rape and a monster."

Not good, Steele thought. A monster raping women. That's how Bianca got involved in this supernatural crap.

"You're saying that the monster killed this guy then raped her?"

"No, Ma'am. I'm saying, rather, she said that the dead guy was going to rape her when the monster attacked them."

Better, Steele said to herself, then asked the officer, "How did she get away?"

The officer shrugged. "Ask her yourself. She's at City of Hope getting checked over."

*

"I hit it," Angela Leonards told Steele. "That guy had a knife on me and was going to, you know. I heard growling then saw this big, black—thing. It looked like a wolf. The guy attacking me went down and it came for me. I didn't know what else to do so I hit it, once with my purse and then I punched it in the nose, er, snout."

Any hopes that Steele had of calling Bianca Jones and telling her that the previous night was nothing to worry about faded when the detective looked at Angela's hand.

"Nice rings, Ms. Leonards. If I can ask, what are they made of?"

Before Angela could reply Steele know that her answer would be, "Silver, why?"

"And the trim on your purse, is that silver as well?"

"Yes. Detective, what's this all about?"

Ignoring her, Steele asked, "This is important, Ms. Leonards, did the ... wolf ... bite or cut you in any way. Any injuries from its attack."

"I have a stab wound from where that dead son of a bitch stuck his knife in me, but no, none from the wolf. Why—oh, you're worried about rabies or something."

"Yes, Ma'am, something like that."

*

Human again, looking in the mirror, his face bruised, his head pounding. That bitch hurt me. He had her scent, thought of tracking her down, making her pay. No, said the throbbing in his head. Better to seek less dangerous prey. Tonight he would roam north.

*

Bianca had most of her team together in her office. Tammy from the Crime Lab had her DNA results as well as a printout from the national database. Beth Steele had her witness statement, the crime scene photos, and police reports. Bianca turned to Tammy first.

"What do you have?"

"The DNA is a mixture of human and canine. I tried to separate the two profiles but couldn't. It's as if they were bound together. The good news is that I got a hit from CODIS. The same mix has shown up in over a dozen cities, and yes, those cities also reported fatal animal attacks that stopped as suddenly as they started." She stopped for a moment then added, "I'll know tonight if the DNA from the second attack is a match."

"For now let's assume it is. Beth?"

"The creature that attacked Angela Leonards and that deserved-to-die rapist was a large, black, wolf-like creature that can be hurt by silver. Now will someone say the word we're all thinking?"

Bianca obliged. "Werewolf."

The other two nodded.

Bianca made a call to the Police Commissioner, telling him what was needed.

"It's done," Bianca told her team. "An order's been sent to the Reid Mining Company for more cartridges with silver-jacketed bullets. In the meantime, all uniformed officers in the Central will be warned to be extra careful when dealing with any wild animal. We can't close downtown and the Inner Harbor entirely, but we're blocking off what streets we can. Patrols will be increased to the point of saturation. That means minimum resources for the rest of Baltimore. They'll just have to take their chances with the usual two-legged monsters."

Bianca sighed and continued. "The three of us are on twenty-four-hour call. We're going to any animal attack where the beast cannot be positively ID'd. Anyone who gets bitten goes into immediate isolation until we're sure they're not infected. Any questions?"

Tammy had one. "What about Lieutenant Greggs? From what I understand, he's got enough firepower to blow King Kong into kibble bits."

Bianca shook her head. "I tried. He's on vacation. His cell's turned off, his home phone goes right to voice-mail. He's probably checked into a hotel under an assumed name."

"What's he doing?"

"Believe it or not, Beth, he's attending a dog sh…. Tammy, check your list of the DNA hits and animal attacks. See if any dog shows or animal exhibits were going on at the same time. We might just catch a break."

The criminalist nodded. Fifteen minutes later—"Eighty percent match."

"So how is this a break? Now we have to find one dog-like creature in a whole convention hall full of them?"

Tammy answered Beth. "The DNA's part human, Detective. I don't think we have to worry about a were-collie or anything like that. Still, there are a lot of people involved with that show."

"I didn't say it was going to be easy." Bianca reached for the phone. "Or popular. Commissioner Williams, Bianca here. No, Sir, we haven't found it yet …Yes, Sir, I do need something. I need the Arena and all its related hotels quarantined …Yes, Sir, I think it is. It's either that or I might have to start shooting pure-breds with silver bullets, starting with the poodles … I don't like poodles … Yes, Sir. Thank you, Sir."

Bianca hung up the phone. "He'd fire me but there's no one crazy enough to take over this job. Tammy, Beth, I'd like to tell you to go home and rest up but that's not going to happen. Good thing this house has plenty of bedrooms. We're camping here until this is over. Beth, if you can, get a list of all those involved with the Alcazar Kennel Club and this show. Do a records check. Tammy, try again to separate those DNA samples. If possible, throw a little aconite in the mix. It might help."

"Aconite? What's that?"

Bianca smiled at the criminalist. "Wolfsbane. Now the two of you get to work. Tomorrow we're going to the dog show."

Alone in her office, Bianca turned toward her window, staring out as if looking for the latest monster to invade her city. All she saw was people walking up and down the street.

"Why me?" she asked herself, not for the first time. She knew the answer—because no one else could or would. She thought back to the first time she had encountered the extra-normal, when she had stopped a creature from another dimension from invading this one. When it was over she had told a friend, "Do a job once and it's yours."

"Damn, sometimes I hate being right," she said aloud in her empty office. She didn't want to be right this time either. She hoped that whatever was out there was nothing more than a crazed animal, something to be caught and put down, that the worse that would happen from here on were a few cases of rabies.

She longed to do what Tavon had done, go off the grid, get away with her husband, and disappear for a month or two. Or maybe forever. No creatures, no monsters, no things after the bodies and souls of the people of Baltimore. Things she was expected to stop at the possible cost of her own life and soul.

At least this one was simple. It wasn't after souls, just flesh. It was pure appetite with four legs and a tail. Infectious appetite. Unless it was stopped, sooner or later one of its victims would survive. And one beast becomes two, and two becomes four. If unchecked, roving packs of pure appetite would make Baltimore a hell even the Devil would envy. The time to stop it was now. And even though Beth and Tammy would help, the one who had to stop it was her.

Again Bianca sighed. She longed to quit this job, go home to Joe and take comfort in his arms. Instead, she called, gave him her love, and told him not to expect her anytime soon. Then she started making plans to disrupt a dog show and catch a werewolf.

*

He tried to leave the Mount Royal, was stopped by a crowd, no, a mob of people in the lobby. Angry people, all wanting to know why they had been confined to the hotel. The harried police explaining that it was just for the night, something about a possible outbreak of something or other. A hotel official announced that tonight's stay would be comped and all room-service and pay-TV would be free. Whatever it was, it had nothing to do with him, except—two nights without feeding. He'd order an extra-rare steak and hoped that would satisfy the beast within.

*

Commissioner Williams was on the scene when Bianca arrived at the Arena early the next morning. "You better be right, Lieutenant Jones. Your lockdown last night cost the city a lot of money and even more goodwill with the hotels, the Arena, and the Alcazar people."

Bianca nodded to show that she understood her boss's position then asked, "Anyone get eaten last night?" Before Williams could answer, she outlined her nightmare scenario of roving packs of appetite to him. The Commissioner turned as pale as a man with very dark skin could.

"You're sure?" Another nod from Bianca. "What causes this—condition?"

"Some take it on willingly, for the power or the thrill. Others are cursed, still others are bitten and infected. Doesn't really matter. What does is detecting and stopping it."

"And you can do that, Lieutenant?"

"I'm going to try, Sir. If not, the next step is to call in the Department of Mystic Affairs and you know what bastards they are."

"What's your plan?"

"Solid police work and a whole lot of luck. We've been on the telephone and computer all night and have managed to eliminate some of the workers, owners, handlers, and judges, mainly those who were not in any of the cities where the other attacks took place. Record checks gave us some possibles. We're cross-checking now and waiting on DNA results."

"And if, when you find the, er, suspect?"

"Depending on the suspect's behavior, I'll take the appropriate action. When I'm done, the city will be safe, for now."

"Do what you have to, Bianca. And God be with you."

"He has been so far."

Record checks and waiting. Not Bianca's favorite kind of police work. She'd rather have a known suspect, someone or something to chase and bring down. She hated waiting, especially knowing what waiting too long meant.

Two nights ago its feeding had been interrupted. Last night it had been forestalled. Could it wait a third night? Bianca doubted it, just as she doubted that the city officials would allow her to shut things down again.

Workers, prep people, handlers, and trainers were trickling backstage of the Arena. Bianca walked among them, wondering which if any was the monster she sought. She knew the so-called signs— eyebrows grown together, fingernails resembling claws, the ring finger being longer than the middle finger. Folklore and legends, probably with some basis in fact but nothing she could count on.

Should I strip them all and see who's wearing a wolfskin belt? I could check their tongues for bristles or force silver on them and watch the reactions. Maybe I should drop my pants and moon them, see who changes.

"Need some help?"

Bianca turned around. Tavon Greggs was behind her. "How did you ..."

"There are reports on TV and the 'net about fatal animal attacks. My hotel goes on lockdown with police guarding the doors. I turned on my cell to find five messages from you, the last two threatening my life if I didn't answer. So I badged my way out and came over. Told the uniform guarding my hotel that I was part of the investigation. Now, what's going on?"

"You carrying your service weapon?"

"Always."

Bianca handed Tavon a clip of ammo. "Silver-jacketed."

Tavon immediately guessed the problem. "I could call my team."

"Already done. If nothing breaks by this evening they're going out. By morning there'll damn few stray dogs in Baltimore."

"And until then?"

The usual—wait, hope, and pray."

Sometimes prayers are answered. Bianca's cell vibrated in her pocket.

"Yes, Tammy."

"Bianca, the wolfsbane worked. The DNA separated and we got a match. Some guy named Terry Britt. He was at most of the shows on our list. No major arrests but got picked up twice for public indecency. He was found walking around naked in Boston and Milwaukee. As a minor sex offender, his profile got into CODIS."

"Good work, Tammy. Can you send a photo?"

Within a minute Terry Britt's picture appeared on Bianca's cell screen. He didn't look like anything special—thin, dark hair, small in stature, sallow complexion. His only outstanding feature was that his eyebrows grew together.

"Got it. What's he do?"

"Whatever's needed. Exercises the dogs, washes cages, cleans up messes. He's probably backstage right now."

"Got it. Get Beth over here then call QRT. I want them at all exits. Send them Britt's photo. If he tries to leave detain him. If he starts changing, shoot him until he stops."

Bianca turned to Tavon, showed him her phone. "This is our guy. We find him, isolate him, and hopefully end this now."

"Bianca, can these things change during the day?"

"I guess we're going to find out."

*

Even in his weaker state, he could feel them. They were hunters like himself. This time, he was the prey. There is no shame in running, no dishonor in fleeing to hunt another day. Survival is what matters. Best exit, through the arena floor.

*

"Bianca, that's him." Tavon pointed to a man in work overalls walking slowly toward the show area. "Exits blocked yet?"

"Don't know. Let's do him now."

Both cops shouted as if with one voice. "Britt!"

Most people would have turned at the sound of their name. Britt just ran, making for the southeast exit. Bianca and Tavon gave chase, the smaller detective outpacing the larger QRT officer. Tavon radioed for back-up. Uniforms began to swarm the arena.

*

Lockers. The lingering odor of sweat and adrenaline from last week's soccer game. No escape that way. Down this hall. Doors at the end. The smell of man from behind them, hunters ready to kill. Must fight, trust the stronger self.

*

Britt was halfway down the corridor when it happened. He stopped and changed, much quicker than Bianca expected. She barely had time to think *Not like the movies* as one second there was a running suspect and the next a large wolf turning her way.

Two hunters faced each other, judging the risk, awaiting their chance. Bianca leveled her pistol. The thing that had been Terry Britt crouched, ready to spring. Time slowed. The world contracted. Even though others were in the hallway, for the two predators only the other existed.

Bianca took cold comfort in the fact that whatever happened to her, Britt was going down. *I've got one chance,* she thought. But she liked that chance. Britt, she realized, had not had time to discard his clothing.

The wolf sprang, and was immediately tangled in its shirt and pants. Falling to the floor, it struggled to free itself.

Coming as close as she dared, Bianca took aim at the beast. Even knowing what it was, what it would do if freed, she pitied it.

Such beauty, such power. What a waste, she said to herself. She thought of all she could do if she had that power, how much better she could protect her city if only—one bite was all it would take.

NO! her better self objected. She'd once had a beast inside her, one worse than this. And it had taken a trip to Hell to rid herself of it. Hell, where as a human she had faced down and beaten the Devil. And it was as a human she had fought vampires and banished demons. She didn't need this power. She had enough of her own.

*

Still struggling, almost free. Not enough time. A look up into the hunter's eyes, seeing death and compassion. So this is how prey felt.

*

Wishing there was some other way, knowing that there wasn't, Bianca took careful aim. Even though the beast was still fighting to free itself, there was acceptance in its eyes. Bianca fired.

*

Beth Steele was in the animal holding area when she heard the shot. When her radio stayed quiet and she didn't hear any follow-up shots, she thought, *I guess it's over.* Then from behind her, she heard yelps of pain, a metal cage coming apart, and a low-throated growl. As she turned, there were the sounds of people screaming.

*

"Bianca, Pet Area. Now!"

Beth's voice over the radio was just on the calm side of panic. Bianca looked at Tavon, he had heard it too. With one last glance to make sure that the wolf was still dead and hadn't changed back, she rushed to the detective's aid.

Frightened people were fleeing the area. Fighting her way through them, Bianca was finally at Beth's side. "What's the prob…" she started to ask, then followed the detective's pointing finger.

Standing in at less than a foot high and weighing no more than seven pounds, Yorkshire Terriers are cute little dogs. They are less so when they are three feet tall and 160 pounds. Which is what Dame Ruth Millicent of Pershing House now was. Some days ago the terrier had nipped the handler exercising her. This same handler was lying dead in the form of a wolf. Somehow, his death had triggered her curse. Already canine, she didn't change, she just got larger.

The animal had stopped growling. And it wasn't charging. It seemed somewhat confused and quite calm and satisfied with itself.

Beth was the first to break the silence. "Now what do we do?"

"Lock, load, and light it up," was Tavon's easy answer.

"Wait," Bianca ordered. "It's not doing anything."

"Yet," cautioned the QRT Lieutenant.

Bianca ignored him. "Beth, get me some doggie treats."

"Like what, a Chihuahua?" Soon she was handing Bianca a handful of kibble.

She had just killed a werewolf. In her fight against evil and the darkness, Bianca had allied herself with mages and ancient gods. She had stood against demons, vampires, the hounds of Fairie, and Satan himself.

And now she faced a were-Yorkie.

Suppressing the urge to laugh, Bianca reminded herself that however cute and ridiculous it looked, the creature was still a predator, with teeth designed to rip and tear rats and badgers. She locked eyes with the beast, challenging it, letting it know that she was not afraid, silently telling it that she was the master. When the dog looked away, she held out her hand to be sniffed.

Behind her, she heard weapons being readied. *Hell of a lot of good that will do me if I'm wrong*, she thought. Extending her other hand, she offered the enlarged dog its treat.

A rough tongue lapped the food from her hand. It then licked up what crumbs remained. The dog would then have jumped up on Bianca but the detective said sternly,

"Down."

Training took over, and the oversized beast sat back on its haunches.

After twenty minutes of petting and stroking, Dame Ruth Millicent of Pershing House was back to her original size and weight.

"So now what do we do?" Beth asked once again.

Bianca thought for a moment. "Tavon, you did say that you'd spent six years in the K9 unit."

Tavon shook his head. "Bianca, you're not thinking …"

"I sure as hell am. Say hello to your new partner."

WEIGHT OF A FEATHER

The Lancer Museum and Art Gallery was, along with the Walter's and the Baltimore Museum of Art, one of the premier museums in the city. Its diverse collections of the antiquities of the ancient and medieval worlds rivaled those in larger cities. So it was no surprise that when the Grand Egyptian Museum decided to send some of its treasures on tour prior to opening, the Lancer was one of the venues chosen.

A wing was cleared out, its exhibits stored. Publicity was arranged. Security was upgraded. Certain legal and diplomatic problems were settled. Two months before its scheduled opening, the exhibit was sold out. A week before "The Splendor of the Two Lands" was due to open, everything was ready and no one anticipated any problems except minor ones.

Expect that the Lancer was in Baltimore—the city of the weird, the strange, and the unexpected. The city that the Lord of Hell had attempted to burn to the ground. The city where a would-be messiah had launched terrorist attacks in his opening bid to remake the world. But these events, among other strange occurrences, had been kept secret from the general public. Had those involved in the exhibition known about them, they may have taken extra precautions, including consulting Bianca Jones and the BPD's Extranormal Investigative Unit. But they did not know about them. And even if they had, they still may not have taken any action. After all, it was only a collection of ancient treasures, artifacts, and mummies from a land famous for, among other things, ten historic plagues. What could possibly go wrong?

*

He was called the Groundhog. No one knew his real name. His childhood had not been the best, he was on the streets by his middle teens, and with all the street names, aliases, and stolen identities he had used, he was no longer sure just what his birth name was. Usually, he answered to whatever people wanted to call him. Lately, whenever he was alone or among his few friends, he'd taken to going by Murray, after the movie.

He was not called "Groundhog" because one day for him was much the same as any other, or because he was afraid of his own shadow, or because he was a weather omen. No, his name came from his chosen profession and the methods he used to pursue it. Groundhog was a thief and he knew almost every underground tunnel, passageway, and storage facility in Baltimore. The subway, such as it was, was his to explore, especially the lines that had been started but were abandoned when the governor cut their funding. He roamed the sewers and the subterranean aqueducts. He knew that in the connected row homes and businesses that made up much of Baltimore, entry into one basement very often led to access to several of them. If it was below street level, Groundhog could get into it. And once the basement was his, the rest of the building was as well.

In the early days of his so far successful life of crime, Groundhog spent his time going over maps and plans in Baltimore's Enoch Pratt Free Library. The internet now made this research easier and more private. No one to question why he wanted the floorplans of the main branch of the First Farmers' Bank of Cockeysville. But it was at the Annual Smith College Spring Book Sale at Timonium Fairgrounds that he found a collection of journals and drawings that detailed the construction of the Lancer Mansion, now the Lancer Museum. The Lancers it seems, were an old Maryland family, one with old Maryland money. They were also secret abolitionists and the station they established on the Underground Railroad was exactly that, underground.

On seeing this, Groundhog smiled and bought the collection. Taking it home, he studied it, made his plans, did some trial runs to make sure that hidden accessways had remained buried and forgotten. And once he was sure of his target, he waited for a prize worth taking, for the burglaries he performed were almost always one and done. Once the points of entry and exit were exposed by his passage, they were no longer any use to him.

When "The Splendor of the Two Lands" exhibition was announced, Groundhog knew that it was time to burgle the Lancer. He would strike a few days before the opening. Yes, there would be security, but mostly structural and concentrated on the known accessible portals. He was sure he could handle the cameras and alarms and as for anyone patrolling the halls, he was prepared to handle them as well, even if it meant leaving injured, unconscious, or even dead rent-a-cops lying on the Lancer's cold, marble floors.

As far as Groundhog was concerned, the ancient treasures of Egypt were his for the taking. What could possibly go wrong?

*

Two before the grand opening, Groundhog had made his way below the streets of Mt. Royal Avenue until he again came to a forgotten door. This was the third time in a week he had stood before the door. The first few times were to prepare the way, clearing the obstacles that time had deposited. All that was left was the door itself and the lath-and-plaster wall with which it was covered after the last enslaved person had passed through it on their way to freedom.

Groundhog did not worry about noise from his forced entry. Late at night and deep in the subbasement, there was no one to hear. He made his hole, one wide enough for himself and the loot he planned to carry away, and entered the bowels of the Lancer Museum.

Sublevel by sublevel he slowly made his way upward. Soon he was in the basement storage area. For a few moments, he was tempted to take what he could find from there, knowing that it would likely be weeks or months before the theft was discovered. But he would have to search for the good stuff and even if he found it, its value would not equal what he could make from the sale of some of the choicer items from the new Egyptian exhibit. He knew private collectors who would pay heavily, never mind that the items they acquired were stolen, never mind that they could never show them to anyone, never mind the damage it would cause to the reputation of the museum and relations between Egypt and the United States. These very private collectors wanted something unique, and he wanted the money they would pay him to acquire it for them. He moved up to the main floor and the special exhibition gallery.

No flash was needed there. The required nighttime safety lights were bright enough. He moved on, his footsteps silent, his ears alert for security.

There, the "clop-clop" of work shoes on a marble floor coming his way. Groundhog hid in the shadows. The guard, who had walked this path many times before, walked by him without looking right or left, without shining the light he carried into the dark places.

Which was good for him. Had he done so, had he found the intruder, well, Groundhog had his knife ready. It was a nasty thing, as nasty as its owner, and what was one more body.

The guard passed him and walked up to the doors of the gallery behind which were the treasures of Egypt. He paused and pressed buttons on a newly installed keypad. Only then did he unlock the doors and enter the hall.

Groundhog cursed to himself. He could have picked the lock but could do nothing about the keypad. Too bad for the guard, the poor bastard. His footfalls still quiet, Groundhog followed the guard into what was, for a time, a small part of Egypt.

Grady Hoffman thought he was alone on the first floor. He was thinking of taking his lunch break after locking up the treasures when the knife sliced his throat. Hoffman died quickly, his life's blood spurting out of him.

*

It was calm in Baltimore, at least in areas of the supernatural. There had been minor manifestations, mostly young fools with old books that they didn't know how to read much less use. Bianca handled these herself without needing to call on the rest of the Extranormal Investigative Unit, freeing its other members to investigate more mundane crimes—Bethany Steele working murders, Tavon Greggs training with his Quick Response Team and getting them used to having a were-Yorkie on the squad, Tammy Dolan back in the Crime Lab preparing DNA profiles. Bianca's husband Joe Russo was working in his Fell's Point bookshop, but even there, things were slow.

Maybe, Bianca dared to think, *it's a good time to close the House and take some time off. Joe could bring in someone to watch the shop and he and I could maybe go down the ocean, check out that new hotel, the one with the disturbing theme, the one I warned them about.*

She shook that thought away. Best to leave that bit of darkness alone. Wildwood was nice, no chain places, and the only "ghosts" were the Doo-Wop motels.

Bianca was about to call Commissioner Williams to request leave when her phone began to play the Twilight Zone theme song. Last week it was the theme from The Nightstalker and the week before the Addams Family. *If I ever find out who's messing with my phone …*

The caller ID said it was Beth. Bianca was tempted to swipe a hang-up, call the Commissioner, and close up the Freak Show but knew that the homicide detective would not have called unless it was important. Bianca sighed and reluctantly swiped to answer.

"Bianca, Beth. There's been a murder."

"Beth, this is Baltimore. There's always a murder, or a shooting, or something."

"This one is in the Lancer Museum."

"That makes it different and a red-ball. Who got killed?"

"Grady Hoffman. White male, fifty, taller than most, heavier than he should have been. He was a security guard, apparently stabbed to death while making his rounds."

Bianca found herself thinking, *Get to the point, Beth. Why call me? What got loose that shouldn't have?* "So?" she asked the detective.

"We've got a suspect. Museum security found him this morning in the 'The Splendor of the Two Lands' exhibit in a confused state. He was standing by a mummy case looking down at Hoffman's body. He had a bloody knife on him. From the evidence on the scene, we think it's the Groundhog."

"Congratulations, you have a dunker and a dangerous criminal in custody all in one. Why did you call me? To brag?"

"It's not that simple." *It never is*, Bianca thought, as Beth went on. "When he was found, he wasn't speaking English, or Spanish, or French, or any other modern language. According to Doctor Akila Hegazy—she's with the Grand Egyptian Museum and is in charge of the exhibit—our killer is speaking ancient Egyptian."

"How ancient?"

"I think Moses might have understood him."

Damn it. "Okay, I'll be right there."

*

When Bianca arrived at the Lancer she walked into the usual chaos that was a high-profile homicide case. While the crime scene itself was secure, the hall outside it was crowded with people, most of whom did not need to be there. There were at least three law enforcement agencies—BPD, FBI, and Homeland Security, the latter two no doubt wanting a piece of the crime for budgetary and prestige purposes. The mayor and his aides were there as well, as was a representative of the governor's office. There were a few officious-looking people Bianca did not recognize, State Department she guessed, and possibly someone from the Egyptian consulate. This was not a way to conduct a criminal investigation, especially not one that might literally go to Hell, or whatever the Egyptian underworld was called.

There was only one thing to do. Bianca pushed her way through the crowd straight to the mayor. His security detail moved to block her, then they recognized her. Knowing who she was and what she did, they quickly parted and began to make plans to evacuate their charge.

"Mayor Brandon," Bianca said, "I'm Lieutenant Bianca Jones of the BPD Extranormal Investigative Unit. You may have heard of me." The look on Brandon's face said that he had. She let the implicit threat of her presence sink in for a moment then continued. "Given that I was called to this situation and given that this building may possibly contain dangerous magical artifacts, it may be a good idea to continue whatever discussions you are having somewhere else, possibly City Hall."

In considering Bianca's suggestion, Mayor Brandon thought about the briefings he'd received from Commissioner Williams about her activities. He quickly said, "You may be right, Lieutenant." He then ordered his security detail to clear the building of all unnecessary personnel and began thinking of what to tell the press and the public should the Lancer suddenly vanish like that house in the southwest used to do.

Soon the Lancer was empty except for the original crime scene team, the security guards who had come across the murder, their prisoner, Doctor Hegazy, Homicide commander Pompey Fredericks, and an FBI agent who refused to leave.

Like most members of the BPD, Bianca did not like having the Feds on her crime scenes. Her interactions with them had never been pleasant and more than once she had come close to shooting one or two of them. She walked over to the FBI man. Reading his ID card, she said,

"Agent Willis, I'm Bianca Jones."

"I've heard of you, Ma'am, but I intend to maintain Bureau presence."

"Very commendable." She took out her phone, called up her contact list, showed Willis one of the names on it. "One call and you will be on indefinite detail to the Freak Show."

Agent Willis quickly decided that whatever was going on at the Lancer did not fall under FBI jurisdiction.

When Bianca entered the exhibition hall, she was confronted by Major Fredericks. Like Bianca, Fredericks was a strong woman who had had to fight her way through the ranks of the BPD. The Homicide Unit was her domain, and she did not appreciate anyone intruding on it. She and Bianca did not like each other, but they each respected the other's abilities.

"What did you tell the mayor, Jones? That the building and everyone in it was about to be possessed by demons."

"I implied something like that, then let their fears take over."

Fredericks nodded. "Fear works. Thank you for clearing out the dead wood. Now, why the hell are you here?"

Bianca looked over to a corner of the room, one far away from where the body of Grady Hoffman still lay. In that corner stood the two museum security guards and two BPD patrol officers, the four of them forming a custodial square around two chairs. On one chair sat a short, thin, red-haired man whose skin was pasty-white from having spent too much time underground and out of the sun. On the other was a professionally dressed woman in her fifties, her light brown skin further darkened by too much sun.

"Your suspect looks like the only Memphis he's heard about is the one in Tennessee, yet Detective Steele tells me he's speaking ancient Egyptian. I thought I'd come and consult."

The Major harumphed. "Consult? See that's all you do, Jones. I've got a closed red ball with a name in black. Don't eff it up."

Bianca had already thought of several ways the case could be effed up. She decided not to mention any of them to Fredericks. The major would not appreciate her insight and, absent of any real evidence of the occult or supernatural, would be within her rights to kick her off the scene as quickly as Bianca had gotten rid of the Fed.

With an "I'll try not to, Major," Bianca went talk to Beth Steele, who waved to the woman who was with Groundhog. After making what seemed to be assurances to the man, the woman came over.

"Bianca, Doctor Akila Hegazy. Doctor Hegazy, Lieutenant Bianca Jones. She's the head of the BPD's Extranormal Investigative Unit."

The two women shook hands. "May I assume that your unit serves the same purpose as my country's Bureau of Occult Affairs. I have consulted with them from time to time. Informally we call them the Medjai, after those awful movies. They hate it."

"You're right, Doctor. And my group is called the Freak Show. I don't like it but I'm used to it."

"Please, Lieutenant, call me Akila."

"And I'm Bianca. Now what can you tell me about …" she looked toward the Groundhog. "…him?"

"He says his name is Amenmose and that he served the Pharaoh Sebkey. That means he would have been alive around 1800 BCE, during what is known as the Second Intermediate Period. As for the rest of his story, I think it would be better if you heard it from him."

"Good idea, then you can tell me if he told you the same thing."

*

Speaking in ancient Coptic, Doctor Hegazy addressed the man. "Amenmose, these women are officials in this land. Tell them your story."

The man nodded and, with Doctor Hegazy translating his words, told Bianca and Beth Steele his tale of life, death, and what came after.

"I am known, was known, to men and to the gods of Kemet, the Happy Land, as Amenmose. I was born in the dirt of uncertain parents but through my own efforts was noticed. I became a Friend of the King's Domain and was named Director of the Dining Hall. Excelling in this humble station, I became known to the King's Chancellor and when he went to the gods I was given his post.

"Although I served my king as best as a mortal man can serve a living god, I also served myself. I used my position to increase my wealth. I used my power over those below me to bend them to my will. I betrayed men and seduced maidens, one of whom was the daughter of the king's sister so it is possible that his nephew was mine by blood.

"When the time of my death neared and knowing that of the forty-two negative confessions I would fail most of them, some more than once, I began to fear the judgment of Ma'at, for I knew that should my heart be weighed against her feather it would tip the scales and be devoured by Ammit, leaving my soul to wander in the darkness.

"This I could not, would not allow. And so to keep my soul from judgment, I stole the wand of my king. I arranged for it to be placed in my hand as I was lowered into my coffin and buried with me. This wand had been brought from the cold north. It was carved from the tusk of an elephant of the ice, inscribed with spells, and anointed with the blood of unwilling sacrifices so that it would hide me from Ma'at's accessors."

"How would it do that?" Bianca asked.

Amenmose hesitated before answering. To Bianca, this was a sign of either fear or guilt, probably both. Finally, he said, "I prepared a confession. Whoever opened my sarcophagus and exposed my coffin would read it and know of my sins. But for them it would too late, for by their actions I would have escaped my fate and again walk in the light.

"I remember little of my dying. At one moment I was conscious, at the next my soul had started its journey. I traveled for what seemed like an eternity before I arrived in the land of the dead. There stood the Assessors of the Dead, each one with their question ready. But they did not ask them of me. Instead, they turned away as if they did not see me. Anubis did not weigh my heart against the feather of Ma'at nor did Ammit devour it.

"*The wand worked*, I thought and moved to enter Sekhet-Aaru. But Osiris blocked my way. "We do not know you," the Lord of the Dead said and turned his face from me.

"Then blackness enveloped me and I fell through it for what seemed like a long time. Somehow the wand that should have saved me was still in my hand. My fingers felt the inscribed spells and, in desperation, my mind recited them. Then there was nothing as my soul, such as it was, slept."

As Amenmose paused for a moment, Bianca looked at Beth and she at Bianca. His story was strange and any other investigators would have dismissed it as fiction by now. But the two women had heard stories just as strange. When they nodded for him to continue he did.

"Something woke my soul. I believe that it was the unintended offering of blood from the poor man who lies dead. Whether it was his blood or something else, a sort of life flowed into my body.

"There was darkness. But that was not supposed to be. The spell I had carved on the wand had cost the lives of four servants. It should have taken the ka of whoever opened my coffin. My spirit for theirs. They would be trapped and I would be free.

"Then I sensed it, the blood on my outer image. It was a connection I could use. In my mind I touched the wand. There was another spell I could use. Before my death I might have prayed to the gods that it would work. But my gods had rejected me, and so I merely hoped.

"My mind reached out and felt the blood on my hard, outer self. I sought its source. On finding it, I discovered that the life of that body had fled and I cursed the gods I had not implored for I believed that I was now trapped in the darkness awake and alone forever. Even if one day someone opened my coffin, the spell had been invoked. It would not work again. I thought then that I should have taken my chances with Anubis. Even the outer darkness would have been better than eternal imprisonment.

"Then I felt…something. A connection to the dead man and his blood. Another man, one with the dead one's blood on him. Blood on a blade in his hand, blood on his body, blood on his soul. He was the killer of the first.

"That was good. The cord of the spell I had cast had not been broken. With what remained of my will and the last of my hope, in my mind I pulled on the cord and awoke to new life.

"I was not in my body. Which was good, for that had been old and fat and this one seemed young and healthy. It held a knife of a kind I had never seen before, the key to my prison.

"Looking up, I saw that I was standing before my sarcophagus. Although it was not mine anymore. It belonged to whoever was now in what had been my body. I felt a twinge of pity for the trapped soul, for it was now facing the eternal darkness that I had thought myself damned to endure.

"Had he been an innocent I would have apologized to his spirit, little good it would have done. But he was a thief and a murderer and so deserved his fate."

Again Bianca and Beth looked at each other. Each knew what

the other was thinking, that Amenmose was a confessed thief and murderer. What fate did he deserve? But a good detective knows not to interrupt the flow of a confession. They let him continue.

"As I looked around I saw that I was in a tomb of wonders, one that contained treasures of which even the mightiest king could only dream. And they were in containers of clear glass, sheets of it, more valuable than that which they covered.

"*What king was it that owned such riches*? I asked myself even as I wondered how long had it been since I died?

"As I walked around this great hall, getting used to my new body, I began to realize that I was not in a tomb at all but in a treasure house, one in which some thief had stored that which he had looted from many tombs.

"For the rest of the night I simply explored my surroundings. From afar I studied the other sarcophagi. I could read what was on them. Some were from dynasties before me, others from ones that came after. I did not get too close to any of them. Others may have set the same kind of traps I had.

"There was light coming from the windows when I heard shouts and saw two men running toward me with raised clubs. It was then that I realized my situation. The men were dressed in the same kind of clothes as the dead man and my hand held the weapon that had killed him. I quickly dropped the knife and spread my hands to show that I was now weaponless. Still, one of them hit me with his club before the other stopped him. I was shackled. I tried to explain how he came to be there, to ask where and when I was, to explain that I had killed no one, but they could not understand my words and I did not understand theirs. Soon I gave up trying and stood quietly awaiting my fate. Then Doctor Hegazy came to speak with me. I told her my story as I've told it to you. I can do no more. I am at the mercy of you and the Fates."

*

"What do you think, Bianca?" Beth asked after Amenmose finished his story.

"Beth, I've been cursed by a witch and licked by a were-Yorkie. A 4,000-year-old mummy is just another day in Baltimore." Then Bianca asked Doctor Hegazy, "Well, Akila, do we believe him?"

The doctor nodded. "I don't know about you but I do. What he told you is consistent with what he told me. He speaks ancient Coptic like a native, his grammar and syntax are perfect. In addition, I was speaking with him before you arrived. He knows things about the Second Intermediate Period only an expert or one who lived through it would know." She paused for a moment then added, "Working with the Medjai I've seen stranger things."

"So have we. So he's the real deal?"

"Yes, he is. He's living history, and he would make a wonderful asset to Grand Egyptian Museum."

"Yes, I suppose he would," Bianca replied distantly. "Would you excuse me?"

At Doctor's Hegazy's "Yes" Bianca took Beth aside. "We have a problem," she told the detective.

"I know. We didn't read our suspect his rights. The confession's no good."

"That's not it, Beth. Akila could testify to what he told her before we got here. If it came to trial."

"Insanity? I could see that."

"No, Beth, innocence. Amenmose didn't kill the guard. The Groundhog did," Bianca looked at what had been Amenmose's sarcophagus, "and he's locked up in there. Or at least what's left of him. Before Beth could respond to this Major Fredericks walked up. "Is there a problem, ladies?"

Bianca quickly reported the situation. Fredericks was not impressed.

"Bullshit. We've got a dead man, we've got a suspect. The rest is between the State and his lawyer. Read the Groundhog his rights, Detective Steele."

There were several ways Beth could have responded to her commander's order. The first, and easiest, was to say "Yes, Major" and take out her Miranda card. The next, and funniest, was to walk over to the sarcophagus and Mirandize it. For a moment she was tempted to do so but decided against being assigned two months of morgue detail. So she simply said, "I don't speak old Coptic, Major."

Pompey Fredericks was not a woman to be denied. She pointed to where Akila Hegazy was standing. "Does she?" Assured that the doctor did speak old Coptic, she led the detective over to her. On her way over, Bianca remembered something she had read about the exhibition and the how and why its exhibits were permitted to leave Egypt.

What the hell, Bianca thought, *it's worth a shot.*

"Doctor Hegazy, I'm Major Fredericks of the Baltimore Police Homicide Unit. Detective Steele is going to read something to the prisoner. I would like you to translate."

Akila's smart, Bianca said to herself. *She knows what's happening and she doesn't like it. And she doesn't want to lose control of the greatest archaeological find since the Rosetta Stone. All she needs is a hint.*

"Just a minute, Major."

"What is it, Jones."

"I'm afraid that we don't have jurisdiction."

"What the Hell, Jones. You were the one who scared off the Feds. If this is one of your …"

"Lieutenant Jones is correct, Major," Akila said. Her voice was quiet and polite, but firm and determined. By the small nod she had given her, Bianca knew that she picked up the hint. "According to contracts and agreements between my country and yours, and between the Grand Egyptian and Lancer museums, the exhibition hall where 'The Splendor of the Two Lands' is displayed has been designated as a temporary consulate. In short, the crime of which Amenmose stands accused was legally committed in Egypt and we will be asserting jurisdiction."

Doctor Akila Hegazy's pronouncement resulted in Pompey Fredericks being rendered speechless, something no one in the history of the BPD had ever been able to do. Being an officer and a church-going woman, the major forbore to say the words she was thinking. Finally, once she recovered, she turned to Bianca and said, "I knew you'd find a way to eff this up." Then she was gone.

Once it was over, once the body of Grady Hoffman had been removed and the person of Amenmose, the one-time Chancellor to the Pharoah Sebkey, had been taken into custody by a representative of the Egyptian government, only Bianca, Beth, and Akila were left in the hall. "Would you two like a private tour?" the latter asked the other two. They would. When they passed Amenmose's sarcophagus they paused and considered the fate of the spirit now trapped inside it.

"He was a killer, several times over," Beth commented.

"And by killing Hoffman he chose his own damnation," Bianca added.

"Which may not last forever." Akila went on to explain. "Amenmose said that the spell he invoked could only be used once. Who knows how long the mind of this Groundhog will remain alive? Today, tomorrow, or thirty-four years from now, he will be dead. And from what you have told me about him, it is unlikely that his heart will be lighter than Ma'at's feather. I wonder which Hell he will face."

BETTER TO REIGN

Milton was a fool, Lucifer thought, as he again surveyed his kingdom. *Maybe once I reigned, but that was eons ago. Now I serve Hell more than I ever served … Above.*

Not for the first time did the unwelcome memory come to him, of the time before the Fall—his fall. He had served willingly then and was happy to do so. No, happy was too mild a word. What mortals feel when they join together, what parents feel when they first see their child, it was that and so much more. It was pure Love, given and received. It was Ecstasy. It was Delight in his role in the maintaining of His Creation.

Then came Pride, his belief that he was Loved more than the others. Most of the others. There was Michael, Raphael, and Gabriel. Proudly he stood with them. They heard the Word and passed it on to the those below them—Uriel, Nika, and others like them.

Envy was his next sin. The Presence loved His mortals more than His angels, more than him. Anger followed. How dare they be asked, no, commanded to serve and protect these lower, weaker creations. He would not, could not.

Finally—Betrayal, Rebellion, Defeat. He and others like him were cast into the depths of Tartarus. There, he rallied the Fallen and sent forth his minions to tempt weak mortals into joining them. He rejoiced over each condemned soul, even as their suffering added to his own. His kingdom grew, and grew, and grew. And it became his curse to manage it—each Hell Lord, each demon, each sinner demanding his attention.

After countless eons, he was tired. But he could not admit it. Not to himself, and not to—Him.

"Better to reign," he reminded himself, sure that he was heard.

Again he looked out over the City Infernal. This time, he noticed a dull greyish light that had not been there before.

Sighing, he could not keep from asking himself, "What fresh Hell is this?"

TAG TEAM MATCH WITH HELL

by
Patrick Thomas, C.J. Henderson, and John L. French

TOP SECRET
AUTHORIZED PERSONNEL ONLY

Report from Agent Barton Karver (formerly Bartholomew Andrew Higgins) on demonic Pact activity in Baltimore, Maryland. Case number: 9781890096-427

CC: Baltimore Police Department, Special Crimes Unit, Sergeant Bianca Jones
The London Agency, Greely Building, New York City, Lai Wan
Consul General of the Republic of Dys, Washington, D.C.

Electronic distribution secured by World Wide Spyder

WARNING: This document is protected by tenth level malisons. DO NOT REVEAL ITS CONTENTS

*

We were back in Manhattan and my partner, Mandi Cobb, was none too happy about it. Not because Manhattan isn't a nice place to visit or anything. In fact, Bulfinche's Pub, the only bar I trust myself to drink in, is there. But we weren't on a social call. We were there because a woman by the name of Lai Wan had called in her marker. That was all right by me, because to be honest, I like the woman. I guess in a sense I could relate to her. She was tortured by memories, too. But at least in her case, they weren't her own.

We had met up with this Lai Wan when she helped rescue Mandi's nephew. Then after helping us with that, she went the extra mile and went to bat for us with Sarge Winston. That made her okay in my book, and in Mandi's. But it didn't mean that my partner was fond of her.

Now, it's not that I have a swelled head, but I'd gone in assuming that whatever Lai Wan needed was something Mandi and I would be able to handle on our own. So, I was surprised to find another woman waiting when we got to the psychometrist's home. In fact, both Mandi and I did a double-take.

"Karver," said the woman on the couch petting a large black dog.

"Miss Jones," I said. The muscles in her shoulders tensed up at what I guess she perceived as a slight. Holding back a grin, I added, "Sorry, it's Sergeant Jones now, isn't it? Good to see you, Bianca."

"You two know each other?" Mandi was justifiably surprised. We'd been partnered since very early on in my federal law enforcement career and since I didn't go out or socialize much, it was reasonable for her to figure very few people outside the DMA knew my new face. This was true. Bianca Jones was one of them.

"Unfortunately," answered Bianca, but I detected a small trace of a smile on the corner of her mouth.

"Miss …" I paused long enough for her mouth to open to protest, then cut her off. "Sergeant Jones and I briefly attended the Department of Mystic Affairs Academy together." A look of understanding crossed Mandi's face.

"You must be your department's paranormal specialist then," said Mandi.

Bianca shrugged, waving a hand absently as she said, "Mostly shit happens and I have to clean it up."

"And you went to the academy with Karver?"

Bianca assumed a slightly sheepish look as she said, "Sort of."

The DMA made a habit of opening up the academy to local law enforcement to better train them to deal with mystic threats. They did this mainly because they have a very limited number of agents and quite simply, we can't deal with everything that comes down the road. The goal was to have at least one paranormal expert in every major local law enforcement jurisdiction in the country. The problem is that the attitude of most departments towards magic and monsters ranges from skepticism to disbelief. Funny thing, but most people don't want to consider vampires and the like as a real possibility until they're in knee-deep and being bitten on the ankles.

Not so in Baltimore. There's been a supernatural protector of one sort or another in that city since before the Great Fire of 1904. Lately, however, Baltimore's had more than its share of mystic crimes, with Bianca in the middle of most of them. So the DMA made her the offer.

"You 'sort of' went to the DMA Academy," asked Mandi. "Ever been a little bit pregnant?"

It was my turn to smile. "Bianca left before graduation. The pregnant thing, I have no idea."

"That's because I was partnered with you, Karver," said Bianca.

"Karver, I never even got a cigar," said Mandi.

"At the academy," Bianca added with more than a touch of irritation in her voice. "I've never been pregnant."

"Well, that explains it then. I can understand why a woman partnered with Karver would want to head for the hills. I've often thought of doing it myself," said Mandi.

"Except back home where you come from all the hill people are related to you and it would have cramped your recreational activities," I said. "Or maybe it wouldn't."

Bianca was now staring, first at me, then at Mandi, unable to tell if we were hurling good-natured digs or mean-spirited ones.

"Never a bad idea to keep it in the family," said Mandi joking back. "Although, I will admit to being a little upset to find out that you had a partner that I didn't know about."

"It was at the academy and just one case," I said.

Mandi started to ask for details but was cut off as Lai Wan came into the room. On seeing his mistress, the black dog jumped from the couch and trotted to her side. The psychometrist took a moment to stroke the fur on his back and give the top of his head a scratching. As she did so, you could actually watch the tension lines that had been straining the flesh around the corners of her eyes relax, then fade.

"Good boy, Stranger," she said to the dog. Her tone lost its friendly lilt as she addressed us.

"I am certain this trip down memory lane is just lovely for the three of you, but I did not summon you here to reminisce." Holding up a DVD with a gloved hand she added, "This is why I brought you here."

"You kept me from going back to Baltimore to have movie night?" asked Bianca.

"And with no popcorn?" I added.

I felt the wisecrack was halfway decent but judging by the lack of movement on Lai Wan's face, I surmised she did not agree.

"What is on this disc is not a laughing matter. You will understand once you see it."

Going over to the TV, Lai Wan pushed a button on the DVD player. A tray slid open and she inserted the disc. A minute later, the screen went from blue to tacky. Very bad music that sounded like it was from some horrid garage bands from the 70s or 80s blasted out and a movie with extremely poor production value started to roll from the point of view of the driver of a car.

"You invited us here to watch bad porn," asked Bianca.

Lai Wan's face remained immobile as she answered, "Yes, the absolute worst."

The scene changed from the view of the driving car to a coed little league game. Where it went from there made even my stomach turn.

"Why the Hell are we watching child porn?" I demanded.

"Because," answered Lai Wan, "despite what you believe you are seeing, that is exactly what it is not."

"If I wanted riddles, I could've gone to our psychic department," snarled Mandi. "I'm guessing you want us to help stop the people who are making this filth, but how does kiddie porn involve the DMA?"

"The people who made this movie," said the psychometrist, her eyes unblinking as she spoke, "are the people starring in it."

"The children are producing it?" I asked. Lai Wan shook her head.

"They are not children. No one you see before you is younger than fifty years of age."

Doing my best Ricky Ricardo impersonation, I said, "Lai Wan, you got some 'splaining to do."

"When this was brought to my attention I made the mistake of touching the disc."

Lai Wan's ability to see various aspects of an object's history was necessarily unpleasant, but as far as I was concerned, this had to be one of the worst things ever she'd had to deal with.

"These seeming children have made a deal with Hell, selling their souls for centuries of eternal youth. As is often the case in these matters, it appears they did not bother with the fine print."

"So," Bianca offered, "literal eternal youth?"

The psychometrist nodded, then continued. "When I heard Sergeant Jones was in New York I asked her to come here because she has a history of stealing souls from what all of you perceive as 'Hell.' Also, these false children are operating in her city. I asked you here, Agent Karver, because of your experience in dealing with demons as well as your talent for sensing the use of 'Hell' magic."

"Why did you ask me?" Mandi asked.

Allowing herself the barest of smiles, Lai Wan shrugged her shoulders, offering, "It was your debt that I had to call in to get Agent Karver here. I assumed while doing the heavy lifting for us, he might require someone to pick on."

Picking up a slip of pink paper, the psychometrist added, "I also thought you could make yourself useful performing menial tasks. Perhaps while we work to clear away this mess, you could fetch my dry cleaning and then prepare afternoon tea."

I had to smile. Lai Wan has a real gift for getting under my partner's skin. Proving my point, Mandi snarled, "You want a mess to clear away, I'd be happy to …"

I put my hand on her shoulder as Mandi started to rise out of her chair. Giving her a playful squeeze that diverted her attention away from Lai Wan for the moment, I said, "Sure we could go that way and have her do that, but you might not want to drink the tea. Mandi tends to mix bodily fluids with beverages when she is upset. Sometimes they're not even hers. She saves them from previous romantic encounters in case she ever needs to plant forensic evidence."

"It was only that one time. And we couldn't get that guy for that triple homicide, but damn it he spent four days in jail for jaywalking thanks to those fluids."

Lai Wan had been exposed to our banter before, but it was easy to see in her face that Bianca wasn't sure exactly how seriously to take what we were saying. Finally, though, she said, "Wow. I had to see this or I never would have believed it. Karver actually grew a sense of humor. He was the biggest stone face I'd ever met back in the day. I was lucky to get a dozen words out of him in a row."

She wasn't wrong. My time in the academy was right after my recruitment by the Department of Mystic Affairs. As many issues as I have now, they were ten times worse back then. I wasn't exactly known for cracking smiles. Mandi is a good influence on me in that respect.

"Well then, if we are not to have tea," said Lai Wan, "then perhaps we should leave for Baltimore."

I've never been a fan of road trips even before what happened to me. With Mandi I don't mind it quite so much; however, with the distinctly different personalities headed for our DMA-issued sedan, I didn't exactly predict a fun trip. I like Bianca and Lai Wan, but Jones is a little too much on the independent side—to the point where she rarely questions her own decisions. That can be a dangerous thing for a cop.

Lai Wan generally comes across as aloof, perhaps even a bit superior. Because of her gifts, she usually is at least one up on whoever she's dealing with. For some people that can make her aloofness annoying, but to me, it's justified. Though it's probably the main reason she rubs Mandi the wrong way. Still, despite everything, including the fact that she tends to use her abilities in exchange for currency, she did right by us, so she's fine in my book.

Getting out of Manhattan by car involved taking the Holland Tunnel to the New Jersey Turnpike. Not an easy trip on the best of days and, as it happens to almost everyone attempting the journey at nearly any time of day, we hit traffic. It was easy to see it was going to add a couple of hours to our trip.

"Anyone up for a round of ninety-nine bottles of beer on the wall," asked Mandi from the passenger seat. I was driving. We could both see Lai Wan's frozen glare in the rearview mirror.

"It always seemed a waste of perfectly good beer to me," said Bianca.

"And an exercise for simpletons in repetition," said Lai Wan.

"Well, with the obesity problem the country is having, even the simpletons need their exercise," Mandi said.

We still had hours to go before we even got close to Baltimore and I wasn't about to let these two start an argument that would last longer than our trip.

"So Bianca, how is wedded life going for you?" I asked.

"Remarkably well."

"Thinking about starting a family?" All three women in the car looked at me simultaneously like I was an idiot. I wasn't, but I figured this was the quickest way to change the subject. I think Bianca realized what I was doing, but she gave me a real answer anyway.

"Joe and I have talked about it, but with what I do—the creatures we fight against would not hesitate to target my child just to get at me. Maybe when the unit I head up can do without me, but until then, no. So what about you and Mandi? You two going to have any little Karvers?"

"Me and Karver? Just thinking about it is giving me morning sickness," said Mandi.

"How do you know that it's not really morning sickness?" As she growled at me, I added, "Of course with Mandi, the problem would always be finding out who the father was. The cost of paternity testing in any given month would be enough to bankrupt a small country."

My partner grinned. "Hey, when you give good service, word gets around."

"And so does my partner. Of course, there is a difference between good service and one that's free and easy."

"True, but at least I can give it away, unlike some people I could mention and am sitting next to," said Mandi.

"Are they always like this?" Bianca had turned to look at Lai Wan who was next to her in the backseat.

"Unfortunately," answered Lai Wan. "Although I will admit I find Agent Karver amusing. Unfortunately, his partner cannot keep up with his repartee." This time it was Mandi giving out the glares.

"I don't know," said Bianca. "I think Cobb is giving as good as she gets."

"She usually does," I said. "It's part of the reason she is so popular."

"This is going to be a long trip, isn't it," sighed Bianca.

Lai Wan nodded, adding quietly, "I believe by the end of it we will all have a new appreciation for the true meaning of eternity."

The road trip actually got better from there, but all attempts at humor stopped once we hit the Baltimore city limits. Besides the ages of the participants, Lai Wan could tell us only certain things about the video. It had been made in Baltimore, of that she was certain. As for the setting, all she could feel was that it had been filmed in something large and empty like a warehouse.

"I can also tell you in what country the disc itself was made. And in what city the DVDs were copied. But beyond that ..." The psychometrist merely shrugged, which meant it was time to get down to some real police work.

Bianca had made a few phone calls to find out where the most likely vacant warehouses might be. Several of them were within a mile radius of each other so that's where we headed. Mandi took over driving so I could concentrate on searching for any Hell or demonic based magic. It was hardly an exact science. It's not as if I can just close my eyes and say, "two miles northeast, that way." In reality, it's more like putting a glass up against a door and listening to people whispering on the other side. Maybe you can hear something, maybe not. After the first search area came up empty we mapped out an inspection grid and began driving back and forth across the city in hopes that either Lai Wan or I would be able to pick up some mystic clue. We were two hours into our grid search when suddenly my stomach flipped upside down like there was a nest of hornets trying to get out from the inside—my vision got much sharper. I felt the urge to beat something to a bloody pulp. I've had a lot of practice controlling not only my emotions but that of my one-time demon hitchhiker, so this was only a medium blip on my emotional radar. Still, I told the others, "Something is nearby. And from the feel, it's not just one person or something else from Hell entirely."

"Sounds like our suspects," said Bianca. "Which way is it?"

I pointed towards a half-finished apartment building. A sign over what would be the front entrance proudly announced, "Coming Soon: The Theodore Hamm Condominiums." Mandi slowed then parked across the street, as I confirmed, "Whatever it is, it's in there."

"We'll need a warrant," said Bianca. "I know a friendly judge. His teenaged daughter unknowingly had a date with a werewolf. The shifter got a little fresh and when daddy went to the rescue, things did not go well. It would have been worse, but I got there in time. I should be able to get the warrant in twenty minutes."

I didn't see how we could get a federal warrant any sooner, so I nodded. Lai Wan shook her head, sighed, and simply got out of the car and walked inside the building.

"What is she doing?" asked Mandi.

"Lai Wan's a civilian, remember? She doesn't need a warrant," answered Bianca.

"We can't let her go in there by herself," Mandi offered.

"I think Lai Wan can handle herself without our help," said Bianca.

"I don't think it is going to be an issue." The others looked at me confused. I told them, "Wait for it."

After a few minutes, a fourth-floor window conveniently opened within our line of sight. That action was followed by Lai Wan leaning out and shouting in mock terror, "Help, oh help."

"Oh look," I said, my sincerity as genuine as the psychometrist's, "We have reason to believe a person is in danger. No warrant needed for that. I'll take the back, you two go in the front. We don't want any of them getting away after this."

"I agree," said Bianca. "But, what exactly are we going to do with them when we catch them?"

I shrugged, answering with more assurance than I actually felt. "We'll think of something. We usually do. Maybe we can get them for trespassing and loitering."

"Or maybe vagrancy and general mopery."

"There you go. That's the spirit."

We split up as planned. On my way in, I discovered a fuse box, which wonderfully had everything in the building clearly labeled. Thanking the fates for the first real break they'd granted me in months, I hit the switch to shut down the elevators, making sure that anyone inside wouldn't be going anywhere except by the stairs.

As I made my way up the stairs, I pulled out my gun, securing it in one hand, one of my blades in the other. At the fourth floor landing, I opened the door and found the ladies waiting for me. One look told me that so far they hadn't found anything—including Lai Wan. I made a move toward a nearby door that was ajar, but Bianca beat me to it.

"Cover me," she said. Mandi and I obliged.

As the door opened all the way we could see the psychometrist standing in front of what looked like a preteen boy waving a metal pipe. Bianca pointed her gun between his eyes.

"Police. Drop the pipe and move away from the lady." The preteen chuckled and smacked the pipe into its opposite palm.

"Or what? What're you gonna do? Shoot a little boy? Now that'd make great TV. Hell, let's record it. Get it on social media, I mean, everyone wants to be a star—right?"

Bianca paced off a tight half-circle, keeping her gun straight-lined toward the pipe wielder, positioning herself between it and Lai Wan. In a low snarl, she ordered; "Last warning. Drop ... the ... pipe."

"Make me."

As good as Bianca is, she's still only human. She had no way of knowing what the thing before her really was. It ripped an amulet off its neck and the cloaking spell was broken.

As Lai Wan and I both screamed warnings, pipeboy blurred, grabbing both of Bianca's wrists, then lifting her over its head. A good trick since they were both about five feet tall. Bianca had stopped growing long ago. The preteen, however, grew until it was a good seven and a half feet tall, sprouting horns and a layer of red scales.

Bianca cursed and the demon laughed. Lai Wan stepped forward. I had no idea what the psychometrist had planned against a demon, but I cut her off by shooting the demon in the kneecap. The Pit creature laughed, but only until the pain kicked in.

We'd come into things knowing we were dealing with Hell magic, so Mandi and I had switched over to special ammo, cartridges with sacred alloy bullets—very effective against demons.

I stepped in and stabbed my charmed blade into the wound, at the same time shooting the wrist of the hand it was holding Bianca's gun hand with. As it howled and let go, she shot its other wrist and dropped to the floor free. Bianca carries her own blessed ammo, courtesy of the Vatican, I believe.

She and Mandi fired into the demon. The ammo hurt it but it's hard to kill demons. Gunshots will slow them down, but they're not enough to stop them. Once the ladies had emptied their clips, I moved in, a blade in each hand. While they reloaded, I did a stab-and-slice, then stepped away to give them the opportunity to empty another couple of clips into it.

During their second barrage, I managed to get around behind the damned thing and sink my left blade six inches into the side of its neck. With it firmly embedded, I used that knife to pull myself far enough up to where I could position my other blade in front of its throat. Since our nasty playmate was sentient, the rules forced me to give it a warning.

"DMA, stand down or be destroyed."

Its response was to reach back, grab the neck of my suit and pull me over its head. I was tossed across the room, but I managed to slice through its throat as I went. The demon's hands went to its jugular to try to stop the flow of whatever it what that kept it and its kind going. Mandi and Bianca fired at the new wound, bringing it to its knees.

"Clear," yelled Mandi, tossing a DMA standard-issue portable ward, which fell nicely around the demon. As soon as the circle touched the ground she intoned the activation words and it flared to life. The demon smashed out at the translucent shield. It held but flickered with each blow. Not a good sign. Still, while it held, the four of us gathered together, catching our breath.

"I've got to get me one of those," said Bianca.

"You can put in for one," answered Mandi, "but they're stingy with them. Very expensive. After we used our last one it took us almost two months to be issued a new one."

"And, they're one use only," I added. "If he'd managed to somehow stop any part of it from making contact with the floor, it wouldn't have worked."

"Will it hold?" Bianca asked.

"With him wounded, it should hold long enough for us to get a containment team here to transport him to Eastern State Penitentiary," I said.

The demon started going berserk, coming at the ward with everything it had in a frenzy that could've torn apart a small herd of elephants and made the ward flicker like a strobe light. Anyone who believed demons were cool had never witnessed anything like this.

"And exactly how long until that containment team gets here," asked Bianca.

"I'll tell them to put a rush on it," answered Mandi.

"An excellent idea," offered Lai Wan, adding quietly, "hopefully a timely one as well."

The rest of us turned and saw what the psychometrist had, namely a group of scantily clad, deceptively young-looking folks huddled together, staring at the demon and us from the set of their latest nasty flick.

"None of you move."

"We didn't do anything," said one boy, looking about nine.

"We're just kids," piped in a girl, playing on an innocence long ago lost.

"You haven't been kids in years, not since you signed away your souls," I said.

"That not against the law, is it?" asked another boy, a poster child for spoiledbrat.com if I'd ever seen one.

"No but cavorting with a demon who just attacked two Federal

Agents is," said Mandi.

"*And* a Baltimore City detective," added Bianca, a touch indignant at being left out of the mix.

"You can all be charged as accessories," I told them. The lot looked shocked. "The federal government has special courts to deal with magic crimes."

"So what? We do a couple of years if that. You'll have a tough time convincing a jury we're not kids."

"Fine. Take that route," said Mandi. "As children who are 'victims' of child pornography, you become wards of the state until you 'grow up,' which won't be for a hundred years or so. Claim you're adults and we get you on the accessory charge."

The youngest looking of the group laughed quietly.

"We all know that ain't going to do a thing. We'll get a good lawyer and come off looking like the victims. We're adults who share a rare growth defect making a living as best we can. How were we to know that that, 'demon' you called it, wasn't one of us?" Pointing at Bianca, he added, "He fooled her, didn't he? So walk out now and we won't press charges for unlawful entry." I started to argue the point when Bianca stepped forward.

"I have a deal to offer," she said, addressing the group of overaged children. "I've stolen souls from the Devil. I've saved people who have had contracts with him. I'm offering all of you the same opportunity. Give up this life and I will do everything I can to redeem your souls."

The boy laughed, but one girl spoke up.

"What would we owe you?"

Bianca focused all her attention on the girl. "What's your name?"

"Jenna."

"Jenna, you wouldn't owe me a thing. You'll have to stop making these movies; even without a contract they give the Devil a claim on your soul."

"I look like I'm eight. How will I make a living?"

"There are enough people within New York City who would hire you on my say so," offered Lai Wan. "The work would not be anything glamorous, but it would be honest."

"Beyond that," added Mandi, "The DMA has a fleshsmith. He can remold your body so you'd look older."

"So, you interested?" asked Bianca.

"Yes," the girl whispered, a glimmer of hope shining in her eyes.

"Jenna, you can't quit. You're our star. If you leave, you're hurting the rest of us. We'll just find you and bring you back."

"No," I said, "you won't."

"How're you going to stop me? The big bad DMA agent going to beat up a little boy?"

I smiled and the 'little boy' took a step back. Behind me, Lai Wan had pulled Mandi aside and was whispering in her ear. Out of the corner of my eye, I saw my partner nod.

"As you have pointed out," the psychometrist said, "it is possible you are beyond the reach of mortal law, a concept for which I hold as much contempt as you yourselves. Still, I have my reasons for what I say next. I will now give you one chance to stop making these films."

"Bite me, bitch," said the boy.

"Are the rest of you in agreement with him?" When the faux kids nodded, Lai Wan said, "Very well. Sergeant Jones, if you would please take Jenna outside." Bianca nodded and left with the girl.

"Karver, you might want to leave, as well."

"I'm not leaving my partner," I said, looking at the raging demon that looked like it might burst out of its warded cage any moment.

"Karver ..."

"Not open to debate, Mandi," I told her.

"What are you going to do? You can't touch us," said the boy, his voice finally breaking, revealing a hint of nervousness.

Lai Wan didn't answer him. The entire room went cold as it dawned on everyone that as far as the psychometrist was concerned, the soul sellers before us had used up their last chance. Not even bothering to look at them, Lai Wan removed one of her gloves, then she and Mandi joined hands. Mandi used her empathic powers to link to Lai Wan and then her propathic abilities to project the psychometrist's vision into the faux kids' minds.

It wasn't pretty, but then, they'd asked for it.

I'd wondered up until that point what had caused Lai Wan to get involved. She's not one to take up a cause, to get involved in something without some kind of monetary reward in sight. But this, this had proven to be different.

She'd come in contact with one of the group's DVDs through a totally random chance, touched it by accident without knowing what it was. Her powers are so strong she usually guards against such things, but well, anyone can have an accident. When her bare fingers had brushed that first DVD she'd shown us, she had seen everything connected to the soul sellers' enterprise. She'd seen it *all.*

Every film they had made had become instantly imprinted within her mind. But far beyond that, she experienced the full depravity of those who watched the films for pleasure. All their lust, all their desire to abuse children, to feel the young bodies they saw—to rub them, lick them, rape them. In that instant, she felt their hands touching her, smelled their sweat and rotting breath and the stale fluids dried on the carpet before their televisions. Every bit of the depravity every viewer felt, from every viewing of every film made, wrapped around her body, stitched to her soul.

And more.

In that terrible, blinding moment she also felt the damage the soul sellers' movies had done to their audiences' families. The divorces, the men who'd used them as inspiration to get up the nerve to escalate their sick fantasies into the real thing. She'd experienced the pain of their victims and their families. From that one accidental touch, her soul had been over-brimmed with a hundred thousand vile tendrils of rotting poison she would never be able to remove from her mind and memory.

And in consideration of the notion that it's better to give than to receive, she gave the soul sellers the same experience, letting them see exactly what their moneymaking enterprise had done to the face of the world. In less time than it takes to blink, the lot of them ended up curled on the floor, drooling and babbling incoherently as their minds shut down from experiencing the full damage they inflicted on others.

Mandi had to go through the same thing she inflicted on them, but she had had decades of practice shielding herself. Still, there was only so much that she could do. The only advantage she had was that it wasn't she who had inflicted the pain, so the pain wasn't attacking her except as collateral damage, saving its worst for those who created it. Regardless, it was still enough to bring Mandi to her knees.

"You okay, partner," I whispered when it was all over.

"No," she told me sadly, shaking her head. "But I will be." Turning away from me, she forced herself to meet Lai Wan's eyes, asking, "You get that every time you touch anything?"

"Yes," the psychometrist answered in an even voice. She began to say more, but her words were cut short by the demon. The thing had finally managed to tear through our binding ward, the mystic equivalent of running through a plate-glass window. The sharded ward ripped its flesh, turning parts of it into hamburger. It was enough to drive it to the floor, but not enough to keep it down for long. And we didn't have the firepower to do much about it.

"Mandi," I shouted, "get everyone moving. Each of you see if you can carry one of the perps out. I'll hold off our playmate."

"Yeah, right," snapped Mandi. "You could carry two or three of those little weasels. It makes more sense for me to stay."

"You expect me to believe you when you tell me something makes sense? I have a better chance. Go," I shouted, adding quietly, "Please?"

"Not leaving my partner."

Our eyes met. It would rip what was left of my heart out if anything happened to Mandi. I knew damn well she wouldn't go, but I had to try. Her eyes told me she felt the same way. Stepping up to my side, Mandi trained her gun on the demon. The thing had lifted its eyes to glare death and things far worse at us.

"Lai Wan," I tried, "get outside. Tell the containment team what's happening. Hopefully, they'll arrive before he gets past us."

"They will not," she answered.

"You're insane. It'll rip you to pieces. You don't even have a weapon!"

Removing both gloves, Lai Wan reached out, taking both our hands as she said, "I require no other weapon when I have the two of you."

The demon had risen to its feet, but I barely noticed. Instead, I was reliving my life as The Carver, feeling the damage the demon that had once lived within me had done with my body, not only to our victims but their families. It was harsh, but I lived with a lesser degree of it every day, so it didn't cripple me. Mandi had taken everything the child pornographers did and only lost her footing. She was vomiting before we were halfway through my dead.

Lai Wan was tough and barely blinked, choosing instead to stare down the demon. She bombarded the thing with all the pain I had caused during my years of possession, but the monster just laughed.

"Thank you," it sneered. "This is wonderful—delicious." The demon savored every drop of both my suffering and that which had been caused with my hands. The only plus I could see in what we were doing was that it had stopped to enjoy, instead of attacking.

Mandi and I were both on the ground, my partner curled into a ball. I started to hate Lai Wan for putting her through this. I hated her more when I realized that Mandi would never be able to look at me again without remembering this. I damn well hoped we at least stopped the demon and that doing was worth the loss of my best and only real friend.

And then, something changed in the vision. Lai Wan went past the pain and horror I had inflicted, feeding our enemy my possessor's exorcism, my recruitment to the DMA. My time in the academy followed, the case Bianca Jones and I handled together, my partnering with Mandi. Suddenly Lai Wan's plan became clear to me. We had saturated the demon with the past evil I had lived through, suckered it into dropping its defenses, opening itself to all the psychometrist had to show it.

Unable to stop the flow, the thing felt the effect on those whose lives I had saved since I became a Federal Agent, the effect that had on their families. Joy and gratitude swamped over the thing, it experienced the tears of parents reunited with their children, the thrill of innocents spared damnation. The peace of a mother who believed her dead daughter had defeated dark magic to save her from a stalker. In its eyes, I could see the mounting horror as emotions such as kindness and simple human decency poisoned its black soul.

Mandi uncurled as I stood, but the demon had dropped to its knees, cursing and screaming, beating its trembling fists against the floor begging for mercy. We had none to give something so evil. My partner and I stood with Lai Wan between us, showering the demon with the burning horror of virtue until the containment team arrived and Bianca led it to us. They got the demon in a much stronger and more portable version of the ward we had.

Only when the thing was trapped beyond any hope of escape, did Lai Wan release her grip on us and don her gloves once more. I stood unmoving until I heard someone calling my name.

"Karver, are you okay?" said Bianca. I stared at her, more than a little confused. I must have looked it too because she added, "You're crying. Are you hurt?"

I simply shook my head. It was all I could manage. I was too overwhelmed to do anything else.

"Agent Karver has had a chance few ever do," Lai Wan said, "to see firsthand the evil and the good that he has done. Karver now knows that the good he has done carries far more weight than he had ever suspected."

"Thank you."

Lai Wan simply nodded. She wasn't ignoring me. Instead, she was giving me the chance to notice that Mandi still hadn't moved. When I asked if she was "okay," she turned toward me, her face pale, hands shaking. Mandi had always been aware of what I'd done when possessed, but now she knew exactly what that meant. I turned away, unable to meet her eyes.

"Karver, look at me," she ordered. I forced myself to comply. "I can feel what you are feeling, remember? So stop it. You know me better than that. Pretty pathetic flashback. I wasn't even in it until the end. And no women. I knew your love life was pathetic, but I didn't realize it was that bad."

"Not all of us need stadium seating to accommodate our lovers," I replied.

"Hell, you couldn't even fill a loveseat," she shot back.

"What'd I miss?" Bianca asked Lai Wan in a whisper.

"Nothing," answered the psychometrist. "And everything."

"Mandi, are we …" My partner covered my mouth with her hand. There were tears in both our eyes.

"Don't insult me by asking," she said. Then she pulled down my head and kissed my forehead.

Seeing that Mandi and I could both use a change in subject, Bianca asked, "So what's going to happen to tall and scaly?"

"He'll be arraigned and jailed to await trial. The ambassador from Hell will undoubtedly try to arrange his release, arguing he is a political prisoner."

"Not in my city he won't."

Bianca was right. For various reasons, most of which she had something to do with, Hell wants nothing to do with Baltimore.

"Hell has an ambassador?" Lai Wan asked.

Despite my surprise that there was something Lai Wan did not know, I nodded. "Human too. Same guy for the US and the UN. A real scumbag, but effective. I think we'll be okay."

"Will you get in trouble for pulling the mojo on the porn peddlers?"

I shrugged off Bianca's question. "Probably. We're not supposed to attack citizens who don't pose an immediate danger, especially human ones. Since they were pushing kiddie porn, though, I think we might just get a slap on the wrist. Thanks for the assist."

"Hey, they were working my town," she said. "Happy to get rid of them." Cracking a smile, Bianca added, extending a hand, "You know, when we first met, I didn't think you had the makings of a cop. Glad to see I was wrong."

"Me too," I said, taking her hand and shaking it.

There wasn't much more after that. No one had realized just how much her stunt had drained Lai Wan. Mandi actually had to help her back to the car. Bianca laughed at the sight. When I gave her a look, she said, "I am so glad I'm in Baltimore."

"What do you mean?"

"Give me a break, Karver. Getting between you and a demon is one thing. Getting back in that car is another." Bianca flashed me an evil grin. Understanding her meaning, I defended Lai Wan and my partner, saying, "Oh, I think those two are all bickered out."

Bianca was about to say something when Mandi came back from the car, grabbing my shoulder as she snapped, "We *have* to go. Say goodbye, Karver."

"But, I ..." The grip on my shoulder tightened.

Say *goodbye*, Karver."

"Goodbye Karver," I replied.

"I wish to be returned to my home and away from this one as soon as possible," said Lai Wan from the backseat of the car. "Please use the siren the entire way."

"Help me," I whispered to Bianca as I was pulled away.

Bianca just laughed and waved.

*

Not quite as I remember it, Lieutenant Bianca Jones said to herself, *but Karver was always one for embellishment and exaggeration.* As she replaced the report in the drawer, she thought back to their time in the DMA Academy—their saving of a kidnapped child, their losing that child to the cult of the Leviathan, their defeat of that demonic monster, the kiss they shared on the beach.

I can't say it was a fun time, but we did some good and I did learn from the experience, so some good came out of it.

Bianca thought about the kiss, smiled, and wondered if Karver remembered it. Then she thought about another of her classmates and looked at the letter she had just received.

What do you want, Herne? What do you need in my city?

THE THRILL OF THE CHASE

For the fifth time in two days, Bianca Jones looked at the letter. It had been delivered to the headquarters of the BPD Extranormal Investigative Unit by special messenger, who, according to the security officer who received it, suddenly appeared, handed over the letter, and just as suddenly vanished.

"Don't worry," Bianca told the befuddled patrolman, "these things happen. You'll get used to it."

The officer's look indicated that he didn't think that likely. As he left Bianca's office she clearly heard him say to himself, "No wonder they call this unit the Freak Show." He then wondered what he had done to be assigned this duty.

The envelope had only her name and address. The letter inside was more of a note. It read,

"My dear Bianca, I am in need of your help. I will be in Baltimore in three days. It will be good to see you again."

It was signed with just an "H," one whose upper posts extended to form the antlers of a stag, leaving no doubt as to the sender's identity.

Herne, God of the Forest, one-time leader of the Wild Hunt, and Bianca's one-time lover.

It had been two days since she had received the note. Herne would arrive the next day. Again she wondered what he wanted and thought back to when she had last seen him. It was years ago, when she was still a detective, just months after she had graduated from the Department of Mystic Affairs Academy.

*

Seven-year-old Emma Ryder did not know what woke her up. She thinks it might have been when the funny man sat on her bed.

Clutching Feliciti, her USA Girl doll, Emma raised her head to see him smiling at her.

Maybe that's why she didn't scream, because he was smiling and, at her age, she still believed that people who smiled did so because they liked you and so would not hurt you.

"He had a funny smile," she told Officer Abby Bowman when questioned in her kitchen later that night. "It was all teeth and no lips."

"How do you know," asked the officer. "Wasn't it dark?"

"There's a nightlight," Emma said. "I don't need it, but Feliciti is still afraid of the dark."

"What else did you see, Emma?" Officer Bowman asked gently.

"He didn't have hair, and his ears were long and funny. And he had very long fingers nails like his mommy had never cut them. And he was white."

"So he was white like your mommy and daddy, and not dark-skinned like me?"

"No, Officer Abby. He was white like this milk."

Albino, Bowman thought. *And he looked bald to the girl because his hair was white too.*

Then Emma added, "He was white all over. I know because he wasn't wearing any clothes."

Damn. Taking a deep breath, Abby Bowman asked the question she had been putting off, the one she and her parents were afraid to ask for fear of the answer.

"Emma, did this funny man hurt you or touch you in any way? Or did he touch Feliciti?"

Emma took a sip of milk and a bite of cookie before shaking her head. "No, he just sat on the bed and smiled and waved. Then he was gone."

"Gone how? Through the door, out the window?"

Emma shrugged. "I don't know. Just gone." Another sip, another bite. "Felicity's tired. Can we go back to bed now?"

Emma slept in her parents' bed that night, while the Crime Lab dusted the window and door of her room and as well as the front and back doors of the house.

"I don't think there's anything to worry about," Officer Bowman told the Ryders. "But to be on the safe side, have all your locks changed and think about getting an alarm system. And have Emma examined by her pediatrician, just in case."

This happened in the Hampden area of Baltimore, a part of town where, in the spring, they hold the "Hon Fest" to celebrate the Baltimorese lifestyle and, at Christmas time, residents of 34th Street are contractually obligated to decorate the outsides of their houses, the more bizarre the better.

There were four more sightings of this "ghost burglar"—another in Hampden and three in other areas of North Baltimore. All the reports were the same—nothing taken and no signs of forced entry, just a naked, funny-looking, white guy who smiles and waves before disappearing.

It wasn't until the fifth victim, Henry Chambers of Old Cold Spring Lane, described him as looking like, "that guy in the old silent horror movie, the one that was Dracula but wasn't," that Abby Bowman, who had taken the lead on the break-ins, remembered hearing about a detective who was said to be interested in the strange and the weird. And so she called the Special Investigations Unit and asked for Bianca Jones.

Bianca brought the case of the "Ghost Burglar" to Major Chester Williams, commander of Special Investigations and one of the few people in the BPD who knew about her "unofficial" job as the city's monster hunter.

"Okay, coordinate with the Sex Offense Unit and work on it when you can this week."

"When I can? You do know this sort of creeping behavior is the first stage of more violent acts?" Bianca not too politely asked.

Williams ignored Bianca's tone, he was used to her by now, and answered, "Which is why you're coordinating with Sex Offense. And yes, the words 'nosferatu' and 'ghost' do make it part of your special assignment, but this week I need you on another detail. Remember our bet?"

Their bet was that if Bianca completed the DMA Academy, she would get a week's vacation. If she left early, she would get a week of pervert duty. Despite officially graduating, she had left before class actually ended.

And so with her small size and slender figure, she became bait to lure the pedophiles who trolled Eastside Park looking for underaged girls.

It was two in the morning on the third day of the detail. Despite a chill in the air, Bianca was dressed in a short, plaid skirt and white blouse and looked very much like a heavily made-up Catholic high school girl. She felt cheap and ridiculous and she hated the assignment, but so far that night she and her surveillance team had made three arrests for solicitation of prostitution and were looking to make a few more before calling it a night, or rather an early morning.

Needing a break, Bianca was about to get into one of the chase cars to warm up for five minutes before going back out but then her phone buzzed. She checked it. It was Major Williams.

"Calling to apologize?" Bianca asked her boss.

"A bet's a bet, Bianca."

"I've told you, Major, the diploma's in the mail."

"And when it arrives you'll get your week's vacation."

"Two weeks, or I'm taking the DMA's offer."

There had been no offer and Williams knew it but Bianca, along with a DMA agent, had saved the world so Williams was inclined to be generous.

"Okay, two weeks, if you have the time. But right now I need you to secure the detail."

Normally that instruction was followed by "Yes, sir. Right away, Sir." But there was something in Williams's voice that made Bianca ask, "What's happened?"

The major hesitated before saying, "I don't want to give out details I'm not sure of. All I know is that it's bad. I need you to go home, clean up, and get what rest you can. You're needed at the Medical Examiners at seven."

*

There were rumors about Dominic Jones. One was that he had helped two drug enforcement agents raise a dead man then let the walking corpse escape. Another was that he had staked and decapitated a dead body to keep it from turning into a vampire. A third was that he had performed autopsies on three fairies after which he had released them to the care and custody of Queen Maeve herself.

Only some of these stories were true. When asked which ones, the tall native of the Dominican Republic would just smile and say, "Jump up on the slab and I'll tell you all about it."

To date, he had had no takers.

Except for Bianca Jones. She had listened to his stories and he had listened to hers. Despite their families coming from different parts of the world, they were relatives by choice based on their last names and the sharing of a secret—that there were creatures loose in the world that cared nothing for humanity except as playthings and cattle. Worse yet, that there were people who aided and abetted these creatures in order to satisfy their own twisted appetites and cravings for power.

"You look tired, Little Sister," Dominic said when Bianca walked into the autopsy arena in the basement of the Medical Examiner's Office.

"I am, Big Brother. All week long I've been chasing ghosts by days and perverts by night. I have had about eight hours sleep since Sunday and other than dinner with Joe, my social life has been non-existent. I could use a long nap and some good news but something tells me that I'm not going to get either. What do you have for me?"

This time of the morning the arena was empty. The support staff would not arrive until eight and the other pathologists not until nine. The bodies that had been brought in since the previous evening were stored in one of the two walk-in coolers just inside the receiving dock. All except one.

"It is a bad one, Bianca," Dominic said as he led her to the gurney at the far end of the room. He unzipped the body bag and spread it open for her to view the remains.

The body had been ripped apart. No, Bianca decided, not ripped but cut apart. Then she looked again and corrected herself. Sliced apart.

"How many blades?" she asked dispassionately, forcing herself to view the body not as a victim but a puzzle to be solved. *And what does it say about me that I can do it so easily?* She asked herself, wondering not for the first time how long she could do her job before falling into the Abyss.

"Several, I would think," came Dominic's quiet voice from behind her, his accent somehow soothing. *This is a man who understands*, she thought. *It's a shame he's married.* Then she thought about the people she had met at the DMA. They too understood. She thought about one of them and a desperate kiss on a beach. Then she remembered one more, a tall agent with literally the body of a god.

Dominic interrupted her thoughts. "Although it is difficult to tell, it appears that first set of wounds occurred simultaneously, the others were inflicted later at a different angle."

"What kind of weapon?"

"Hard to say, Little Sister. All that comes to mind is that wolf-like person from the comics my son reads. I prefer Superman myself, but I suppose you like Batman."

Batman doesn't kill his monsters, Bianca thought but didn't say. Instead, she asked, "Retractable claws then?"

"Something like that, maybe. I will know more after the autopsy."

Something like long, retractable claws. Maybe a human then. Then Bianca remembered the statement of Emma Ryder, "He had very long fingers nails, like his mommy had never cut them."

Maybe not nails but claws. "Damn," she said aloud.

"Is there something wrong?"

"I don't know, Dominic. Maybe. I'll let you know later. For now, I'm going to catch another hour or two of sleep and then I'm off to see the wizard."

*

Morgan's Rare Books and Collectibles was a small shop on the recently named Lisbon Street, which had once been an alley. Yielding to the need for more specialty shops, the backs of many stores had been converted to storefronts. This being the case, there was no explanation this side of reality as to why the bookstore was twice the size it should have been or why it had a back door. And no one had ever dared ask Morgan where this door led.

Morgan was a small, wizened man, not much taller than Bianca. In addition to running the bookshop, Morgan was one of those who fought for the light against the darkness. His body and soul bore many scars acquired in this fight and if one looked into his eyes too long they would see the price he had paid in earning them.

It was Morgan who had revealed to Bianca what he called the preternatural, the other dimension in which dwelt Old Ones and banished gods, who, aided by corrupt humans, constantly sought to return to this world to devour it. It was Morgan's duty to keep this from happening. And ever since Bianca had fought and defeated a monster on Federal Hill, it was hers as well.

"Morgan, are you here?" *A stupid question, Bianca*, the detective thought. *Of course he's here. He's never anywhere else. And his door is open.* She looked around at the piles of books that, having overflowed their shelves, were now stacked on chairs, small tables, counters, and the floor, anywhere there was open space.

She had once offered to take a few days off to help him sort and organize what she viewed as a chaotic mess but the old man had declined.

"A proper bookshop should be messy. Part of the fun, no, the joy of going into a bookshop is searching its stock to find the book you always wanted but didn't know existed. The thrill of the chase so to speak."

"Back here, Miss Jones," came Morgan's voice from a room, which, according to the official floor plans, could not and should not be there. She followed the voice and, found him at his desk, carefully perusing the pages of a very old book that was written in a language that no longer existed.

"It about time," he said gruffly.

"Time for what?" Bianca asked.

"Time you came and told me about this casper of yours."

"Casper?"

"The friendly ghost you've been chasing. The naked one who smiles and waves."

Bianca was not surprised that Morgan had heard about her ghost hunt. If there was a whisper about a supernatural occurrence in Baltimore Morgan heard about it, sometimes even before the whisper had been uttered.

Bianca moved some books off a chair and pulled it up to his desk. "Maybe not so friendly," she said as she sat down. Then she described to him what she had seen at the Medical Examiner's. Morgan listened quietly and when she suggested that what Emma Ryder had described as long fingernails were really claws that could have inflicted the wounds of the dead man, he simply nodded.

"It's possible," he finally said, his voice somewhere remote as if part of his mind was already working on the problem she had set him. Then, without a word, Morgan stood and walked over to a long bookshelf that was against a side wall. He stood there for a long time, his eyes searching the shelves as he muttered to himself. "No, not that one. No,

that's not the one. How did that get there? I thought I had locked it up."
Finally, "Ah, that's it."

Disdaining a nearby ladder, Morgan climbed the middle set of shelves and took a volume from the top shelf.

"You have a lot of books here, Morgan."

The old man looked up from the book he had started reading. "They're not mine, Miss Jones. I'm more their guardian than their owner. When I'm gone someone else will be entrusted with them. Much like some of Adam Soto's books came to me after that case of yours in Pennsylvania. Now then, where was I?"

The book Morgan had pulled from the shelf appeared to be one of the newer ones. Bianca looked at its title—*The Encyclopedia Cryptozoological*. Again she heard him mutter.

"Oh, it updated itself again. More discovered every time I look at this. Mmm, that one's new. My lord, I hope we never have to face that one. That's not right, those aren't species variations, they're gender-based traits. Ah, here it is."

As Morgan read quietly to himself he began to frown, His frown grew deeper as his face darkened. Finally, he closed the book and said, "This is bad. Have you ever heard of a rake?"

"I assume you're not talking about the thing that gathers leaves."

"No, Miss Jones, although that is how this creature received its name. Its long claws are similar to the tines of a garden rake. It is a nocturnal predator, Miss Jones, a monster of pure appetite that seeks only blood and flesh. Its description is identical to that provided by the young girl and other witnesses. It is quite dangerous."

"That doesn't fit in with its reported behavior."

"No, but there are three stages to the rake's life cycle. The first is, let's call it childhood. It is new to the world and the world new to it. It explores, it seeks out beings that resemble it. It enters buildings seeking warmth. Why it smiles and waves no one knows. These actions no doubt mean something different to it than they do to us. It does this for a time until it becomes, for want of better term, an adult.

"Then it feeds. It feeds on flesh and blood, using its long claws to rend its victims. Your "brother" at the Medical Examiners will no doubt find less blood than expected and some of the organs partly or mostly devoured. At first, it takes what it can find, but once it tastes human flesh that becomes its preferred prey." Morgan paused to allow Bianca to take in what he had told her.

"What about the third stage?"

"What else? Reproduction. The rake might look human, Miss Jones, but it is not. You tell me that some of your witnesses described it as male. If so, its penis is for the elimination of fluids only. When it is time, it attacks but not to feast. Instead, it forces its victim's mouth open and inserts a proboscis in a manner similar to what the French called *baiser amoureux*, a French kiss. The proboscis releases a protozoaire which lodges in the body cavity and feeds off its host. When it gets old enough it eats its way out of the body and the cycle begins again."

"How soon does it start reproducing?"

"Given the timeline, Miss Jones, I would say a month or two, more or less. And before you ask, once it is infected, the only thing that can be done for the host is a quick, painless death followed by cremation."

Morgan was right. This was bad. The city was looking at multiple violent deaths followed by rape-like attacks that were even worse. There was only one way to handle the problem.

"Can be it killed?" she asked.

"Anything can be killed, Miss Jones. For the rake, I would recommend your shotgun to bring it down followed by high explosive incendiary bullets. Or, if you like, I can teach you some simple but deadly fire spells. But killing it is not the issue. The problem is finding it. I know no spells for that."

"Don't worry, Morgan. I know who to call about that."

*

In her cubicle, her hand near to but not quite touching her phone, Bianca told herself that it was the right thing to do, the smart thing to do. Herne the Hunter was the best tracker the Department of Mystic Affairs had. His senses were sharper than a bloodhound's. He was the perfect choice to find a creature that so far had left no trace.

That Hunter was tall and good-looking had nothing to do with her decision. Neither did the fact that he had complimented her on her perfume when she wasn't wearing any.

"Must be your natural scent," he had told her. "It's quite pleasant."

Bianca had found his scent "pleasant" as well. More than pleasant actually. She had found it arousing.

Having left the Academy before classes ended, she did not have the chance to follow up on her feelings for Hunter. *For the best,* she had told herself. She had her life, he had his. And then there was Joe Russo.

Bianca had come to care for the Crime Lab Technician who had become involved in her fight against the darkness. He had made his feelings toward quite clear. As for her feelings toward him—they scared her. Despite having looked into the Abyss, Joe was still an innocent, a pure soul. She could not bear to have such goodness destroyed or corrupted and so she kept him at arm's length.

Bianca stared at the phone for a long time. Finally, she thought of Emma Ryder and the others to whom the Rake had appeared as a "friendly ghost." She thought of the still-unidentified body that was cut to ribbons and now lay on a cold metal table in the morgue. *Maybe he was scouting,* Bianca asked herself. *What if he returns for more than a smile and a wave? What if he goes after Emma?*

Taking a deep breath, Bianca picked up the phone and punched in the number of the Deputy Director of the Department of Mystic Affairs. "Sarge," she said when he answered, "Bianca Jones here. I need Hunter." When she told him why, the man she called "Sarge" immediately agreed to send him.

As Bianca broke the connection and put her phone, she thought, *It was the right thing to do.* Then, in a moment of honesty, she added, *Besides, I have to know.*

*

"Who are you waiting for, Miss Jones?" Morgan asked the day after Bianca had called the DMA. "Is it your young man?"

"No, Morgan, it's … someone else. And he's not my young man."

"That's a shame, Miss Jones. I like him."

"So do I, that's why I don't want him involved in what we do any more than necessary."

"Involvement in 'what we do' is not always our choice, Miss Jones. Now just who is …"

Just then the door of the bookshop opened and a man walked in. He was tall and wore a baseball cap emblazoned with a rainbow pouring into a shot glass. As he walked toward the back he moved with a predator's gait—purposefully, intent solely on his target. As he came to the doorway to the back room he paused, as if sensing something wrong.

"This should not be here," he said, more to himself than anyone else. Then he shrugged and walked through, confident that the person he was seeking would not lead him into a trap. Passing through the doorway, he turned and saw Bianca sitting to his right.

He smiled. "Bianca," he said softly and as she replied "Hunter" he grabbed her out of her seat and pulled her into him for an unsought but not unwelcomed hug. Their embrace was more than that of old friends and it went on for longer than either had expected, Bianca clearly feeling Hunter's excitement at their meeting. Herne, for his part, sensed that Bianca's excitement matched his own.

Finally, their embrace ended but with a promise that it would soon be renewed.

"You forgot to tell Sarge where I could find you."

"I didn't think I needed to."

"You were right. Your scent …"

There was a discrete cough. Her cheeks red with a rare blush, Bianca turned toward Morgan.

"Morgan, may I introduce …"

But Hunter was already lowering himself to one knee. "My Lord Morgan, it is an honor."

"Arise, Cernunnos, we are equal here, each of us answering only to the title of friend." Morgan then looked toward Bianca. "This is about the rake, isn't it?" At her nod, he said, "You made the right choice." And to himself he said, *And I understand why you did not want to involve your young man.*

Bianca then told Hunter about the rake.

"I've heard of them. The Academy offers advanced classes on cryptozoology—rakes, hyotes, snallygasters, dwayyo, and other such creatures. Some of these cryptids want only to be left alone, others hunt men even as they hunt other game. Some are easy to find, others less so. The rake is one of the latter, I'm afraid."

"Does that mean you cannot track him, Cernunnos?"

A look of wounded pride passed over the forest god's face before he answered, "Friend Morgan, I assure you that ever since my ascension I can hunt and find anyone, or anything. But I will need a starting point. Bianca, is there any physical evidence from this creature?"

"None that we found."

Hunter thought for a moment. "Then I will need to examine the body of the victim, and the homes he broke into."

Bianca nodded. "I'll need to go back to Headquarters and make the arrangements. We can start tomorrow. You stay here with Morgan and drink and tell each other lies. I'll meet you at my place later tonight. Do you need the address?"

Hunter just smiled.

Later that night, in Bianca's apartment, appetites of all kinds were satisfied. There was eating, drinking, and loving. Passions long-anticipated and delayed were expressed in many ways. It was well after midnight before the two were sated.

And now I know, Bianca thought as she lay in the arms of a sleeping god.

*

After breakfast, Bianca and Hunter went straight to the Medical Examiner's Office to meet with Dominic. The ME was taller than most men but still had to stare up to meet Hunter's eyes when Bianca introduced them. When he did, he recognized the god's spirit if not his name.

"Ogou!" he said in surprise.

"No, he works the Caribbean," Hunter said with a smile, "but I've shared drinks with him in a bar in Manhattan." Hunter pointed to his baseball cap. "If you're ever in New York, just follow the rainbow. Now then, where's the body?"

"In here."

"Here" was a small, refrigerated unit off to one side. It was where special cases were maintained—those not yet identified or were being held for further investigation. The rake's victim was both.

The body lay naked on a metal tray that was itself on a gurney. Despite the coolness of the air in the unit, decay had already begun. Hunter looked past this and the damage done to it and examined it and examined it carefully.

"I do not see, or sense anything but that which belongs to this unfortunate. If you were to take me to his murder scene, I could lead you to where he lived. But as for his killer, I sense nothing. However ..."

Hunter sighed, his breath coming out in a cold cloud. "Bianca, watch the door. Dominic, my new friend, you are not to speak of this to anyone."

"Understood, Hunter."

Slowly, Hunter took off his shirt. Standing bare-chested by the gurney, he took off his hat. Suddenly, many-pointed antlers grew from, no, appeared on his head, extending his height by at least two feet. Dominic, who in his youth had never been sure that gods truly existed, fought back the urge to kneel as Hunter faded and the god Herne appeared.

Watching from her place at the door, Bianca thought back to the night before and smiled. She had seen all this and more. *If Dominic only knew*, she thought.

This time it was Herne in his full aspect who examined the body. To his god's eyes, the victim glowed, the light reflecting the nature of the man he had been. It was mostly red and purple mixed with yellow and green.

Herne started at the feet, worked his way toward the head. The colors varied but did not change their basic pattern, that is, not until he focused his awareness on the chest cavity. On the left side, on the lowest rib, lowest rib, was a hint of black. Herne remembered this and moved on but did not find anything else like it on or in the body.

"Turn off the lights, Bianca," he said in a commanding voice, the one she had willingly obeyed several hours ago. She did and the room was lit only by the light of the body. Through his power Herne allowed Dominic to see through his eyes.

"That spot on the rib, that small piece of corruption. Do you see it, Dominic?"

"I do, Herne."

"Carefully take it, bottle it, and give it to me. For that is what I sought." And his face glowed with the success of his quest.

"Lights please, Bianca." By the time they came on, Herne had given way and was again Hunter, his shirt on and his antlers concealed with a baseball cap.

"What did you find?" Bianca asked Hunter after they thanked Dominic and left the morgue.

"As always, what I was looking for. During the attack, one of the rake's claws scraped against a rib. A tiny piece broke off. White against white, concealed by blood, it was all but impossible to find. It is not enough, but it tells me what I must look for. Now, if we have the time, take me to where this man died and I will take you to where he lived and maybe we can give him a name."

They had the time, and Hunter used what he had learned from the victim and the scene to find his home. Bianca called in the address and learned that a missing person report for Davis Powell had been filed four days ago by his wife Amelia.

"I hate this part," Bianca said as she and Hunter left their car and walked toward the house.

"Which part is that?"

"Notifications of deaths. 'Sorry for your loss' seems so inadequate."

The house, a single-family dwelling on West Rogers Avenue, had a nice lawn that was just short of needing mowing. There was a well-maintained fence around the property. The house itself was fronted by a large porch. It was the kind of home Bianca would have liked for herself one day. But she did not see herself living in such a house anytime soon. For that to happen, Baltimore would have to become a city free of the evils she now combated. And a house, no, a home like this required someone to share it with, a life partner. She thought of Hunter, he was not one to settle down with. Gods were mercurial and never settled down. Then she thought of Joe Russo and suddenly felt guilty about the previous night.

Hunter saw it a second or two before she did. Daily papers on the front porch, envelopes and circulars sticking out of the mailbox, the front door ajar. Bianca drew her pistol.

"Hunter, around back."

As he left her side she called it in. "5801, possible break-in at the home of a homicide victim." She gave the dispatcher the address. "This unit and a federal officer on the scene. Requesting back-up."

Drawing her pistol she went inside. There was movement behind her. Hunter came through the front door. "Back door locked," he told her. Then looking toward the stairs he said with sad certainty, "Front bedroom."

There was the sound of approaching sirens, patrol units responding. "You go up," Bianca told Hunter. "I'll talk to patrol."

The responding officers recognized Bianca—short cop, shorter temper, bad attitude. Unpleasant things happened to people who crossed her. But the word was that she was a good detective who broke cases no one else could and she had Command's ear.

"What's the problem, Detective Jones?" the uniformed sergeant asked.

Before she could answer they heard, "Federal agent coming out." Hunter appeared in the doorway and shook his head.

Without having to be told Bianca said, "Better call Homicide. Tell them they have a bad one."

Amelia Powel had suffered the same death as had her husband, sliced to death by a monster called the rake. Of the officers who viewed the body, only the sergeant was able to remain in the bedroom and he stood by the door facing out.

"So who called in the missing person report?" Bianca asked.

"She did," Hunter replied. "Her body's fresh, dead less than twelve hours." As the Lord of the Hunt, he would know. "The rake did the same thing we did. Tracked its first victim back home to choose its next victim."

"Damn. Sergeant?"

"Yes, Detective?"

She handed him her card. "Tell homicide that Agent Hunter and I had to leave due to an emergency. They'll have our report by tomorrow, maybe."

"Begging your pardon, Detective but you found the body. You're supposed to remain on the scene." Bianca then gave the sergeant the look she used when staring down demons and other such creatures. He paled and said, "But I'll give them your message when they get here."

Bianca and Hunter quickly fled the scene, Bianca driving much too fast with one hand while working the radio with the other. Using authority she did not have, she commanded the dispatcher to send Quick Response teams to surround and protect the homes of the families who had reported the ghost burglaries with orders to shoot any "milk-white naked men with extremely long fingernails. And tell them to keep shooting it until it's library paste or they run out of ammo."

To Hunter, she said, "Did you get anything from her?"

Knowing what she meant, the god replied, "More than I had. I have a better sense of him but not enough to track him."

"That's what I thought." She sped up. Hunter's view out the side window blurred.

"Where are we going?" he asked, silently wondering if they would arrive in one piece.

"To the scene of the first sighting. I'm hoping a little child can lead us."

*

Children responded well to Bianca, mostly because her small size made her seem less like an adult but also because she listened to them and took what they said seriously. So it was that Emma Ryder happily explained once again what the ghost looked like and exactly where he sat on her bed. This while her parents worried about all the attention the police were paying to their daughter and why armed men were standing guard outside her house.

"Are we in any danger?" Mr. Ryder asked when Bianca and Hunter appeared at their front door accompanied by four officers wearing tactical gear—two for the front and two for the back of the house.

"Just a precaution," Bianca lied smoothly, seeing no reason to upset the Ryders any more than they were. "We've received information that the 'ghost' Emma saw may be less than friendly. So until he's caught, we want to make sure that you two and Emma are protected."

"Are you going to put the ghost in a proton pack?" Emma asked as she showed Bianca and Hunter around her room, introducing them to Felicity and her other dolls.

"Don't worry, Emma, we're going to put him someplace safe," Bianca told the child.

Back in the car, Bianca asked Hunter. "Did you get what you need?"

"I could use more, but yes, I've got what I need. Let the hunt begin."

As Hunter said this, Bianca could see his Herne aspect coming to the fore. His eyes shone and he appeared to grow larger. An animal musk filled the car, one similar to but different than the one the detective had smelled last night.

As Hunter's excitement grew, Bianca remembered something he had told her back in the DMA Academy, "The chase is the best part of the hunt."

A hunter herself, Bianca understood this. There were the clues, the discovery, the identification of the quarry. Then came the rush, the adrenaline charge as the pursuit began, the thrill when the quarry was brought down. Then, of course, came the inevitable letdown, for the thrill and its afterglow never lasted as long as it should. Then everything was different.

Like last night, she thought as she started the car and began following Hunter's directions.

There's no emergency, Bianca told herself as she slowed down to better listen to Hunter. *It's a predator that hunts by night. It fed last night. There's no rush.*

Her eyes on the road, Hunter's words in her ears. "Turn here … Straight for a few blocks … Take a right, now a left … Bear right, down this ramp."

Bianca knew this area. South of Hampden and the Avenue. The abandoned buildings off Clipper Mill fronting the Jones Falls. There had been talk of redevelopment but for now it was derelict factories and an old roadhouse from the 1940s. A good place to dump bodies, and a better place for a monster to bring one for a late-night snack.

"It's getting dark," Bianca observed as she parked the car outside the roadhouse.

Hunter smiled. "Makes for a better hunt."

Bianca and Hunter got out of the car. She was carrying a Mossberg 500 shotgun with a flashlight strapped to its underside. Hunter was armed with a pistol containing incendiary cartridges.

The roadhouse showed all the signs of its advanced age. Animal scat surrounded it. From inside came the odor of death and decay. Slats covering the windows had broken free and were hanging from rusty a rusty nail or two. Of the grand double doors that had once welcomed patrons, one was hanging on its hinges and the other was missing.

"Is it inside?" Bianca asked.

Hunter nodded, then removed his shirt and cap. "No reason to take any chances," the god-man said.

Slowly the two approached the front entrance. Herne took point.

"Wait," Bianca said, taking something from her pocket. "A flashbang. This monster is nocturnal, this will slow it down."

"Good idea."

Then from the corner of her eye, Bianca saw a white shape emerge from the nearby factory. It was as tall as Herne and much faster than she had expected. It rushed toward them, "Herne, behind you," she shouted. He turned but not in time to prevent the rake from reaching him. Had Herne been human, its claws would have been his end. With the speed of a god he pulled away, but not before the long claws cut him on his gun side.

Herne dropped his pistol, but he did not need mortal weapons to face this monster. He lowered his head, and antlers locked with claws.

For what seemed like hours but which was only minutes, they stood there seemingly frozen. They struggled and strained, the rake trying to free its claws, the god shifting to catch them even as they slipped and cut into his antlers. Finally, the rake freed one arm and would have plunged his blades into the hunter but then,

"Hey ugly!"

Bianca did not wait for it to turn. She pulled the trigger of the shotgun. The rake's head disappeared and its body collapsed before the tips of its claws could reach Herne's abdomen.

Covered in monster blood and brains, they looked at each other and smiled. It was the climax of the hunt and they were feeling it even as they felt the ones they had shared the night before.

"You cut that rather fine," Herne said.

"It would have cut you finer," Bianca replied indicating their fallen quarry. "Then, why did you think it was in the … Dammit!"

Without waiting for Herne, Bianca ran toward the roadhouse. Kicking down the remaining door, she swept the large, main room with her gun and its light.

Had it been any color but milky white she would have missed it, but there it was in a corner. Beside it were two sets of remains, both were clearly human but whether male or female would be up to Dominic. The rake itself stood in front of the fresher body. It was no larger than Emma Ryder and was covered in the blood and gore of the host from which it had emerged.

Newly born into this world it first blinked at the light then it smiled and waved at Bianca. She easily resisted the urge to wave back.

"This is our chance to capture and study one," came Hunter's voice from behind her.

"Yeah, right," Bianca said then turned the light on the rake and, when it blinked, fired twice, spattering it over a back wall.

"The DMA can have the other one after Dominic finishes with it."

"I was going to call a recovery team."

Bianca shook her head. "My city, my monster, my kill, my body."

Bianca called it in. Then, like with Amelia Powell, she left when patrol arrived, promising to send Homicide her report in the morning. That, with Dominic's help, would give her time to come up with an explanation of events that did not involve monsters.

On the way back, Bianca said, "You can clean up in my apartment before you go. I'm sure Sarge will be waiting for your report. There's at least one more rake out there and you're now the DMA's expert on him."

"What makes you think there's not another one in Baltimore?"

"If there were you would have sensed two diverse trails."

"Makes sense, but why call it 'he'?"

"He came into town, made some babies, and left without a trace. Of course it's a male."

They were quiet for the rest of the ride. When they were almost back at Bianca's apartment, "Bianca." Hunter's voice was sweet and seductive, "Earlier you said something about your body …"

Keeping her eyes on the road Bianca replied, "Hunter, back in the academy you said that the chase was the best part of the hunt. We've had our chase, we caught our quarries. Let's leave things at that. Two successful hunts."

"Two, but there was only one … oh." He was quiet for just a moment. "You're probably right."

"I usually am," she said.

THE WILD HUNT

It was in the time of good King Henry, when Anne Boleyn was queen but before we started slaughtering monks and killing good men like Bishop John Fisher and Thomas More. Although, to be an honest fool, the latter did nothing to discourage his martyrdom, perhaps seeing it as a shortcut to Heaven. But on this day More and the others were alive and well, and it may be that more would be alive had they just signed the Act with one hand and crossed their fingers with the other. But Thomas did not, as so More became less by a head.

But on the day in question, all were alive. His Majesty was on the hunt in Windsor Woods, looking to bring home a stag or a boar. Many were hoping for a stag, since there were already too many bores at court. The hunting party was made up of the favoured members of his court, including myself, Charles Brandon, Thomas Boleyn, Doctor William Butts, and the royal magician Gregory Absalom. The ladies of the Court stayed behind, no doubt seeking their own favoured members among those courtiers who remained.

It was Absalom's duty to summon the game for Henry and his party so it may be pursued and slain. However, his magic, which he disguised as prayers to avoid confrontation with Cardinal Wolsey, worked too well that day. A marvelous stag almost immediately sprang from the woods, one with horns more impressive than those Henry had placed on many a husband's head.

The stag was sighted and the horn was blown, but before the King's party could advance and give chase, the stag rushed forward, straight towards the King.

So fleet was the beast that Henry had no chance of escape. Anne would have been left a widow and would have kept her head but for the actions of one of the gamesmen. This man, call him Robert Horne, interposed himself between his king and the stag, thus drawing the beast's attention and saving His Majesty. But alas for Horne, he was trampled by the stag and sorely gored by its antlers.

As many men and some women would be in the years that followed, the stag was executed for the sin of following its nature. It was quickly brought down by crossbow and flintlock. The king, as was his right and duty, administered the fatal blow with his lance. With the beast dead, Henry turned his attention to the brave man who had saved his life.

"Butts," Henry called from his horse, "save that man for he saved both us and England."

And indeed he had, for Henry had no male heir. There is no doubt that the surviving Plantagenets would have arisen and plunged the country back into civil war.

Doctor Butts has already unhorsed and rushed toward the fallen man. He knelt at Horne's side but one look at the wounds told the physician that his skills would be to no avail.

Butts stood, looked toward the king, and shook his head. "There is nothing I can do, Your Majesty."

"The man is useless, Butts by name and an ass by nature," Henry uttered quietly to Suffolk. (A jest he stole from me, I should add. But Henry was king and like all kings, could steal with impunity.)

Then Henry shouted out, "Absalom. Do what you must but save that man."

Riding up to the king, the magician said, "Your Majesty, I don't think ..."

"Your duty, Absalom, is not to think but to obey. Now use your arts to save him or I shall turn you over to Wosley's mercy, and you well know that the cardinal has none when it comes to your sort. And for good measure, he can have Butts as well."

"Very well, Your Majesty, but I must ask that all save yourself depart from here for what I must do is not meant for most men's eyes."

With a "Speak not of this to anyone," Henry ordered us gone and when we had departed he stood by the fallen Horne while Absalom knelt at the man's side.

"There is still the breath of life in him, Your Majesty."

"Then fan that breath into a healing flame that will revive him, good magician."

What spells and incantations the sorcerer Absalom chanted over the one called Horne no one knows. Nor was the knowledge of what potions and oils he applied to the man's body passed down. What is known is that there came a time when he said to the king,

"If Your Majesty will, cut the antlers from the stag and bring them to me."

"Can you not ..."

"It must be done by the hand that slew the beast, Your Majesty."

So Henry cut the antlers from the stag and gave them to Absalom, who placed them on the head of the fallen man.

"Now, Your Majesty, place your hands upon this man and invoke your royal power of healing, for it is only right that you save the life of the one who saved yours."

And so the king did, and although he prayed to the Almighty that the man be healed, it was another power that heard him. Cernunnos, the god of beasts and wild places, entered into Robert Horne and claimed him as his own.

Slowly, the one called Horne opened his eyes. On seeing the king kneeling beside him, he quickly got to his feet, as did the king. Then it was Horne's turn to kneel, his last human act.

"Rise, man, so we can properly reward you for saving our life."

Rise he did and in doing so grew until he was taller than Henry. His antlers, which were now a part of him, made him seem even taller.

"Robert Horne is gone, Henry Tudor, and in his place stands Herne, Lord of the Forest and Master of the Wild Hunt. Do not venture here again, lest you and yours become the hunted."

And with that, the newly crowned Herne the Hunter turned from the king and claimed the wild places as his own.

All this I know this because while I made to depart that day at the king's command I circled round and hid myself to as to witness what foul deeds might be done. And thanks be to St. Genesius that I was not caught doing so, not by king or magician, although the Horned One did glance my way and smile.

Never again did I enter that forest, and thank God and Genesius for that, for some who did so did not return and those who survived swore that they heard the baying of hounds and the galloping of horses as the Wild Hunt passed them by.

from the diary of Will Sommers, the Tudors' Fool

*

"My dear Bianca, I am in need of your help. I will be in Baltimore in three days. It will be good to see you again. H."

Bianca's first thoughts on receiving the note from Hunter was of a case years ago, of a hunt for a creature that should not have existed, and of a night of passion that should not have happened. Her next thought was, *I have to tell Joe.*

Neither Bianca Jones nor her husband and lover Joe Russo had ever discussed their past affairs with each other. Neither had been an innocent when they first physically expressed their love in Ocean City but then, as now, they cared only for the present and looked forward to the future. But a part of Bianca's past was now going to intrude into her life and Herne the Hunter was many things, but discrete was not one of them.

That night, after dinner but before going to bed, Bianca showed the note to Joe. He read it calmly then said, "From the antlers growing out of the H I'd guess that this is from … Herne the Hunter? You know him from the DMA Academy, don't you, Bianca? Do you know what he wants?"

Bianca shook her head. "No idea, but Joe, Hunter and I were once … close, physically close. But only once."

Bianca watched as pain, disappointment, worry, a bit of anger, and, finally, resignation quickly passed over Joe's face. "When was this?" he asked, his voice as calm as he could make it.

"It was during a case. After the academy but before Ocean City." She smiled at the memory of her and Joe's first time together and was pleased to see that he did too.

"Then it's in past. When Hunter arrives we'll give him what help he needs."

"I'm glad you understand, Joe."

"Of course I understand. Why wouldn't I? We love and trust each other. Besides, if need be, I know how to kill a god. Now let's go to bed."

It was early yet but neither cared about that. Once in bed, they expressed their love for each other over and over until sleep and satisfaction claimed them.

*

It is said that in the time of Arthur there was a beast that was much pursued but could never be captured. Until it was, of course, but that came much later, in the last of the days that came before the awakening of arts and science. It happened before Richard charged Henry, lost his crown and his life, and was buried in a quiet, unmarked grave.

But while such a beast may finally be caught and killed the idea of it can never fully pass from the minds and tales of men, and so it continues on, brought into being time and again by the curse that first formed it and nurtured by stories and belief.

The Beast returned after the second Catherine lost her head over Culpepper. Since then, it is said that at night the countryside echoes with the baying of dark hounds and the sounds of horses as the Wild Hunt rides in its eternal quest of the Beast, which, or so it is said, can only be captured by one as powerful as it is.

from the diary of Will Sommers, the Tudors' Fool

*

It was in the mid-1760s. He had been a member of the family Chastel when he learned of his fate, that he was forever damned to be pursued but never captured, not until he was found by one like himself. But unlike the ones who came before him, he was more or less mortal and so was compelled to do those things that would cause him to be pursued.

For him, disowned by his family who purged his name from their history, the Curse of the Beast proved a blessing. He was born with an urge to kill, and so kill he did, knowing that he would not be punished for he could not be caught. For years he terrorized the region of *Le Gévaudan* until he grew bored and moved on. He later learned that to preserve what little honor his family had left, Jean Chastel killed a striped hyena and declared it "the Beast."

He killed throughout the continent and into Egypt and Asia. Always pursued, never caught. He was, for a time, Fantômas. He bedeviled the consulting detectives of England, and when he tired of that, terrorized London as he ripped his way through Whitechapel. He was Nikola, the Opera Ghost, or whomever he had to be to get the authorities to pursue him. And when he grew bored with Europe, he took ship to America.

He liked it, the thrill of taking lives, of being the hunter even while being hunted. He would kill just so many, enough to put the authorities on his scent, then move on. Sometimes he would remain in the area just long enough for them to almost catch him, but like Houdini, he would always escape. It was in his nature.

So he killed, varying his methods, his patterns, his choice of victims. He would leave clues or mail codes or letters to the media. Or not, as the mood struck him. There were times when he needed a rest, and so would settle in an area for a time, killing only once or twice a year, just often enough for the police to keep searching for him as so satisfy the curse. Eventually, though, they would give up or arrest the wrong man and the hunt would be over. Then he would move on and begin again somewhere else.

But now he sensed a challenger, a foe that was older than his curse. A hunter, no, The Hunter, who had pursued the spirit of what he was centuries ago and who was once again aware of him.

That was good. He was getting tired of the old game. It was time for a new one. He had killed many men and women. Now it was time to kill a god. Why not? He was the Questing Beast and could never be caught for there was none like him.

*

Hunter flew into the Baltimore area in a private plane that landed at Martin State Airport in Middle River. From there he drove a rented car into the city. He was very much looking forward to again seeing Bianca Jones.

Once in Baltimore, he lowered his windows so as to find her. He searched for her by scent. He could never forget how nice it was when he first met her, and how she smelled when she was on the hunt or in bed with him.

It should have been easy, just a few particles of odorants was all he needed, even in a city of almost 100 square miles. But he could sense no trace of her. He drove around but—nothing. How, why? She had known he was coming.

He got on I-695, the interstate that encircled the city and drove its full circumference. Still nothing.

I should call, he thought. *The BPD will know where she is. But how would that look if word got out?*

Desperate, he drove to one of the two places where they had met years ago. First, her apartment, the scene of a very pleasurable night. *If she's still there …*

But she wasn't, only traces from long ago remained. That left the bookstore.

Joe Russo was busy stocking and rearranging books—mysteries with mysteries and biographies with biographies. He wondered briefly if he should separate the fantasy and science fiction sections but decided to leave things as they were. He was looking at a book written by a former member of the Baltimore City Council and was thinking, *There are lies, damned lies, and the memoirs of politicians* when the front door opened.

Joe looked up. He knew the man although they had never met. Bianca had described him perfectly. The man was tall, good-looking, and wearing an Orioles baseball cap.

I should be jealous, Joe thought. *But then why? She loves me and not him. Might as well start off friendly.* "Greetings, Herne."

"You know me?" Hunter asked in surprise.

Joe nodded. "I know of you. Bianca told me you were coming."

Now he looked confused. "Bianca's in the city?" Then, more to himself than Joe, "Strange that I can't sense her."

"There's a reason for that," Joe explained. "Bianca's done a lot for this city. She's risked her life for it again and again. She protects it and in turn, the Spirit of Baltimore protects her as best it can." Joe smiled. "No one can easily find her—not demons, not angels, not even gods."

There was slight anger in Hunter's voice when he said, "I don't know who you are, but you say that you know me. So you know that as the God of the Hunt I can find anyone. And if I want to find Bianca I will. I need her help." His voice softened. "And I hope to renew our personal relationship." The smile Hunter gave Joe left no doubt as to what that relationship was or how he intended to renew it.

Joe smiled back. "I'm just a bookseller and heir to the mission of Morgan. I'm also Bianca's husband."

"I didn't know that she had married. Not that that matters. I am Herne, and I always get what I go after."

Joe ignored the smirk on Hunter's face. "As I said, Herne, I am Morgan's heir. And as such, I am guardian to the books he left me." Joe went into the back, came out with an old book. "This is the journal of Will Sommers, the Tudors' Fool. It is written in his own hand. The copies that were made from it changed certain names. This book," Joe held it up, "contains true names."

Joe reshelved the book. He came back with a slip of paper and handed it to Hunter. "Do I make myself clear, 'Robert Horne'?"

Hunter looked at the name written on the paper. It was not "Robert Horne." It was instead a name Hunter had not been called since before he was trampled and gored by a stag. He paused and thought for a moment. Finally, he quietly said, "Very clear, eh, how shall I call you?"

"Call me 'Joe.' Now would you like me to tell you where Bianca is?"

"Yes, please."

*

On his way to the house that was the headquarters of the Freak Show, Hunter talked to himself. "I swear that I do not know why I said what I did to him. I swear that I did not know that Joe was her husband. I swear I did not even know she was married. And I swear that when I get back to the DMA, I am going to punch Karver in the face for not telling me. No wonder he was smiling when he wished me, 'Good luck in Baltimore.' Karver hardly ever smiles. I should have known something was up."

Hunter had his car windows opened just enough to allow air to circulate. He was still hoping to pick up a trace of Bianca. She might not be where Joe said she was. He was, after all, Bianca's husband and so had reason to misdirect him. *That's what I'd do*, Hunter thought.

But then another scent wafted through the air. It was new to Hunter, but it wakened ancient memories. Memories of riding with the hounds through Windsor Forest at the head of the Hunt, in pursuit of that which could be found but not caught.

How could this be? After 100 years both hunter and hunted had tired of the game and moved on. He later heard that a knight of the Crescent had done what he could not do, brought down the Beast and with the help of his version of the One God. Hunter remembered feeling jealous at the knight's accomplishment and consoling himself with the fact that the man had cheated by calling in an outside expert.

Isn't that what I'm doing now? The man-god asked himself as he turned the car, circling one block than another as he tried to determine the direction from which the scent was coming.

Yes, it is, he admitted, *but I'm much older and a little wiser now. Besides, my association with the DMA has taught me how to play well with others. And speaking of playing, I wonder if Bianca is as married as Joe thinks she is. After all, what he doesn't know won't hurt him. But if he finds out, I could find myself fully mortal again.*

Hunter considered the consequences of the many actions he could take and decided that his past relationship with Bianca Jones would remain in the past, just a pleasant memory. After all, there were plenty of other women in the world.

But damned few who were able to ...

He broke off this thought as he caught the essence of his quarry. That it was his quarry he had no doubt. A new scent, a different body but this he knew and had expected it. But he had not expected the spirit of the Beast to remain in a tangible form, a detectible ghost in the machine as it were.

Hunter was torn. Should he continue to the headquarters of, what did Joe call it, the Extranormal Investigative Unit and enlist Bianca's help? Having "tasted" it, he could always pick up the scent again with her and her team at his side. Or should he follow the trail, confront the Beast, and bring it down himself? He felt he could. Wasn't he a god, one that had grown in power over the centuries? Had he not fought greater foes than the Beast? How nice it would be to drive up to the Extranormal Investigative Unit with his kill in the trunk and say to Bianca,

"I thought I needed you but I did the job myself. Congratulations on your marriage. I'm sure we'll meet again. Just remember, we'll always have the rake."

With this in mind, he turned his car in the direction of the scent.

He drove where the scent, where the urge, where the certainty led him. His search took him from southeast Baltimore, through the city, and into its western part. He found himself on Windsor Mill Road and took this for a sign, especially since it would take him through a large, wooded area with the odd name of Leakin Park.

Windsor, a forest, it began there and it will end here. As it was, so let it be.

With that thought, Hunter followed the road until he could go no further. It was blocked. There were a parking lot and a turn-around to his left. A large sign in front of him read, "Road closed for repairs."

Hunter parked and got out of his car. The scent led into the forest anyway, as it should. He would continue on foot. No, not on foot but on hoof. He took off his hat, his shirt, and his shoes. He grew in size. Antlers appeared on his head as his full power emerged. Hunter no more, he was Herne. As he entered the woods, Herne sensed spirits gather around him. They were the dead, he realized, murder victims who had been dumped in the woods. Some had been found and had been given the proper rites. Others remained undiscovered, their bodies still buried deep. None of these had moved on, their thirst for justice and vengeance keeping them on this plane.

He dismissed them all. He was not here for them. Picking up the scent of his quarry, he followed its trail thinking, *Let the Beast feel the true power of the Stag God.*

*

After Hunter left the bookstore, Joe called Bianca.

"You were right. He came here. He's on his way to you now."

"What story did you give him?"

"The one about the spirit of Baltimore protecting you. He seemed to have believed it."

"Well, that was better than him finding out that, after the last time and without telling me, Morgan put some kind of ward on me to keep me from being tracked by people like Herne. How did you find out about it?"

"I think Herne stopped being 'people' centuries ago. Anyway, Morgan had left notes in a jester's journal about it."

Ninety minutes later, Bianca called the bookstore.

"Hunter isn't here yet. You didn't give him the wrong directions accidentally on purpose did you?"

"You know me, Bianca. I only lie in a good cause. I may have threatened his immortality but I didn't lie to him."

"He should have been here by now. Given his nature, he would not have gotten lost. That can only mean one thing, Joe."

"Yeah, I know. I'm on my way, Bianca."

"I'll call Tavon and ask him to bring Millie."

"What about Beth?"

"She's on that serial killer task force. They just found the fourth body floating near Middle Branch Trail. A lot of knife work but nothing for us, she says. She'll be busy with that."

When Joe arrived at Freak Show headquarters, Hunter still had not arrived. Tavon Greggs and Millie the were-Yorkie were with Bianca in her office.

"Any word?" Joe asked Bianca.

"None. I put a citywide description out on him in his usual form. And we'd get a call if anyone reported finding an eight-foot-tall man with antlers. Something's happened to him."

Joe found himself wondering if there was more than just the ordinary tone of concern in Bianca's voice for a colleague who might be in danger. *She cared for him once*, he told himself. *It would be natural.* Then he shook this thought away and asked, "Did he tell you why he was coming? That would be the place to start."

Bianca shook her head. "Just that he would be here today and he needed my help. If he doesn't show up or we don't find him soon I'll call the DMA and ask what he was working on. They may or may not tell me. You know what they're like."

"I know this Herne," Lieutenant Greggs said. "I met him at the DMA Academy. He worked with Millie and the other were-beasts with their tracking. She followed his scent a few times in training. She's no bloodhound but if we knew where to start she might be able to find him. But we'd need something of his."

"All we have is the note. I don't think that's enough." Tavon shook his head in agreement.

"It might be, since it's written in his own hand and not printed out." Joe said. "but we'd need more. Tavon, would you and Millie excuse Bianca and me for a few minutes?"

Tavon Greggs was naturally a perceptive individual who was sensitive to people's moods. His work with Bianca and his training with the DMA had made him more so. Sensing that there was more to the situation than appeared, he said, "No problem. Millie needs to be walked anyway."

Tavon and Millie left. Joe closed the office door behind them. Placing a chair next to Bianca's desk he sat close to her.

"Bianca, I have to ask this. Do you have anything of Hunter's? Something from your past relationship?"

Joe's voice had been calm, steady, and devoid of emotion. Just from that Bianca knew it had hurt him to ask. You only keep things from people whom you were close to, who meant something to you, that might still mean something to you.

"Joe, it was one night." *One very long, intense night*, she thought but didn't say. "All I have from that night are memories. And they're mixed with the memories of the two of us hunting the rake. And those of killing the monster are stronger." *A white lie but in a good cause.*

"Bianca, before Ocean City I had girlfriends and loves, and although I love you more than anything, I still remember them fondly and can smile when I think about them, even the ones who dumped me. Which, to be honest, was all but one of them and the one who didn't dump me moved away. If we're to help Hunter, we need your memories."

Quietly, Bianca said, "What do I have to do?"

"Take out the note, hold it tight against you, and think about Hunter. Think of everything you know about him, everything you felt about him, even everything you did with him. But to yourself, please."

Bianca closed her eyes and did as Joe asked. He busied himself with some string and a paper clip. After about ten minutes she opened her eyes and let out a long breath.

"That brought back some powerful memories and feelings. When this is over and we're alone you just might be thanking him. What do we do now?"

Taking the paper from Bianca, Joe turned it over. Herne was a god, and gods could be summoned or, at least, traced. On the back of the note, Joe drew a few summoning runes, incorporating Latinized versions of all of the hunter's names, including the one that had not been spoken since King Henry's fateful hunt.

He returned the note to Bianca. "Make a paper airplane out of this."

"What are you going to do, fly it out the window and follow it?"

"No." He held up the string and paper clip. "That's what these are for."

With Bianca driving and Tavon and Millie in the back seat, Joe rode shotgun and watched the movements of a paper airplane that was hanging from the rearview mirror by a piece of string. With Bianca following her husband's directions, they soon found themselves on Hilton Parkway winding through Gwynns Falls Park.

Suddenly Joe recalled Will Sommer's journal and knew where they were going and why.

"Turn left on to Gwynns Falls Parkway," he told Bianca. "Follow that on to Windsor Mill Road."

"Through Leakin Park. Joe, will you be okay?" Bianca asked. Joe had once been shot and left for dead in that park.

"I'll be fine. That was years ago." *And besides*, he thought, *I beat you bastards. Even if you had killed me I still would have beaten you.*

They came to the same dead end as had Hunter. When they stopped, the paper plane turned and pointed into the woods.

Bianca had parked next to an out of state rental car. On its back seat were shoes and socks, a shirt, and the baseball cap Hunter had been wearing.

Another memory from the fool's diary, his story of an endless chase through the wild forest, and Joe knew who or rather, what Herne had been after.

"Take your shotgun, Bianca. And, Tavon, say Millie's trigger word now. If you find what Herne was after, or it finds you, there may not be time to say it then."

"What is it, Joe?" Tavon asked.

"The Questing Beast, only I don't think this one runs away."

"Right," Bianca said as she checked her sidearm then got her Mossberg 500 from the trunk, then loaded and checked it.

"Joe, when we go in, call for QRT backup," Tavon said after checking his own weapon and triggering Millie. "Tell them to bring the heavy stuff. When they get here, direct them in. Bianca, let's go."

Joe understood. A non-combatant, he'd be more hindrance than help in a fight. And so he stayed back and watched his love, his friend, and a pony-sized Yorkshire Terrier enter the woods, guided by a paper airplane.

*

That there had been a fight, a clash between two powerful forces, was clear. The ground was torn up. Trees had been partly uprooted. There was clothing, blood, and fur all about. And that was just at the scene of the initial meeting between the two ancient foes. The devastation led deep into the woods of Leakin Park, a trail so clearly marked that Joe's airplane was no longer needed.

Despite all this, the forest was eerily silent. Whatever had happened was over. There had been a winner and a loser, or maybe both had fallen and were now injured, dying, or dead.

Bianca wanted to rush forward to the end of the torn-up trail, to find her friend, to either save him, treat him, or mourn him. But she held back. That was not the way of the hunter. Move stealthily, approach quietly, do not alert your prey. With Millie on point, Bianca in the center, and Tavon watching the rear, they moved cautiously through the woods.

Millie was the first to find the body. Recognizing its scent from her training, she ran to the fallen figure of Herne.

He was lying unmoving beneath a tree. Bianca resisted the urge to run toward him. Herne might just be a Judas goat, left as bait for those that might follow. With Tavon and Millie on guard, she slowly and carefully approached the fallen god.

Herne's pants were in tatters. His body, now more beast than man, was broken and bleeding. A piece of antler had been torn away. He was still and did not appear to be breathing.

Bianca knelt by her friend. She felt his neck and breathed a sigh of relief when she found a pulse. It was weak but it was there. *But for how long*, she asked herself.

Tavon came up behind her. "Area seemed to be clear. Millie's still patrolling. She'll let us know if she finds anything. Although I don't know what she could do to something that can bring down Herne."

"Call her back, Tavon. If that beast is still out there we'll have a better chance together. Right now Hunter needs a doctor."

"Should we call DMA?"

Bianca shook her head. "I don't know if they'd get here in time." She thought for a minute, then got out her phone and called her husband.

"Joe, Hunter's down but alive. Cancel QRT then call for medical transport. Then call Dominic. Tell him to we'll need a room and privacy. We're bringing him a live one.

"Tavon, contact the district. Tell them we'll need Windsor Mill closed at Gwynn Falls. Tell them it's a Freak Show case and that no one is go into the woods. You and your team can bring Tammy Dolan out here tomorrow to see what she can find."

When Herne was carried down to the road and loaded into the ambulance it took a few minutes to convince the two paramedics that, yes, the Medical Examiner's was where he was to be taken.

"You sure about that, Lieutenant?" one medic asked. "'Cause he ain't dead. And it looks like he should be taken to a vet instead of the morgue."

The other medic winced. She'd heard stories about this small cop and from what she had her partner had just carried out of the woods it appeared that at least some of them were true. She knew that this Bianca Jones was quite capable of commandeering their ambo at gunpoint and driving this ... whatever it was, to the morgue herself. "Forgive him, Lieutenant," she said. "He's new and doesn't know how things work here in Charm City."

The ambulance sped off, the older medic telling the new guy the stories she had heard about the head of the Freak Show.

"Are you sure about Dominic?" Joe asked her as they headed for the ME's. They had taken Hunter's car, leaving hers for Tavon and Millie.

"He's the best chance we've got. He's got experience with the strange and interned with Shock Trauma."

"Well, I just hope he doesn't start an autopsy out of habit."

*

It was a tense few hours as Bianca's brother-by-choice Dominic Jones worked on Herne with Joe assisting. Bianca remained outside the room, scaring away the curious. Finally, the door opened and Dominic and Joe came out.

"He was already healing when you brought him in. I guess it's good to be a god. But he was severely beaten and cut several times. Some of them were deep. I stitched him up as best I could. He's still unconscious but I think he'll be okay. Would you like to see him?"

Cleaned and stitched up, Herne was already looking better than he had in the woods. He lay there naked and Bianca made a note to bring him some clothes.

Looking over her shoulder, Dominic said, "He certainly has an ... impressive physique." Herne did, his body was godlike in many ways. "As I said, I guess it's good to be a god."

Conscious of Joe standing next to her, Bianca said, "It's not the size of the wand but the magic within." Then, having arranged for a room in University Hospital and a guard, she and Joe drove home. On the way, all she said to her husband was, "You, Joe Russo, are an extremely skilled magician."

Joe blushed and smiled, then replied, "Who would be nothing without his lovely partner."

Bianca smiled back. She knew she was far from lovely, but when she was with Joe, he made her feel that way.

*

He found himself drifting, awake in a void. At first, he was aware, but that was all. He did not know his name, his nature, or his reason for being. Slowly he recalled himself.

He had been a hunter, a gamesman, a servant to the king. A king he had saved, a king he had died for. He was rewarded, and cursed, and blessed. He became something else, not a hunter but The Hunter.

He was a god, or had been. He was not sure if he was alive or dead. If dead, he hoped this was not Heaven. Maybe God had no use for minor deities. What was it He said? "Thou shalt not have strange gods before Me."

And I am a strange god. I have antlers and chase things. Well, at least I'm not Egyptian. Antlers are bad enough, I wouldn't want a stag's head.

I was chasing—something. Or it was chasing me. Either way, I caught it and it caught me. And hurt me, hurt me badly. If I hadn't already died once it would have killed me. I should have killed it. I was bigger and stronger. But no, it just laughed, and dodged, and when I did it hit it, it laughed and stabbed me again, and again, and again. And then it beat me, and beat me, and beat me.

Hell of a god I turned out to be.

The void faded and the blackness again took him.

When Hunter truly woke he found himself in a hospital bed. He was in a gown with tubes in his arm and elsewhere, putting fluids in and letting them out.

Something was beeping. He looked up, it was him, or rather, his monitor. He checked his vitals. Had he'd been human he would be dead (again). Good thing he was a god.

He lifted his cover and checked things out. Everything was there and hopefully still in working order. His head felt funny then he realized he was wearing … he reached up and felt it … a baseball cap. Good, the antlers were hidden.

Maybe they shouldn't be. Maybe if I take off the cap. No, better not.

Hunter tried to extend his senses, to learn exactly where he was. That made his head hurt. He decided he'd had enough exercise for one day and went back to sleep.

When he woke up he felt better, almost as good as new. The tubes were gone. There was no beeping. He was still wearing only a gown and his cap was still on his head.

And he was not alone. A small woman was standing just within his field of vision.

"You stood me up, Hunter. Don't you know that it's impolite to keep a lady waiting?"

Bianca Jones.

"Something came up." There was a joke there but he was too tired to go for it. Besides, her husband knew his true name. And he wasn't quite sure it would come up, not with having had that tube in.

"I know. And to save you the trouble of asking, you're in the secure ward of University Hospital. You're here because you got your godly ass kicked. Now get up and get dressed." Bianca pointed to a pile of clothes at the foot of the bed. "We've got work to do." She turned to leave the room.

"You don't have to leave. Nothing you haven't seen before."

"And there's nothing I want to see again."

"But I might need help getting dressed."

"If you do you're no use to me. Get moving, Hunter. We have a monster to catch."

*

Later that day, they met in the conference room of the Freak Show—Hunter, Tavon and Millie, and Bianca. Joe was also there but sat away from the others and listened.

"Tell us a story, Hunter."

"It's your fault, Bianca. The way you managed to ID Karver as the Carver using his DNA. That got some people thinking. There were others like him out there. So they created their own version of the Combined DNA Index System and started looking, first in this country and then in others. They found matching DNA of some killers they knew about and others they didn't. And they found—him.

"His profile appears all over this country and in Europe. Knowing this, the DMA got their pattern people and their psychics to work with the real evidence. They traced him back to the mid-eighteenth century in someplace called Gévaudan but at a cost. Two of the psychics quit. One went catatonic but not before shouting out, "The Questing Beast," before shutting down. He's better now, retired and on full pension and with carefully planted false memories.

"Someone got the idea that the ultimate hunter should go after the prey that could not be caught. So here I am."

"And why here? Why now?" Bianca asked then answered her own questions. "The serial killer Beth is working on. The second victim fought back and marked his killer. Bit him and shot him. The DNA profile generated from the killer's blood and skin cells were entered in CODIS."

"And hit in our database," Hunter said. "Your serial killer is the Questing Beast. And I don't know how you're going to stop him because I certainly can't."

Hunter fell silent. Bianca wanted to wait him out but finally said, "Tell us about it."

He shrugged. "It's like you said, Herne the Hunter got his ass kicked by his prey."

"It happens, Hunter," Tavon said. "So tell us what happened before you got your godlike ass kicked."

Hunter looked in the faces of those in the room—Bianca, Joe, Greggs, and a dog. No judgment from any of them. So Hunter put his shame aside and made his report.

*

I should have gone to Bianca. (Hunter said.) But when I caught his scent I followed it. I thought I could handle him. And when I found him in the woods I knew I could. He was just a man—white, thinning brown hair, medium height, medium build, a little overweight—and I was a god.

We were in a clearing when I caught up to him. On reflection, I think he may have been waiting for me.

Feeling that thrill that comes at the end of a hunt start to build, I smiled and said, "I found you, Beast."

He smiled back. "Finding me is one thing. Capturing me, killing me is another. You're not as strong as I am."

I remember smiling again and saying, "No, I'm stronger." Then I moved toward him.

And the next thing I remember is waking up in a hospital bed with tubes running in and out of me.

*

"So how do we stop him?" Bianca asked when Hunter had finished.

"You can't," the god replied. "It's his nature to be always pursued and but never caught. That must mean that he can counter any force that goes against him."

"Shotgun to the head would work," Tavon offered. "Better still, cut his damn head off with that sword Bianca has hanging in her office."

Hunter shook his head. "The gun would jam or the slug, pellets, or flechettes would be deflected. The sword would probably break."

"There's no problem in this world that can't be solved by a suitable application of high explosives," argued Tavon.

Hunter was about to say that it was worth a try when Bianca spoke up.

"He's not the first Questing Beast, is he? So how were the others defeated?"

Joe then spoke up from his chair in the back. "There were two others." With all eyes now on him, he went on.

"While Hunter was healing, I was busy in the bookshop and with Tammy at the Crime Lab. According to my books, the first Questing Beast was an Arthurian creature. It was a true beast, a chimera with the head and neck of a snake, a leopard's body, and the haunches of a lion. A geas placed on King Pellinore compelled him and his family to hunt it until it was caught. According to the *Chronicles of Seejay*, centuries later a knight of Scotia named Conor assisted the last remaining Pellinore in capturing the beast."

"Does it say how he did it?" Hunter asked.

"He's not clear. All Seejay wrote was that Conor defeated the beast 'not with a sword but with words.' Another beast arose after that. This one was taken by a Saracen knight who was a descendant of Sir Palamedes of the Round Table. Again, no details in any of the books I have, except that the Holy Grail might have been involved."

"So how does that help us?" Hunter asked. He was anxious, no, desperate to return to the hunt, to avenge his defeat, to reclaim his honor, but he was smart enough not to proceed without a plan. "There's no one here worthy of the Grail, and we don't know what words this Conor used. So what do we do? What do I do? Keep chasing him, trying to minimize the damage until one or both of us gets tired of the chase, as I did with the second beast when I led the Wild Hunt? No, this time I won't quit, and I'll bring this creature down if I have to strap on a bomb vest and blow myself and it to Hell. I don't see any other choice."

As Hunter raved, Bianca glances over at Joe. From the look on his face, she could tell that he was experiencing the same thrill that a hunter does when he's nearing the end of his hunt.

He knows, she thought, *he knows*. Then she recalled that there was a price to everything, especially magic, and worried because her husband was the kind of person who would willingly pay that price for the greater good.

"There is a way," Joe said calmly. He paused, enjoying the moment, then went on. "Hunter, tell us again what the Beast said to you just before you attacked him?"

"That I was not strong enough."

"No, his exact words."

"He said that 'You're not as strong as I am.'"

"In Will Sommers's diary, the fool said that the Beast can only be captured by one as powerful as it is. Not more powerful, not less powerful, but just as powerful."

"So how, Joe, do we find such a person?"

"You already found him, Hunter. The Beast himself." Reaching into his pocket, Joe pulled out an evidence envelope. Breaking its seal, he showed that it contained bloodstained swabs. "It's blood found on the Beast's second victim here in Baltimore. The Beast's blood," he explained.

"I don't need his blood to find him," Hunter protested. "After what he did to me, I will always know where he is." He closed his eyes and thought for a moment. "He is still in the park, waiting for me."

"The blood isn't to find him, Hunter. It's to kill him."

Hunter grew angry. "Don't you see, you foolish man, I can't kill him. All I can do is find him and fight him and be beaten by him. Maybe this time, or the next time, or the time after that, he'll manage to kill me. If so, I pray that the spirit of Cernunnos rises from my dead body and finishes the job. He probably created the Beast, let him destroy it."

"Bullshit."

Everyone looked at Bianca. When she was sure she had their attention, or at least Hunter's, she went on.

"What's happened to you, Hunter? I thought you were Herne, God of the Forest and leader of the Wild Hunt. Now you seem to be a despairing coward, god of those afraid. I can't believe that I once thought you worthy of my bed."

The angry god grew angrier. As he sprang from his chair to confront Bianca, Joe readied a dagger on which he had inscribed a certain name. But this was Bianca's play, and so he held back. She too knew how to kill a god.

"You cannot speak to me like that."

"I just did, now shut up and listen, or I swear I will snatch that cap from your head, rip off your antlers, and wear them myself. I've been a god once and if need be I will again. Besides, I wouldn't mind being two feet taller."

As god and mortal started each other down, Greggs unsnapped his holster. Millie began to grow even without her trigger word. Joe clutched his dagger.

Hunter blinked first. Smiling, he said, "I don't think Joe would mind a perpetually horny wife. It would probably kill him but what a way to go, going from one heaven to another." He sat back down, and after everyone breathed a sigh of relief, and Greggs snapped shut his holster, and Millie grew smaller, and Joe sheathed his dagger, Hunter asked, "So what's the plan?"

"Tonight," Bianca replied, "Herne will gather his strength and ready his bow. He will call up the spirits of the vengeful dead and at his command, the Wild Hunt will ride through Leakin Park."

*

It was night, the only time for such a hunt. A half-moon hung in a cloudless sky. Bianca was in place, Joe's prayers and the sword named Tromluí with her.

"I'd feel better if you had your shotgun," he had told her. Actually, he would have felt better if she were not involved at all.

Bianca shook her head. "Shotguns have no place in this, Joe. Tonight's the night for the old ways."

"Just don't get naked and paint yourself with woad."

She smiled. "Maybe later, if you're good."

So Joe sat in his car in the parking area while Tavon and Millie stood in a clearing with Herne. He was the old god now, in his old form. Easily nine feet tall, more beast than man, and like a beast, he was clothed in only what nature had provided.

His mind searched for and found his foe waiting for him a few miles away. The thrill of the chase ran through him. It was a feeling he had not felt for hundreds of years.

It has been too long, the god thought and with this thought he loudly proclaimed,

"Attend me, creatures of the wood. Hear me, spirits who seek vengeance. I am Herne, Lord of Forest, and I summon you. Tonight is our time. Take what forms you will on this night of the Wild Hunt."

There was the baying of hounds as stray and wild dogs obeyed Herne's summons. House pets whined and barked until their owners sent them outdoors where they pushed open gates, leaped fences, and ignored the pain of electric barriers to answer the call with their wild cousins. Coyotes, fox, a few wolves, and even a hyote who lived undetected in the woods joined in.

Herne had his pack.

An antlered buck appeared with his does. Approaching his lord, he bowed his head in honor and submission. *Tonight*, the forest god sent, *we are the hunters*. The deer stood by his side.

Herne had his attendants.

The spirits of the dead, those that were killed and left in the park, awakened and arose. As Herne had commanded, they abandoned their human forms and took the shape of beasts. Tigers, lions, bears, boars, and rams. There were also dragons, unicorns, dway, and the like. They gathered in the rear, behind the pack, awaiting the word.

Herne had his hunters.

We are coming for you, you bastard. Herne sent this thought to the Beast, hoping it would be heard. *Let him be afraid. Let this succeed*, he prayed to the God that was greater than he, adding, *and please keep Bianca safe*. Adjusting the strap of the quiver that hung on his back,

Herne raised his bow and shouted to his wild ones.

"Let the hunt begin!"

Millie whined and looked up at Greggs. He knew what she wanted. Unable to join in himself, he could not deny her.

"Oh, okay. Talbot."

At the trigger word, the one-foot, six-pound dog was suddenly three-foot tall and 160 pounds. Yelping in delight, she ran to the head of the pack. A few growls established the were-Yorkie as the alpha and, at Herne's command, she led them into the woods.

*

He heard Herne's *We are coming for you, you bastard* in his head before his ears picked up the baying of the pack and assorted growls, roars, and other noises from Herne's hunters. The spirit of the ancient beast that was inside him knew these sounds, it remembered them from centuries ago and was afraid. But he that was now the Beast dismissed them.

Let them come, he said to himself. *They can't hurt me. They can't be as strong as me.*

Yes, said the spirit within him. *But while one is not enough and all are too many, just a few may prove to be your equal. Run, and keep running until the coming dawn banishes the Wild Hunt.*

So he ran. He fled south, hoping to leave the park and go east on Franklintown Road and into the city. Millie and her pack cut him off and chased him past the sports fields and nature center, and across Windsor Mill Road. He ran north and west, hoping to escape through the grounds of the maintenance yard, but the cries, growls, and roars of the hunters drove him back into the woods.

His pursuers drew closer, the pack and the hunters merging to encircle him, leaving him only a small arc through which to escape. He was driven north, towards Wetheredsville Road and a maze of apartment buildings where he could perhaps hide and wait for the day.

He was almost there, the hunters and dogs behind him. From the path he was on he could see the road through a clearing.

Safe, said the ancient spirit, *soon we will be safe. For the Hunt may not leave the forest and should its leader pursue, he is not as powerful as we are.*

This thought and his fear drove him on. He was almost at the clearing. The way to freedom was on the other side. One more burst of speed.

Then *she* stepped onto the path and blocked his way.

She was a small woman, dressed in hunter's camouflage. Her head was uncovered. On her face was a predator's smile and in her hand a sword with a crimson tip. The Beast halted and as he did, realized that the hunters and the pack were silent. They had done their job; he was now where he was supposed to be. They waited, blocking his retreat, as he faced his final test.

"You are not Herne," The Beast said to the woman.

"He had his chance," Bianca replied. Then, using the name she had taken in Eire, "I am Bán, and I am your doom."

The Beast laughed. "You are not as strong as me. That sword will do you no good."

Bianca's smile grew wider. "I am as strong as I need to be. As for my sword, like me, it is just a distraction."

Before the Beast could think the word *trap* there was the twang of a bowstring, the whoosh of an arrow, and a thock as that arrow embedded itself in the back of the Beast. Three more arrows followed, and then another two, each shot perfectly placed.

The Beast moaned, wavered on his feet, then fell forward and lay still. From the trees, the pack and the hunters waited for word from their master and when it was given, rushed forward and savaged the body. They were not called off until there was little left of the Questing Beast.

Putting aside his bow, Herne called "Enough. The Hunt is over." With this the pack dispersed. Those that had homes went to them, but, having tasted the wild life, were no longer the calm, domesticated pets they had been. They were now guardians, protective of their territory, and woe to anyone or anything that threatened their homes or families.

Millie went to find Tavon. Her adventure at an end, she shrank down to her natural size and looked expectantly at her partner and friend as if to say, *I was a good dog. I need a treat.* And so she got one.

Most of the stray and wild dogs, along with the coyotes, fox, wolves, and the hyote returned to wherever they had been before Herne's summons. Most. Just as most of the spirits of the dead, their need for vengeance having been slaked, moved from this plane to whatever fate awaited them.

The small herd of deer again paid homage to their lord and disappeared into the woods, no longer easy prey for would-be hunters.

Bianca and Herne stood alone over what remained of the Questing Beast. Herne was still in bestial form. Bianca tried to ignore his obvious exictment.

"The Beast's blood on the tips of the arrows," Herne said, "I would not have thought of that."

"Only the Beast was as powerful as the Beast," Bianca replied.

"Your husband was right."

"He usually is," Bianca replied.

There was one thing left to do. Dipping their hands into the blood of the Beast, they smeared it on each other's face.

Looking down at the remains, Bianca said, "I'll have Tammy Dolan come out and recover what she can from—this. We'll need some evidence so that Homicide can close their serial murder case. You can stay behind and meet her." It took a moment before Herne realized that this was an order and not a request. Then Bianca added, "And put on some clothes. She won't be impressed."

"No?"

"Not even a little bit. Now, if you were Diana ..."

"Ah, I see. Oh well. Does she at least have a sister?"

Bianca scooped up some more blood, left Herne with his kill, and walked out to meet Joe. Before he could react to the blood on her she smeared his face with what was in her hand.

"It was your kill too," she explained.

"And now what?" Joe asked.

"What do you think?"

The two smiled at each other, then they rushed home where they released the built-up passions of the hunt and washed the blood off in the morning.

*

"Leakin Park is likely to be haunted," Hunter told those who had gathered at Clancy's Pour House the following night to celebrate the end of a successful case. "Some of the Hunt remained behind. Those woods will no longer be a safe place for those with ill intent."

"So no more bodies in the park?" Tammy Dolan asked. Bianca had been right. Tammy had not been impressed with Herne, paying more attention to what remained of the Beast than to him.

Hunter shrugged. "I didn't say that. The Hunt may occasionally leave one or two behind as a warning to others."

Homicide Detective Bethany Steele came in. At first, she was mad because she had missed the hunt. Then she forgave them all when she learned that she'd officially get the credit for closing the serial killer case.

"Of course," Tavon said, "that means you buy the next round."

Drinks were poured. Pub food was eaten. The celebration went on.

Tavon was the first to leave, shortly followed by Beth and Tammy. That left Hunter, Bianca, and Joe.

"We need to talk," Bianca said to Hunter.

"Those words are never followed by good news," he replied. "Okay, let's have it."

Joe went first, handing Hunter a package. "It's the diary of Will Sommers, the original. I still have one of the first copies, one in which a certain name was changed."

"Thank you. I'll keep it safe."

"You should. Only you and I know that name. It would not be good for you should anyone else find out."

"Again, thank you, Joe. I … I don't deserve it."

"You're right about that," Joe said without a smile. He turned to his wife. "Bianca …"

"Herne, you know the Beast will return. We killed its host but not its spirit."

Hunter nodded. "It's the nature of the Beast, I'm afraid."

"When it comes back it may be worse than this time."

Not sure where the conversation was going, Hunter said, "It may be."

"Unless someone of good intent takes it on," Bianca said. Then she and Joe both looked at him meaningfully.

"You aren't suggesting …"

"You are the god of the hunt," Bianca told him. "And for you, that hunt is for peace and justice. A never-ending battle. And what is that but an eternal quest?"

There was silence at the table until Hunter finally said, "I don't know. I don't know if I want to or if it's even possible. But I'll think about it."

He looked at the wall clock next to a TV on which a hockey game was playing. "I should go. My plane back to the DMA is waiting at Martin's Airport."

Goodbyes were said, handshakes and hugs were exchanged. Soon it was just Joe and Bianca.

"Any regrets," Joe asked her.

"None at all. How about you, are you okay?"

"I'm good and getting better."

They smiled at each other, two people in love. Then Bianca asked, "What if Hunter becomes the Questing Beast and things go wrong?"

Joe thought about a dagger on which was inscribed a certain name. A dagger that was locked in his safe. "I don't think that will be a problem."

"Neither do I," Bianca said. "Come on, it's time for my favorite magician to take me home. He's got magic to do."

SEX AND DAMNATION

It was the twilight hour, the time when the light of the day gave way to the darkness of the night. It was the best time, according to some books, for those who worshipped the dark powers to hold their ceremonies.

Just outside Ellicott City, a combined Baltimore City/Howard County task force prepared themselves. It was led by Baltimore City Police Lieutenant Bianca Jones, a specialist in things occult. She had the knowledge. Her team had the weapons and experience. The Howard County Police Department had the jurisdiction.

Worshipping evil in any of its myriad forms was not against the law. Every adult was free to seek and choose their own form of redemption or damnation—unless there were unwilling participants or demons were to be summoned. According to information received by the HCPD Special Victims Unit, the ritual that was to be conducted at the Hell House Altar in Patapsco State Park involved both.

"Lieutenant Tavon Greggs, his team, and I will go first. Sergeant Serrano, have your team surround the altar. Take any person who tries to escape into custody. Use deadly force against anything that doesn't look human."

Sergeant Jarvis Serrano did not like taking orders from members of outside jurisdictions, particularly in his own county. He especially did not like taking orders from a woman who did not look any older than his youngest daughter. And what was this "Doesn't look human" crap?

"Listen, little lady," he said, ignoring all courtesy, protocol, rank, and common sense, "This ain't our first time doing this and this is our woods and our case. So why don't you and your Freak Show just stand by and let the real police do their job?"

There was a time when Bianca would have responded physically to this, leaving Serrano rolling on the ground, clutching his groin while gasping for breath. But that was back when she felt she had something to prove. She was now calmer, more in control, and had learned more efficient methods of payback.

Bianca took out her phone, pressed a few buttons, then put Howard County Police Chief Felicia Spencer on speaker. "Felicia, Bianca here. Sergeant Serrano has something he wishes to discuss with you." Smiling, she handed Serrano her phone.

"What's the problem, Sergeant?"

"No, no problem, Chief. Just wanted to let you know that we're about to commence operations."

There was silence as Chief Spencer decided whether or not to believe her man. Finally she sighed and said, "Very well. Proceed as Lieutenant Jones commands. She has full authority." Then, after a significant pause, the chief added, "We'll talk about this later."

Apparently resisting the urge to "accidentally" drop Bianca's phone on a rock, Serrano handed it back to her. He looked angry. Bianca didn't care. There was a job to do.

"We go as planned. Serrano, you're with me and Tavon. If there's any shooting, try not to get any blood on the altar."

They moved in when the music started, heavy bass and drums. Still, the raid team moved as quietly as they could.

Lights came on in the distance. Guided by them and the music, the team easily found their way to what was known as the Hell House Altar on the grounds of the old Saint Mary's College.

The area was lit by portable LED lights. A camera was set up, recording the scene. Eleven robed and hooded figures stood in an arc around the altar on which a naked, young man was strapped down. Bianca knew him; he was James Loft. He was their informant. He had wanted no part of what his cult was planning. "I was only in it for the sex," he admitted. Now he was the sacrifice.

They were almost too late. Two medallion-wearing robed figures were about to thrust daggers into the chest and groin of their victim.

A ritual designed to summon a demon of the Fallen angel Moloch, Bianca thought. *Joe told me about this.*

"Stop! Police!" Bianca shouted.

The knives continued to descend. If they drew blood, it would be all over.

"Do it," Bianca said and fired, with Serrano and Tavon discharging at almost the same time.

The two hooded figures dropped to the ground, their daggers falling from their hands. The victim was not cut, but a bullet from Bianca's pistol went through the hand of one of the priests before striking her chest. A single drop of blood fell on the altar.

There was a cloud of smoke and the roar of rushing air. From the cloud there emerged a very naked, very male, horned demon, at least seven and a half feet tall with a layer of red scales.

In each hand he held a priest, both of them suspended by the medallions that were now around their necks.

"Who summons Zeng, Demon of Moloch?"

The question was rhetorical as Zeng was staring at Bianca when he asked it.

"I did. I'm Bianca Jones. I think your boss has heard of me."

Zeng snorted. "Morningstar has no hold over me or Moloch, Bianca Jones." Then, because even Hell has rules, the demon asked, "What are your commands, oh Summoner?"

This last was said without enthusiasm, for the name Bianca Jones was known in Hell and so Zeng knew what her answer would be.

"Return to Hell. You make take the souls of the scum you hold with you."

Zeng smiled, revealing black and yellow teeth. "They are already there. I leave you their husks."

The bodies fell as the demon vanished. Bianca turned to the remaining cultists. "Anyone want to play follow the leader? I can call Zeng back." None of them did.

As the cultists were being taken into custody, Bianca again called Chief Spencer. "Felicia, me again. Two down, none of ours … Yes, a demon, so we follow protocols."

Bianca checked her team, saw Tavon comforting Serrano. Members of the BPD's Quick Response Team were doing the same for the other Howard County officers. The knowledge that absolute evil exists is hard to take.

"I'll call the DMA and have them send some crisis counselors," Bianca told Chief Spencer. *And next week this time*, she thought, *they'll be more focused on having helped stop a cult and saved a young man's life than they would on the demon.* She looked over at the surviving cult members, decided that they could live with what they saw. Maybe it would scare them into repentance.

Based on the presence of the video camera, warrants were obtained and the homes, vehicles, and workplaces of those involved in the ritual were raided. Occult paraphernalia and video recordings were seized. From the latter it was learned that this was not the first attempt at a summoning, only the first that had been successful. It helped that the other three attempts had occurred inside Baltimore City limits. Thanks to Bianca Jones, Baltimore was a charmed city. No demons were allowed inside the protective circle of Interstate 695.

Other than the failed summonings, the recordings showed the usual sex, drugs, and occult rock music. Bianca forced herself to watch them all. What she saw was mostly adult children playing with Hellfire at the risk of their souls, each of them willingly taking their turn on makeshift altars as that session's "sacrifice," some of them crying out "Hail Satan" each time they were used.

What Bianca did not observe was any sign that any of the cultists had any knowledge of the occult or Satanic rituals. Not at first. She had been watching the recordings in order, from first to last. Toward the end she began to notice a robed figure directing the activities from the shadows. It was only after this figure appeared that the attempts at true summonings began.

Whoever, or whatever, this figure was took great care not to be shown in any of the videos. They hugged the darkness and did not take a turn on the altar. All she could tell from the recordings was that they were much shorter than the others.

"Nothing wrong with being less tall than all the others," Bianca said to herself as she wondered why this person had not been among those in the park.

Or maybe she had. Maybe she slipped away just as the raid started. Of course she was there, Bianca realized. Something had bothered her about the setup and she finally knew what it was. One on the altar. Eleven around it. That made twelve. The magic number was thirteen.

Reviewing some of the previous recordings Bianca saw that it was always thirteen people. *Little bitch got away*, Bianca thought in disgust, *and she was the most dangerous of them all.*

She continued watching the videos, hoping for a break. She got one. Almost at the of the second to last video, one of the cultists who had just had her way with the "sacrifice" climbed off the altar and bumped into one of the lights. The light shifted and for a second, the short shadow's face was illuminated. One second was all that was needed. Going back and forth, Bianca managed to get a clear screenshot of their face. A face she knew.

On the screen, Alison Yates looked about twelve. Bianca Jones knew she wasn't. She knew her from an old case, one she had worked with the Department of Mystic Affairs. Several people, adults in age but children in appearance, were making pornographic movies that were sold as kiddie-porn. Bianca helped put an end to their business.

Six of them—four women, two men—had been involved. They had promised their souls to a demon for eternal youth. The demon had, as demons do, taken them literally. They become forever young, ranging in physical age from eight to thirteen. To survive they did what they thought they had to do—cater to the twisted desires of perverse men and women.

When confronted, one of them, an apparent eight-year-old named Jenna, surrendered, repented, and was given help—a new name, a new job, and magical flesh-shaping to make her appear older. The others suffered various forms of mental anguish when they were confronted with the consequences of their actions. Until now, Bianca had believed them to be in the custody of the DMA.

Bianca thought back to what DMA Agent Karver had referred to as "the tag team match from Hell."

That explains how Zeng knew me, she realized. *He was the demon we battled that time. Some people never learn.*

Bianca considered the situation. The DMA still owed her a few favors and they had the biometrics on Yates. She was their responsibility anyway. Let them track her down.

*

It's gotten bigger, Lucifer thought as he looked out at the dullish grey light in the far reaches of Hell. He now knew what it was and what it meant. It had taken time and many souls were sent to the deepest pit to obtain this knowledge, but this was Hell, where souls were plentiful and time had no meaning. He had given the task to the Detective, that mostly forgotten god who was the chief of those who enforced what order there was in the eternal chaos. The Detective, in turn, had sent his minions to investigate—fallen police all, who had earned their damnation by breaking their solemn oaths, forgetting that it was the public they were supposed to "protect and serve," not themselves and their friends.

So many of them, the Morningstar thought. *Still, they are far outnumbered by the hypocrites who make the laws. Quis custodiet ipsos custodes?* he asked himself. *I do, and scoop up their souls when they finally fall.*

The Detective sent many fallen cops into the Grey, only a few escaped it to report that it was yet another attempt at rebellion, some damned fool who wanted to rule Hell in his place.

It had been that way since Hell began. They had all rebelled against the Presence, why should they not fight among themselves. Lucifer beat them all, but from time to time there were attempts to supplant him—Mammon, Beelzebub, Belial, Moloch, and the others who had fallen with him—they had all tried more than once. Even the Rhymer had rebelled, as had the Dancer.

And it was not just the Fallen. Damned souls, some of whom believed themselves to be heroes, raised armies and battled demons. Would-be conquerors—kings, emperors, generals— from all ages fought and failed.

For that was the nature of Hell. Whatever your desire, no matter how badly you wanted it or how well you planned to attain it, you would eventually fail to achieve it. Sometimes you came so close you could almost see it, touch it, taste it, and then it slipped away and however high your hopes had risen you would fall twice that far in your despair.

If any creature knows that it is I, Lucifer thought. *It's not we who abandon Hope, it is Hope that abandons us.*

"So why do you keep trying?" asked a voice in his head. The voice, which sounded very much like a certain Baltimore Police Detective, had been there ever since she kneed his mortal form between his legs. "Why keep beating yourself? Don't you know how good it will feel when you stop?"

"Enough," Lucifer shouted out loud, even though there was no one to hear him, "Thou shalt not tempt the Lord of Hell."

The voice fell silent, although Lucifer imagined it chuckling before it did.

The Lord of Hell returned to his consideration of the Grey, which seemed to be getting brighter as it grew in size. *Of course it does*, he thought, *considering who is behind it.*

The identity of one at the center of the Grey was known to Lucifer. It was not one of the Fallen, nor was it a king, emperor, general, or politician. No, this one was the recently damned Apollonius of Tyana, a onetime god and would-be messiah, who, when he walked the mortal plane, called himself the Bright One, and who was brought down by, who else, Bianca Jones.

Once damned, he had begun gathering those of his followers who had preceded him to Hell. Since then his army had grown with many new souls going straight to him. Lucifer knew that this should not be, but he did not know how he was managing it. Not until one of the Detective's officers returned with the secret.

Genius, Lucifer thought when it was told to him. *I am ashamed that I did not think of this myself.* He spent some time thinking of ways he could co-opt the scheme and came up with several. He even considered letting the game play out and seeing how far Apollonius could get. *Or maybe I'll let him win, let him serve Hell for a few decades then take it back.*

For some reason, this last thought lingered, and it bothered him more than the pains of the damned he eternally suffered.

"Still, it's not quite playing the game is it?" he asked himself, or maybe he asked that annoying voice. Then he decided on a way of frustrating the Bright One, a way that for some reason amused him, even as it went against his very nature.

*

It was years ago when Glen McKay was seventeen. They had snuck into this Goth club—him, Zack, Leon, Justin, and Emily. It was her idea really, to go someplace daring and forbidden. So of course they went along. The four of them and Emily. She was small and cute, with short, black hair and deep green eyes. She always wore black and sometimes didn't wear a bra, not that she needed to. She always seemed happy and vibrant and had a way of looking at a person as if they were the most important thing in her life. The four boys were all in love with her and would do anything for her. And she, in her way, was a bit in love with each of the boys. She would do almost anything for them. Not *that* of course, nothing like *that,* but as needed she was their sister, their confidante, their guide, and their inspiration and the five of them were happy as only those who were seventeen could be.

The bar didn't have a name. It was just another dark place with a reputation. Emily charmed the doorman who let them in despite none of them except maybe Zack looking old enough to drive much less legally drink.

They sat in the back and sent Zack for the drinks. Four beers and a Coke for Leon who was driving. It was his turn. Just as it was Glen's turn at shotgun. Zack and Justin got the back seat with Emily. She'd sit between the two of them and hold their hands. That much she would do.

Glen, Justin, and Zack were on their second beers. Emily had switched to Coke. "Don't want to get drunk and have you guys take advantage of me," she joked, knowing that none of them would.

Then it all changed. A man appeared, that was the only word for it, in front of the bar. He was the most beautiful man anyone there had ever seen and like most everyone there he was dressed in black. But his black was not of the night, or the dark, but of the Abyss. They had never seen him before, but they all guessed his name. and when he made his offer, they were sure of it.

"What would you give for your heart's desire? Your souls, small though they be? I think not. Whatever their worth, they are not mine to buy nor yours to sell. You must give them away, as some here already have. What then? A year of service? Ten years of your life, five of the life of a loved one? Maybe a child's beloved pet? Or a simple favor, one to be named later and payable on demand?"

There was someone else, a small woman named Jones who turned out to be a cop of some sort who kicked the ass of the man in black and sent him away. Then she turned to the crowd and figuratively and literally scared the Hell of them, but not before it was too late for some.

Emily had not wanted anything. At that time she was happy just being seventeen. As for the boys, well, they all wanted the same thing.

Make out with Emily. Do it *with Emily. Have Emily love only me.*

They were primal wishes made by boys who could not help but be young and stupid. And once they were made, they were instantly withdrawn. But they *had* been made. But Glen had made his first—*Marry Emily.*

The dark place cleared out. The cop Jones followed one of the crowd as he left. The rest went home, to worry and wonder about what deals they may have made.

For once Glen and his friends were quiet. There was no laughing, joking, talking, or hand holding on the way home.

Leon had only had his license for six months. He'd had nothing to drink and was driving slowly and carefully. He even waited a second or two after the light turned green before entering the intersection.

Eddie Jackson had had his license for decades. He'd been drinking for hours. His driving was neither slow nor careful. Despite being a half-block away he sped up when he saw the green turn to yellow. He was at full speed when he hit the Honda with the five teens in it. He did not survive the crash. Neither did Leon, Zack, or Justin. Witnesses who saw the crash and those who responded to it said that it was a miracle that Glen and Emily survived, that God had been with them.

Maybe God had. But so had a certain man in black. He'd been frustrated once that night by a certain Bianca Jones but was pleased to collect the soul of Eddie Jackson and bank a favor to be claimed later.

Some years later, Glen and Emily married and moved to York. Glen was a licensed plumber. Emily put her business degree to good use and opened a tea shop. They had a child on the way. To everyone, it seemed that they were likely to live happily ever after.

Except that sometimes before dawn, one of them would dream of the accident and wake up screaming or in a cold sweat to be held and calmed by the other. And there were nights when a memory would not let Glen sleep—the memory of a dark man in a dark place and the wish to marry Emily. But mostly they were happy.

It was one day when evening was fading into night, when Glen came home from his last job. Emily's shop was open late so he thought he would be home alone. He was not expecting to be greeted in his living room by a tall blond man wearing a suit as black as the Abyss.

The man was sitting on Glen's couch. He had apparently been waiting patiently, or else he had timed his appearance to coincide with Glen's arrival. Either way, Glen flashed back to the dark place and knew the man's name—Satan, Lucifer, the Devil, the Lord of Darkness. As for his purpose...

"It's time to pay up, Glen. For this house, for your child, for your ... wife. That is what you asked for, wasn't it?" Then in perfect mimicry of Glen's voice, he said, "Marry Emily. Remember?"

"Every day," a shaken to his soul Glen replied. His knees went weak and he would have fallen but instead collapsed into a chair opposite. "Bu, but…"

The Devil smiled and explained quietly, "But you thought you've been doing all the right things to save your soul—confessing your sins, never missing Mass, performing acts of charity and mercy. I'm sure He's pleased. But as I told you back then, your soul was and is not for sale. Those inclined to sell theirs are already mine. No, we had a deal, an arrangement, favor for favor. Now the bill is due."

Glen's shock had worn off. Only fear remained. What would he be asked to do, and what might the cost of refusing be?

"Much too high, Glen," Satan said calmly, reading his thoughts. "Like Job, you would lose everything."

"Justin, Zach, Leon, weren't they the price?"

The Devil laughed, no, chuckled. "No, I am afraid not. Their deaths were truly an accident. Although I do recall whispering in the mind of a very intoxicated Eddie Jackson that if he floored it he could probably beat the light. I really didn't expect him to T-bone the car you were in. After all, *I'm* not the Omniscient One. But when I saw what had happened I took steps to save you and Emily. After all, we had a deal and dead men can't pay."

"My friends, did they…"

Satan knew what Glen was asking. "Like all souls, they went to whatever fate they were expecting and deserved. I'm still not sure what He does with the atheists. But no matter, you called the tune and now it's time to pay the fiddler."

As the Devil reached into the inner pocket of his suitcoat, Glen tried and failed to imagine what horror he'd be asked to commit. Satan then handed him an ordinary, white business envelope. There was no stamp but the name written on it was "Bianca Jones" and the address was in Baltimore.

"Please deliver this as soon as possible."

Glen looked at the envelope, then at Satan. "That's all, just deliver an envelope?"

Smiling at the man's relieved astonishment, the Devil replied. "That's all. As you may or may not recall, the now Lieutenant Jones was there that night. She kneed me in my—Pride and has been a pain there and elsewhere ever since. She's the reason you're getting off so easy. Because of her, neither me nor mine can enter the Charmed City. Do this for me, Glen, and it will be over. Even the dreams will stop. I've afraid the guilt will remain. For that, you'll have to forgive yourself."

And with that, the man in black disappeared, just as he had years ago in the club. Only the envelope remained. Glen looked at it, knew that tomorrow morning he'd be driving south on I-83 toward Baltimore.

"She's never going to believe me."

*

"Of course I believe you, Mr. McKay." Bianca looked at the envelope Glen had given her, then back at Glen, who was seated in front of her desk. "I don't think either one of us will ever forget that night."

"I didn't think you'd remember me."

"I remember you because of the accident. Four dead. Were your friends the price of your happiness, Mr. McKay?"

Glen quickly shook his head. "The Dev…" Bianca shot him a look. "I mean, he, the man, told me they weren't. That he was after the other driver."

"And of course, he would have no reason to lie." Bianca let Glen think about that for a moment, then let him off the hook. "But in this case, he probably didn't. Otherwise, he would have used a different messenger. You may go now, Mr. McKay. Your job is done. Go back to York and Emily, and may your child be gifted with beauty, wit, grace, dance, song, and goodness."

Glen looked at Bianca in surprise. "How do you know about…"

"I know about you because I made it my business to know about as many from that night as possible. There was a young man named Roger. I managed to save him. Others were not so lucky. I encountered them later under…difficult circumstances. What they had asked for, what they did, the price they paid." Bianca shook her head. "Their souls may be suffering in Hell right now. As for the rest, well, I still pray for them, hope for the best, and prepare for the worst."

*

Bianca sat looking at the letter for over an hour. Glen McKay was back in York and replacing a toilet by the time she decided to open it. She was not afraid. Morningstar would not, could not attack her, not in her city, not in her place of power. That wasn't how things worked. Bianca had no illusions about living long enough to get old. But somehow she knew that when it was her time for her last battle it would be with some monster other than the Devil.

Joe would want to run a dozen magical tests on this and even if they all came up negative he'd still tell me to burn it. The rest of the squad would call me six different kinds of crazy for even thinking about it. And each one would offer to open it for me. Good thing I'm alone then. Still, there's no sense in taking chances.

Putting on gloves and a mask, Bianca picked up a silver-bladed knife that had been blessed by two popes and the Rabbi of Jerusalem and opened the envelope.

A single sheet of paper was inside. Bianca was disappointed that the letter was computer printed rather than in the Devil's own hand, and even more disappointed in that he had chosen Times New Roman rather than some more esoteric font. Chiller or Creepy would have been nice, or possibly Deutsh Gothic. *You'd think the Lord of Hell would show more imagination.*

"My dear Miss Jones," it read,

"At the bottom of this letter you will find a website address. It leads to a site that contains the worst sexual deviances, fetishes, and perversions ever conceived by man or demon. Actually, it contains them all—all ages, all sexes, all genders, all preferences. It ranges from mildly erotic to grossly disgusting. Whether it is simply a naked celebrity, a loving couple, or an act for which one may be eternally damned just by considering it, one can find it on this site. The site may be found by one of any number of searches and one does not need a credit card, a declaration of age, or even a username and password to log in. It does, however, require that one read and agree to the terms of use before accessing the site.

"But, Ms. Jones, as both you and I are aware, nothing has ever been free, especially sin. There is always a cost. As for the cost of this site, well, I would advise you to read the Terms of Use carefully. Doing so will answer your many questions. Above all,

"DO NOT AGREE TO THE TERMS OF USE. DO NOT ENTER THE SITE.

"Secure in the knowledge that you will be capable of handling this problem to our mutual benefit, I bid you good day.

"*Morningstar, Dominus de Inferno.*"

*

Bianca assembled her team—Beth, Joe, Tavon, Tammy. They met in the conference room where Bianca passed the letter around.

"Comments?" she asked.

"Other than you were crazy as crap for opening it alone and without Joe's protection, no?"

"Thank you, Beth. Anyone else? Yes, Tavon?"

"Sexanddamnation.dys. Not trying to hide anything, are they? Just who in the …world would be stupid enough to go to a site like this." He waved away the comments everyone was about to make. "Never mind, I forgot. There's a whole lot of stupid on the 'net."

"Agreed. Let's see what it is."

Bianca accessed the site on an old laptop. The Freak Show usually kept several of them around, for dealing with possibly demonic activity in cyberspace. They were "use and lose", to be destroyed according to protocols established by the Department of Mystic Affairs. They were down to their last one, having burned through several when a digital version of *The Necronomicon* was loosed on the world.

The site came up.

"Welcome to Sex and Damnation. Below are the services offered on the site."

There followed a summary of the site's contents that matched with what was described in Lucifer's letter.

"If the above interests you, read and agree to our terms of use, then enter freely and of your own will. Once you do, you will find a world of sin and desire. Anything you want, anyone you want is here for your pleasure. Do what thou wilt."

The terms of use that followed were the usual boilerplate of rules, conditions, and disclaimers. Until one scrolled to the middle.

"By clicking on 'Yes' the user agrees to serve Apollonius of Tyana in whatever capacity Apollonius or his representative requires in life. Furthermore, unless this contract is specifically voided by petition to an appropriate deity, this obligation will continue after the user's life has ceased."

The remainder of the terms was more the usual legalities and denials that, like everything else in a terms of use agreement, most people never bother to read. This was followed by,

I AGREE TO THE ABOVE TERMS AND CONDITIONS
	YES		NO

Bianca quickly clicked NO, left the site, and turned off the computer. "Hell."

"Exactly, Joe," Bianca said. "It looks as if the Bright One has decided he'd rather reign than serve and is gathering an infernal army to launch a coup. I can understand why our friend Nick told us about it. It won't stop the revolution but it might slow it down."

"Plus he's probably pissed that he didn't think of it himself."

"That too, Tavon. The question is, what should we do about it?"

"Who says we should do anything about it, Bianca?" Beth asked. "Why should we help him? The Bright One can fight for a thousand years and not win. He'll never win, that's what Hell is all about."

"And how many souls will be lost because of this website?" Tammy Dolan asked. She was the team's forensic specialist and she knew how easy it was to fall. During the war Apollonius had waged against Baltimore, she had betrayed Bianca in order to keep her family safe. She had repented and all had been forgiven and mostly forgotten.

"Hardly anyone reads terms of use," Tammy went on. "They scroll past them and click "Yes" or "Enter." The ones using this site won't know that they've damned themselves."

"Too bad," Beth said. "If you ask me, anyone going to a site this sick deserves anything that happens to them. Let the sick bastards go to Hell."

"Except," Tammy argued, "what about the young and curious who just stumble on the site. Or the lonely and desperate looking for self-release? They try out the site, are repulsed and disgusted by what is on it, leave, and never go back. Yet they'll still be damned."

"Not if they repent," Tavon replied.

"They may repent the deed but if they don't revoke their agreement they'll still be damned."

"Yes, but …"

"Tammy, Tavon, enough," Bianca said sharply. "You too, Beth. Like it or not, everybody, there are souls at risk and it's fallen to us to save as many as we can. Joe, any ideas on how to shut this site down for good?"

Joe Russo had been considering the problem since his wife had told the team what it was. There were rites of exorcism in the books back in his shop. And yes, in time he could adapt them. But …

"It could be done," he finally said. "But there are a couple of problems. Remember, nothing is ever truly destroyed on the Internet. The hunter bots that were unleashed against the cyber Necronomicon are still finding and destroying copies of that. To take out Sex & Damnation might require the equivalent of a digital EMP." He explained the possible consequences. "But I think I can account for that."

The team thought about what that would mean. Finally,

"I'm good with that," Beth said.

Tammy agreed. "The world could use a rest."

"Gonna piss off a lot of people." Tavon smiled. "Hell, it's gonna piss off everyone."

"There being no objections, let's do it," Bianca decided. "But Joe, you said there were 'a couple' of problems. What's the other one?"

"To do this, someone has to access the site. So who's going to offer their soul to the Bright One?"

No one spoke up. Everyone pointedly did not look at Tammy. After a long silence, Bianca spoke up.

"That's easy," she said. "Someone who's already damned."

*

The DMA had yet to track down Alison Yates. There had been demonic outbreaks all over the country, with demons fighting demons using the mortal plane as their battlefield. Finding Yates was not a top priority.

Behind her desk in her office, Bianca teleconferenced with Tammy Dolan in the BPD Crime Lab and Joe at his bookshop.

"Tammy, what have we got on her?"

"Fingerprints from when she was arrested. The DMA pulled her and her friends out of Juvenile Detention before we could swab her for DNA."

"Right. What's time and procedure when you have gods working for you? I'm surprised they didn't delete the files."

"What makes you think they didn't, Lieutenant? But if you remember, you had me do the booking. I went old school with ink and print cards then fed them into the system."

"Isn't the procedure to shred the paper copies after entry?" Joe asked.

"That's the procedure, Joe," Tammy replied. "But who says I followed it in this case."

"Good job, Tammy," Bianca said. "Where are they now?"

"You have them, Lieutenant. They're in the file room. I brought everything I had to the House when we moved in."

"Joe, is that enough for you to find her?"

"Definitely."

"Good. Bring what you need and we'll find her from here. And bring lunch."

Joe Russo had his own workroom at Freak Show Headquarters. It was equipped with a table, a few chairs, a bookcase with reference books, grimoires, and tomes, and a state-of-the-art fire suppression system in case one of his "procedures" went awry. Also, in addition to the magical wards Joe had placed on the House itself, his workroom was heavily shielded to keep nasty things from getting in, or out.

With his workroom locked and secured, and just him and Bianca present, Joe picked up the card on which were the inked impressions of Alison Yates's fingerprints. He scraped a bit of that ink from the fourth finger of the left hand, the traditional *vena amoris*, or heartline. He had no basis in science in choosing this finger, but Joe Russo wasn't working with science. He then carefully transferred this scraping to the stylus of the 22-inch tablet that was lying flat on the table. He then hooked the stylus to a silver chain and held it over the tablet.

"You know the risk?" Joe asked Bianca.

"Yes, I do, but I doubt if the DMA is watching. Its agents are too busy with this Hellish Civil War that's going on."

"Maybe we should tell them the reason?"

"When this is all over," Bianca said.

"Or if things go wrong."

"That too. Do it, Joe."

"Funny, that's the same tone you used last night."

"Just shut up and do it."

"That too."

Then Joe got serious and invoked his spell of sympathetic magic, like calling to like. He once had to move an indicator over large, highly detailed paper maps. Now he used a high-resolution, large-screened tablet and a mapping program.

With the stylus hanging over the screen, the display started to move. Soon it stopped over a section of southeast Baltimore. Joe zoomed in and the image on the screen moved again. Joe did this over and over, until the stylus was hovering over a rowhome in Brewer's Hill, not far from where Yates and the rest were first taken into custody.

Joe read the address of the house to Bianca. In turn, she called Tavon who had his Quick Response Team at the ready.

"Here's the location. Fill in the address on the warrant and hit it now. And just in case, use blessed ammo and take Millie. Nothing puts the fear of God into a person like an angry were-Yorkie."

Thirty minutes later, QRT hit the house—two officers and a dog through the front, one each through the kitchen and basement doors. Nothing on the first floor or the basement, but there were sounds of panicked activity on the second.

"Millie, Talbot."

On hearing her trigger word, Millie changed into her were form and, at her partner's command, launched her 160 pounds up the stairs with Tavon right behind her.

Yorkies are normally cute, but not when they're three feet high and growling. There were screams of shock, surprise, and terror. Tavon followed them into the front bedroom. There he found Anita Yates dressed only in panties and a girl's undershirt. Two men were with her, both over forty and overweight. One of them was wearing jockey shorts that were too small for him. The other was naked. A video camera was pointed at the bed. From the looks of the bedclothes, whatever activity it was meant to record was over.

The men started protesting, declaring their rights, demanding their lawyer, and denying that anything went on. Yates just stood there looking young and innocent but the bored look on her face said, "I've gotten away with this before. I'll do it again."

Tavon called in. "Yates is secure, Bianca. There were two men with her." He described them and told her about the video camera. "What do you want me to do?"

"By now all of the neighbors are watching, most of them with their cell phones ready to record. Get Yates dressed. Cover her face and put her in a patrol car with a female officer. Perp walk the men, give the neighbors a good show."

"Should I let them get dressed?"

Bianca sighed. "I guess you'll have to. But cuff them from behind and don't let them hide their faces. Strap them in a patrol wagon and bring them and Yates to the House."

*

With Yates in the House's basement holding cell, Bianca dealt with the men first. As soon as Donald Henry and Kenneth King were led into the interview room they again began demanding their rights, threatening lawsuits, and complaining about their treatment.

"Shut up," Bianca said firmly.

Both of the men knew that there should be no reason to be afraid of the small woman sitting across the table from them, but there was something about her attitude, her manner, the way she looked at them as if she had examined their souls and found them wanting that made them obey her. They shut up.

"I watched the video you two made with that young girl. You should be ashamed of yourselves. Hell, I'm ashamed to be of the same species as you two."

King opened his mouth as if to say something. At a look from Bianca, he did not.

"Here's what's going to happen. If you two cooperate, there will be no charges in this matter, no statements to the media, and that video stays locked away. Refuse to cooperate, or lie to me, or go public with your own version of today's events and threaten legal action, then the video gets released along with all your personal information and you two will be charged with everything I can think of or make up. Is that understood?"

Bianca hoped that King and Henry would not realize that by now they were probably already all over social media. They'd been recorded being led out of a house where they'd been in the company of what appeared to be an underaged girl. By now the speculation had begun. Once they were identified their lives would be placed under the social microscope. In addition, their information had been given to the BPD's Sex Offense and Child Abuse Units. Bianca had said that *she* would not charge them *in this matter*. She had made no promises about anything or anyone else.

After Bianca's, "Is that understood?" Henry replied, "Yes." King nodded and asked, "What do we have to do?"

She handed them pen and paper. "Names and information. How did you find out about the girl? Who else is involved in your perversions? The more you tell me, the better for you. And one other thing. Have either of you ever accessed that Sex & Damnation porn site?" They hesitated. "Full cooperation, gentlemen, or warrants get served on your homes and offices and you two never see the light of freedom again."

"I was on it a few times," King admitted.

"Me too," Henry said, adding, "I know I have … a problem, but that site is, well, too much for me."

"Did either of you ever read the terms of use?"

Henry and King looked at each other. What kind of question is that? Their expressions seemed to ask.

It's a hint, she thought, *and a warning. If you're smart enough to take it.*

"No," they both said, with Henry asking, "Should we have?"

Bianca just smiled.

*

Her business with King and Henry finished, Bianca had Anita Yates brought in.

"What do you want, Jones," the woman asked.

"I need your help."

"Well, screw you. I'm not doing anything for you, and you can't make me. You can't even hold me. Summoning demons is part of my religion and you were the one that shot those priests. And that Dys Ambassador got me off the DMA hook. Now call me a ride or my lawyers will be all over you and the police for harassing a minor child."

Bianca listened calmly to Yates's demand and rant. Then she replied just as calmly.

"I don't give a damn about your lawyer, your rights, that ambassador from Hell, or even the DMA. I really don't give a damn about you. I just need you to do one thing and you can go about your business."

"Why should I?"

"Ever hear of a Faraday cage, Anita?" The look on Yates's face said that she hadn't. "It's something that blocks electromagnetic fields such as cellphone signals. That cell you were in is a magical Faraday cage. It blocks spells, magic, anything supernatural. I got the idea from the owner of a bar in Manhattan. And when spells are blocked they tend to rapidly reverse. You're now about a week older than when we threw you in there. I figure after a few months in that cell you'll qualify for Medicare."

"You can't do that," Yates protested in a voice that was not as cocky or confident as it was minutes before.

Bianca laughed. It was not a pleasant sound. "Get this straight. I'm Bianca Jones and I have a license to do anything I must to get rid of supernatural menaces like you. I could keep you in that cell until you die of old age. I could drop you in the middle of Leakin Park and let the things that live there hunt you. Or," Bianca reached down and pulled her .40 caliber pistol from its holster, "I could just shoot you in the head and send you straight to Hell. No one will care. Not about you. And soon, you'd be less than a forgotten memory."

Bianca put her weapon away. "Or you could me a favor and walk out of here a relatively free woman. What's it to be?"

Looking into Bianca's eyes, Anita Yates saw nothing but the truth. She thought back to that night in Ellicott City and how easily Bianca had dealt with the demon. She thought about how she liked looking young and liked the power it gave her over certain kinds of men. She liked the money she got from these men, both upfront and from blackmail later. And she had no desire to fulfill her part of the demonic pact anytime soon. There was only one thing she could do.

"What do you want, Jones?" she asked again, this time in surrender.

"Have you ever heard of a website called Sex & Damnation?"

"Heard of it? I make good money uploading my videos to it."

*

"Are you sure about this?" Bianca asked.

Joe nodded. The two of them were in the conference room The old laptop was open on the table next to a portable hard drive. "I designed a spell that would have downloaded every ritual of exorcism found in my books, regardless of faith or belief. Then I got an idea and called our contact in the Vatican."

"How is Father Lawrence?"

"It's Bishop Lawrence now. Inquisitor General of the Holy Order. It turns out that his office had been working on the same thing, only theirs is more targeted. Less collateral damage, more of a tactical nuke than a digital dirty bomb. He overnighted me this." Joe tapped the hard drive.

"Nice that he trusts us, especially after the whole Bright One thing."

"He trusts me, Bianca. He's still upset with you for not telling him. Anyway, I added a few rituals of my own and one from Doctor Hegazy's new translation of *The Book of Emerging Forth into the Light.*"

"Is that out already? I heard she and Amenmose were working on it."

Joe shook his head. "She sent me an advanced PDF copy."

"Okay. Bring that bitch in here and let's do this."

Anita Yates was brought in. At Bianca's command, she sat before the laptop. Joe handed her a jeweled pendant. "Please put this on," he told her.

"What's it for?"

"It's for your protection. You know the forces we're dealing with." Bianca told her. "Now put it on and do what I told you."

Yates entered sexanddamnation.dys and hit "Enter." The welcome screen came up, followed by the Terms of Use page.

"Should I log in?" Yates asked after hitting YES. Bianca nodded and watched as she put in her username and password.

WELCOME, appeared on the screen, DO YOU WISH TO UPLOAD?

Again, Yates hit YES.

PROCEED

Joe plugged the hard drive into a USB port.

RECEIVED. UPLOADING…

As the digital exorcism ran through the site's coding there came the sound of a wounded beast. If HTML could be said to have a soul, this one was in agony. Curses in languages that were old when the Earth was new spewed from the speaker. Then, as the holy rite finished with its first target, it entered cyberspace in search of further prey. For 600 zeptoseconds, a blink too fast for the human mind to register much less imagine, every computer device in the world was affected.

On the laptop's screen appeared ERROR 777. It then went blank, as did every other pornographic or hate-filled website all over the world. Bianca knew that soon back-ups would kick in and that within weeks most of the sites would be restored, with one exception. Sex and Damnation was gone for good.

"That's done," Bianca said. "Thank you, Anita."

Yates started to take the pendant off.

"I wouldn't do that," Joe warned.

"Why not?" she asked.

"Because," Bianca explained, "you just helped us destroy the site created by agents of Apollonius the Bright One, the damned being you pledged yourself to every time you entered the site. He's going to be mad and looking for revenge."

"Wearing the pendant will protect you from magical or demonic attack, even outside of Baltimore," Joe said. "But take it off or use magic of any kind and your soul will shine like a beacon. He'll send his agents after you. Leave it on and you'll be safe from him."

"Until you die, then you're his for all eternity," Bianca added. "Unless you renounce your allegiance to him and repent your sins."

"You bitch. Damn you, Jones."

"You're the one who's damned, Anita. But you can change that if you want. Thank you for your help. Joe, would you ask Officer Winder to take Ms. Yates home?

*

Lucifer Morningstar stood atop the highest tower of Dys and looked toward the patch of greyish light that was the domain of Apollonius of Tyana, once known as the Bright One and now as Hell's Rebel. Earlier Lucifer had felt some within that domain cry out in agony as they realized how they had been tricked into damnation. Their souls rebelled against the Rebel. A few even considered their actions and truly repented. Lucifer felt them as they ascended out of their assigned circle.

"Feels good, doesn't it," came a voice from behind. Lucifer turned and saw ...

She was dark-skinned with long, black hair. The feathers of her wings were ash-grey except for the ones on the tips. These were blackened as if burnt in a fire. She was an angel of power and majesty.

He had known her before his Rebellion. They had last met at the Birth of the Child and before that in the battle for Heaven. He saw that her arm still bore a scar from his sword.

He did not trouble himself to wonder why one of His Messengers would be in Hell. Angels such as she went where they wished without fear.

"Watching my enemy brought low, Nika? Yes, it does."

"I was referring to doing the right thing, freeing souls from torment and saving others from damnation."

"I was stopping a rebellion from growing stronger, that is all."

"A rebellion that, like the others, is doomed to fail. I think not, Lightbringer." She came close to him, stood next to him as she once had. As they looked out over Dys, she asked, "Have you ever wondered what it is like to be one of them?" Before he could answer she went on. "Truly one of them, and not just using their bodies. That boon could be yours, if you wish it. Call it a reward for doing the right thing."

Lucifer turned toward the angel ready to again object, but she was gone. Just then, another repentant soul ascended.

Damn it, the Lord of Hell admitted to himself, *it does feel good.*

A GIFT FREELY GIVEN

A few days before Christmas, a man approached the guard at the front door of The BPD Extranormal Investigative Unit, aka The Freak Show, gave his name, and asked to see Sergeant Bianca Jones.

"She's a lieutenant now, Mr. Patton," Officer Thomas Winder said, "But I'll let her know you're here. Is she expecting you?"

"No, but I'm sure she'll see me."

Winder keyed his radio. "LT, there's an Anthony Patton here to see you. Do you want to see him?"

The reply was terse. "No. Send him in."

Bianca Jones's office was on the first floor of the old house. Officer Winder showed Patton in.

Bianca knew Patton of old. She had once cleared him of a murder that his now-deceased wife had committed with the help of a genie. The genie, too, was deceased, killed by Bianca when he attacked her. During the investigation, it was discovered that Patton had a large collection of child pornography—magazines, photographs, DVDs, and video images. He should have been arrested. He was not. Instead, all charges against him were dropped and Patton was seemingly forgotten by everyone.

Everyone except Bianca Jones and the people who worked with her.

"What do you want, Patton?"

"I have a message, Lieutenant Jones."

"From?"

"I'm not allowed to say the name, but I was told to remind you about Genny Starr and a rest stop in Virginia."

Genny Starr was the current America's Sweetheart, a wholesome actress who had once made a very bad deal with a very bad being. That told Bianca who had sent the message and why the charges had been dropped against Patton. "What time?"

"Six in the morning. Luci…" Patton choked on the name he was about to say. "That is, he said he wanted to get an early start."

"An early start at what?"

"Ruining my life, I think."

"Good."

*

Nika, messenger of the Divine, sat atop the dome of the Basilica of the Assumption. She was comfortable there. The December sun was warm on her face and the cold wind felt good as it flowed through her wings. She had no worries about being seen. Humans lived in a mostly two-dimensional world. Few of them looked up. As for those that did, well, who would wonder about an angel on top of the church.

Shifting slightly, Nika looked out over the Charmed City. Baltimore had its problems, just like any city in any country of the world, but it lacked the pervasive influence of the Fallen One. Because of that, it shone a little brighter than the rest.

But things change, she thought in the language of her kind and recalled the words of Ecclesiastes and thought of how she was to be an agent, His agent, of these changes. But that was for another time, another season. For now, she would simply enjoy the day. There would be time later to seek out Bianca Jones.

*

Every Sunday and Wednesday, Josiah Harris, pastor of St. John's Christian Baptist Church, preached on sin. He was against it, against it in all its forms—the greater ones, the lesser ones, the deadly ones. There was too much of it in the world, too many ways to fall, too many ways that the Devil could lure God's children into temptation. And so twice a week, he preached against it.

Pastor Harris also preached on Love. He was in favor of that. Love of one's self, love of one's family, love of one's neighbors and friends. But mostly he preached on the Love of God, and the love for God, and how this love can help us overcome sin.

For Pastor Harris knew sin. In his youth, he had committed lots of it in its many forms. Later, he tried to combat it as a member of Baltimore's police department. But though he, like many of the men and women who wore the shield of the BPD, was a good and decent person, he felt there had to be a better way. And one night, after investigating a burglary in a small, storefront church, he stayed and listened to the minister's sermon and found that better way.

And so Josiah Harris preached on the Bible—the Old Testament and the New. He preached on the Gospels and the Acts and the Epistles. He preached on love and he preached on sin. He preached against immorality, against bigotry, against corruption, and against illicit drugs.

And his sermons were heard by those who came to his services. And maybe his congregation acted on what they heard and maybe they didn't. But as he read the papers and listened to the news, as he attended meetings and conferences, and as he spoke at too many funerals of young men barely out of their teens, and some who never left their teens, Pastor Harris decided that more needed to be done.

So unlike many of his fellow ministers, Pastor Harris decided to preach against those whom he saw as spreading sin—dealers, racists, corrupt cops, and crooked politicians. Every Sunday he would name their names and call them out from the altar. He would demand that these "purveyors of sin" repent. Failing that, he prayed to God and demanded of public officials that these sinners face the Judgment of both Earth and Heaven. And failing that, he wished them luck in Hell.

*

The December sky was clear and winter's chill was in the air as Bianca Jones drove south into Virginia. She pulled into the rest stop ten minutes early. Anthony Patton was already there.

Bianca sat down opposite the man and looked into his eyes. In them, she saw not the pedophile who had made a deal to escape child pornography charges but the creature with whom he had made the deal. She greeted him by name.

"Morningstar."

"Good morning, Miss Jones." Lucifer turned and looked at the rest stop building.

Someone had made an attempt to decorate for Christmas. Lights were haphazardly hung from the roof, on top of which had been placed holiday inflatables—Santa going down a chimney, a team of reindeer, a Frosty who had no business being on a roof. All three were partly deflated, Frosty looking like he'd been placed too close to the chimney and, magic hat notwithstanding, was now melting.

"Pathetic, isn't it?" Satan asked. "Not just their efforts at decorating, or lack thereof, but the fact that more and more, He is not represented on what has been designated as His birthday. Would you like to know the correct date, Miss Jones? I know what it is. We were there. We tried to stop it. But someone was there to stop us."

Morningstar paused as if in contemplation. "I really did admire the man, Mary's husband. Your Joseph reminds me of him. Both would do anything for the woman they love."

Bianca listened patiently for as long as she could. Then she asked, "What do you want, Morningstar?"

Patton's shoulders shrugged. "Maybe I've missed you. It's not like I'm allowed to visit your city. After losing to you three times I can't go within the circle formed by I-695. Or maybe it's to thank you for your latest gift. The would-be messiah you sent me is causing all sorts of trouble. He acquired a lot of followers over the centuries and half of them wound up in Hell. You may have depowered him but their worship is slowly restoring that power. Or maybe I just wanted to wish you a Merry Christmas."

"I would think you'd be the last one to wish anyone that."

The Devil smiled. "And why not? This is my favorite time of year. Greed and Gluttony abound. Envy when someone gets something you wanted but didn't get. Nothing says Sloth like being too lazy to shop and giving cash or gift cards. There's Anger all through the season. And let's not forget Lust. Who needs incubi and succubi when there are stores like Toria's Secret and Love Craft and websites like Santa's Naughty Elves.com? That's a current favorite of Patton here. So, I love this season. I even send the Pope a Christmas card every year."

"Again, what do you want, Morningstar?"

Patton's head shook. "If Patience is a virtue I don't know why Impatience is not on the list of Deadly Sins. What do I want? To give you a gift, Bianca Jones. A gift freely given with no strings attached. And this is it. Come the Eve an exhibition opens at the Lancer Museum and Art Gallery. Given its nature, you are probably aware of it."

Bianca nodded. "The Parker Avery collection."

"The very one. The majority of it is fake or of no consequence. Most of the arcane objects have lost their power. Most, but not all. And there is gold among the dross, including one very special item."

"Which is?"

Another devilish smile. "That would be too easy. Just try to keep it out of the wrong hands, hands attached to those who will no doubt try to steal as much of the exhibit as possible."

"We'll be ready for them."

"Of course you will. Now if you'll excuse me, I plan on driving Tony's car as far west as I can until it breaks down or runs out of gas. Then I'll leave him stranded. I've already stripped him of cash, ID, and credit cards. It should be fun. Unless you want to save him."

A shake of her head. "He had his chance. This one's yours. But one question."

Satan leaned forward. "Sorry, I already have a date for New Year's Eve."

"So do I. Why the gift?"

Satan stood. "To be honest, Ms. Jones, I don't really know. Maybe it's because you make my damned existence interesting and cause me to think otherwise forbidden thoughts. Now we must be off. Maybe we'll run into a blizzard."

If anyone deserved to be left to his fate it was Anthony Patton. But Bianca had offered people worse than him a second chance. "You can always repent, you know."

"Now there's the Bianca Jones I know."

"I was talking to both of you."

"Of course you were. Or you would not be Bianca Jones."

To this Bianca had no reply. Instead, she got back into her car and headed north. On the way back to Baltimore she'd stop for breakfast then take advantage of the fact that most of the mall stores had early openings. She still had some Christmas shopping to do.

For his part, Satan headed west, the unfortunate Anthony Patton a prisoner in his own body. "It's your own fault, Tony. When I said I wanted a week of your life I didn't mean you'd die seven days early. Now sit back and enjoy the ride for as long as you can."

*

It was no surprise that Pastor Josiah Harris had enemies. There were drug dealers, neo-Nazis, extremist groups from both ends of the political spectrum, self-appointed activists who claimed that Pastor Harris had gone too far and other activists who claimed that he had not gone far enough. When he supported police officers whose only offense was doing their job too effectively then he was a lackey of the authorities. When he called out cops who used force beyond that which was necessary or politicians who used their positions for their own benefit the pastor was then labeled a tool of radicals.

Josiah Harris did not care. He had a message and a mission and he would serve the One who had given him both. But there were those who did care, members of his parish who worried that one day the various forces of sin would join together to silence the pastor's voice. They felt the need to do something. But did not know what to do.

Lieutenant Tavon Greggs did. Officially, he was a squad leader in the Baltimore Police Department's Quick Response Team. He was also a member of the Freak Show, whose job it was to identify and combat extranormal threats to the city. He had done things of which he was not proud and things that had left stains on his soul. But thanks to him and his teammates, Baltimore was generally safe from the monsters that hunted humans from the shadows and who would ravage their souls just for the fun of it.

A recent encounter with one of these creatures resulted in Tavon acquiring a partner, a six-pound, one-foot high Yorkshire terrier with the formal name of Dame Ruth Millicent of Pershing House. Most people called her "Millie." Millie was a cute dog that only looked harmless.

When he could, Tavon attended service at St. John's. While he was gratified to hear someone preaching against crime and sin and in favor of love and personal responsibility, the QRT Lieutenant began to worry when Pastor Harris started to name names. Some of these belonged to very dangerous people, people who would shoot their brother if it would bring them an extra hundred then kill their mother if she witnessed the crime.

Tavon knew it was a matter of if and not when. He called in favors and used his connections both in and out of the department to make sure that if there were a real and imminent danger to the pastor or his church that the QRT lieutenant would hear of it.

Tavon attended services on the Sunday before Christmas. He was, of course, accompanied by Millie. At first, there were objections to his bringing a dog into the church. But Millie was more than a dog, she was a member of the BPD K9 Unit so she was tolerated. And once people realized that she was quieter than most of the children and some of the adults, she was accepted.

After services ended, Tavon was approached by someone on the street. He knew this someone, a drug user and sometime informer. The man greeted Tavon then bent down to pet Millie. Then he left without a word. It was only after he was gone that Tavon saw the piece of paper in the dog's collar. On it was written a phone number and when Tavon called it the person who answered said,

"The dealers are tired of the pastor. So are the Nazis and the other right-wing nuts. Some of the left-wingers as well. They all want Harris quiet so they're doing a one-time team up."

"When?"

"Christmas Eve. They're going to take down the man, the church, and maybe the congregation. The dealers will show their power, the right and left will blame each other, and everyone's biggest problem will be gone."

Tavon reported this threat. No one believed him. Other than the word of an anonymous informant there was no evidence of any threat or collusion between the disparate groups.

So Tavon went to Pastor Harris, asked him to request protection.

"I will not have my church turned into an armed camp, not on what you've shown me, Brother Greggs. The Lord will provide. The Lord will protect. You and Millie are, of course, welcome. But remember, Christmas is a time of peace, the Lord's Peace."

So Tavon went to Bianca Jones. As head of the Extranormal Investigative Unit, she had broad latitude to fight monsters and supernatural threats. She also had virtual *carte blanche* on how she did it.

"I would call people out to destroy a church and its congregation monsters," he argued.

"So would I, Tavon, but the department calls them suspects, and right now there's no evidence to suspect them of anything."

"So there's nothing you can do?"

"All I can do is approve your leave request so you can attend that Christmas Eve party you were talking about. That goes for anyone else you may have invited to attend."

"What about you?"

Bianca shook her head. "Joe and I have to attend an opening at the Lancer. It's business. There's information from a credible source that there's going to be our kind of trouble there."

Tavon was not happy. "And if there's trouble at St. John's?"

"I'll make some calls, have units ready. As soon as someone lights the candle call it in. And use Millie if you have to."

"Are you sure about that?"

"Who's going to believe it?"

*

"Bianca, tell me again why we're going to a museum on Christmas Eve," Joe Russo asked his wife.

"You'll see when we get there. As I told Tavon, there's a potential for our kind of trouble."

"After that mummy episode, the Lancer is one of the heaviest warded buildings in the city. I know, I set the wards myself. Nothing and no thing is going to get inside."

"It's what already inside that worries me."

"If this has something to do with your meeting in Virginia why isn't the rest of the team with us?"

"Tammy's not a fighter, and Tavon and Beth are in church. Tonight it's just me and my favorite bookselling magician."

There was a banner hanging over the entrance to the main exhibition hall.

"Welcome to *Treasures and Wonders: The Parker Avery Collection*." Below this banner, there was a sign on an easel. It was a quote from Parker Avery.

"Please enjoy these mementos of my travels. As you view them you will no doubt wonder which if any of them are truly what they seem to be. The secret is: It doesn't matter. They are as real as we want them to be, just like the myths and legends from whence they came. Seeking proof only robs us of our dreams and in the end, dreams are sometimes all we have."

Bianca and Joe went into the hall.

*

When he was assigned to the security detail of the Extranormal Investigative Unit, Officer Thomas Winder was told about the building's notoriety. It was what had been called by some "The Ghost House" and it had had a habit of appearing and disappearing at random. But that was in the past. Now, he had been assured, it was nothing more than an old house with a colorful history. Still, he was warned that strange things were apt to happen.

He did not believe any of what he was told. The EIU, he told himself, was nothing more than another specialized unit that used specialized techniques to go after gangs, terrorists, and major dealers. Look what they did, he told himself, to the Bright One Gang. There were hardly any of them left. Yes, the FBI took the credit—they always did—but everyone in the BPD knew that it was Lieutenant Jones's crew who really brought them down.

No, Officer Winder did not believe any of the stories about the Freak Show. He did not believe in vampires, fairies, old gods, or werewolves. Those things did not, could not exist.

Then a bright light appeared in the sky. It made Officer Winder think of the Christmas Star. He wondered if the star meant that a new messiah was being born or if the One whose birth was being celebrated that night was returning.

The shape this city is in, he thought, *we could use one or the other.*

Then the star fell from the heavens and Thomas Winder became a believer. It landed in front of him and, at first, looked like a large bird. Then he saw that it was a woman, one with dark skin and grey wings that appeared burnt at the tips. *An angel*, Winder thought, adding, *Why not? It is Christmas.*

"Bianca Jones," the woman said. "Is she here?"

"N-No, Ma'am," Winder managed to stammer out. Then without thinking and against all procedure and protocol, he told her where Bianca was.

The woman smiled when Winder mentioned the name Parker Avery. Then she spread her wings, rose up, and flew toward the heart of the city.

He had seen an angel and having seen her, Thomas Winder realized that everything he had believed did not, could not exist—vampires, fairies, old gods, and werewolves—did. A sudden chill that had nothing to do with the weather ran through him and only then did he think of calling Bianca to warn her of what was coming.

*

The Avery exhibits were objects of pulp, myth, and fantasy. After Joe checked his wards and made sure that they were strong and active, he and Bianca walked through the exhibit. In one section there was a sword in a stone, which according to an explanatory note, was not Excalibur. There was a so-called magic lamp, said to have one wish left. There were Hippolyta's girdle, the chain that had bound the Fenris Wolf, a flying carpet, Joseph's coat, a Valkyrie's spear, and a hammer that only the worthy could lift. There were also several pieces of eggshell, mostly white but with faded streaks of yellow, red, and orange through them. These were housed by themselves in a glass case. The explanatory card stated that they were pieces of a phoenix egg.

"Do you think any of these could cause trouble?" Bianca asked.

"Well, there are some comic book fans who would like to have that hammer."

"It looks too small to do any good," Bianca observed.

"If you rub it, it gets bigger."

"If you're lucky I might but I'm not talking about the hammer. Any readings from the lamp?"

"If there's a wish there I don't sense it. Want to rub it and find out."

"Is that all you men think about it?"

"When I'm with you it is. What one would you pick?"

"Those eggshells once cost a man his life but that was a long time ago."

They moved on to the next section. In it, there was a mask believed to have been worn by a vigilante who had protected New York in the Thirties.

"Do you think that was the Nightmare's?"

Bianca shrugged. "From what I've read he and Parker had some adventures together, so it's possible."

Next to the mask was a cloak—black on the outside, pink on

the inside-that was worn by a different crime fighter. There were pulp magazines—*the Shadow, the Spider, From the Shadows* and its companion book *The League of Shadows.* There was a brace of .45 caliber pistols and several beer mugs that bore the name "Moran's."

Religious items were in a third section. There were pieces of wood, not from the True Cross but from the one on which St. Peter had been nailed. There was a rope with which a betrayer may have hanged himself. There was a cup that may or may not have been the Holy Grail and driftwood said to have come from Noah's Ark. There were three jewelry caskets, one of which may have held gold, the other two spices or incense. Also in this section were a rough wooden box which was presented without any explanation other than a small card that read "Feed Holder, circa 4 BCE," three pieces of silver, and relics of various saints, including those of St. Anlee, patron of the graphic arts and of St. Guinefort, a very holy greyhound.

The religious exhibits held the most potential for trouble. Sacred objects were things of power, fueled by belief as much as by fact. The sword that was not Excalibur also worried Bianca. Should it be real, and should it be drawn, it could spark a revolution that would split Britain apart. The rope and the coins, the gifts of the Magi (maybe), the cup—any of these could be trouble. Bianca decided to wait and see who came for them.

She turned and looked for Joe. He wasn't there. Then she remembered that along with the Parker exhibit there were very old, very rare books on display. Joe had said he wanted to inspect them in case there were ancient grimoires like the kind he kept in his bookstore, the kind that in a way talked to him. Bianca tried not to worry about what they might be telling him.

Her phone buzzed. It was Officer Winder. He warned her about the flying lady. She thanked him and turned back to the exhibits.

There she saw a dark-skinned woman standing by the feed holder. As Bianca watched, the woman reached out and touched it gently, almost reverently.

Due to her sensitivity to the supernatural, Bianca recognized the woman as something *other*. It took but a second for her she realized the woman's nature. It was, after all, hard to miss the wings, even if she did wear them like a cloak.

Wondering why no one else saw he for what she was, Bianca

walked over to the woman. "Another word for feed holder is manger. I'm Bianca Jones."

"Yes, I know. And I am Nika."

"It's not …"

"No, it is not His, but it could have been."

"And you would know."

"Yes, I would," Nika admitted. "I was there. It was my duty and pleasure to protect the Family."

"And your duty now?" Bianca asked, knowing that angels never appeared without a reason.

Before Nika could answer, Joe ran back into the exhibition area.

"Those fools have a copy of *The Necronom* …."

That's when hell broke loose.

*

Christmas Eve services at St. John's were held at six-thirty in the evening. Knowing that there were parents with small children in his congregation, Pastor Harris kept his service short. They had more than enough to do when they got home, making things ready for Santa Claus. Unlike some ministers, Pastor Harris had no problem with the concept of Santa. He saw his mission as making sure that the people of his parish concentrated more on the Presence than the presents.

Tavon Greggs did not listen to Pastor Harris's sermon, although the choir was loud enough for him to hear the Christmas hymns through the doors. They were loud enough for the people across the street to hear them.

Tavon spent his Eve outside the church. As he looked up and down the street, his eyes searched the shadows for movement and he wished that he had rooftop snipers covering all sides of the church. He did have backup, though. Homicide Detective Bethany Steele and three members of his QRT team had given up their Christmas Eve to help protect the church. They were the perimeter guards; their mission was not to engage but to come up from behind in case there was trouble.

Beside him, Millie was off her leash, sniffing the air for trouble. Due to her special condition, she had been trained in a very special way. She had the senses of a wolf and occasionally, when Tavon said the word, the size and strength of one. Those with ill intent would not escape her nose. Tavon often wondered what Pastor Harris would think if he knew that he had welcomed a creature of dark myth into his church. Tavon hoped the pastor would never find out.

Services ended at seven-thirty. As the congregation departed Tavon let out a sigh of relief. One hurdle passed. Now if things went sideways there was only the pastor and the church to protect. Maybe the informant was wrong. Maybe he just heard guys spouting off in a bar, maybe he …

Beth Steele's voice came over the radio. "Tavon, there's a crowd coming your way and they're too ugly to be elves. About twenty of them."

"Another fifteen coming from my end," reported one of his men. "Like the detective said, they ain't elves and they are ugly enough to be the butt end of a reindeer."

"Okay, let them come. Millie and I will meet them and try to talk sense. If you hear gunshots you know what to do. Try not to hit the church or any houses."

Tavon got on his phone. "Bianca," he said, "send help. We got some Christmas evil coming our way."

*

The attack was threefold. The main force attacked the museum lobby, rushing past the guards. A smaller group came from inside. They apparently had hidden in the museum earlier. A third group was already there, having mingled with the crowd. Some of them had pistols, others had knives. Thanks to Joe's magic, the guns would not work. Knives, however, always worked.

The invading mob targeted the feed holder, the sword, the cup, and the coins. It fell to Bianca and the two detectives assigned to the exhibit to stop them.

Joe was not a combatant. His job was to maintain his wards while getting as many people to safety as he could. The detectives were fighters. Unable to use their guns, they did best they could but soon were in danger of being overcome as the thieves went after the treasures.

Nika joined in. She was more than a fighter; she was the Lord's warrior and had faced far worse than this crowd. She moved quickly towards the invaders and whomever she touched she broke. Bianca, too, was more than she appeared. She had brought down gods and demons and the short sword she had with her was more than a match for any knife.

The sword could not be removed. The cup could not be picked up. The coins could be, but burned the hand of the one who did. No one reached the feed holder.

The gangs were almost subdued when there came the breaking of glass from the book display. The case that had held the dread tome of Abd el-Hazred had been smashed and the book stolen.

"Joe," Bianca said, "The attack on the treasures was a decoy. The real target was *The Necronomicon*."

Joe nodded. "I thought that might happen. So before I came running in here I took it out of its case and hid it. Then I cast a glamour on another book and put that one in its place."

"But they still got away."

"No, they didn't. You've heard of the bait money banks use. This was a bait book. Just about now," Joe looked at his watch. It was about seven-forty. "My second spell on the book just went off. The detectives should find the thieves passed out on a sidewalk within a block from here."

Nika came over. "Your husband is very smart, Bianca," she said.

Joe blushed as Bianca said, "Yes, he is and he's due for a very special Christmas present tonight."

It was just after the would-be thieves were taken away for questioning when Bianca's phone rang. It was Tavon.

"Bianca," he said, "send help. We got some Christmas evil coming our way."

"It's Tavon," Bianca told Joe. "He needs help. He's called a Signal-13 but there may not be enough time."

"This Tavon is a friend of yours?" Nika asked.

Bianca nodded, adding, "He's defending a church and its pastor."

"Then he is a friend of mine. How do I find him?"

*

Tavon watched as the gangs of dealers, Nazis, and other extremists came toward the church. He knew that Beth and his QRT team men were behind them. He didn't know how much help they'd be. He called in a "Signal -13 Officer Needs Assistance" but knew that backup would probably not arrive in time.

"Well, girl," he said to Millie, "looks like it's just you and me."

"And me," came Pastor Harris's voice. The man of God was standing behind him holding a pump-action shotgun. "I preach the New Testament, Brother Greggs. But sometimes you have to go Old Testament on the heathens and unbelievers."

"Amen to that, Pastor."

"No offense, but how much help is that little dog going to be."

"Wait and see, Pastor, and trust in the Lord."

"I always do."

By then the two gangs had merged and had gathered in front of the church. The sight of two armed men had given them pause.

Might as well try, Tavon thought.

"I am Lieutenant Greggs of the BPD. So far all you men have done is exercise your right to assemble and no crime has been committed. If you're here to praise God on this blessed night then I'm sure Pastor Harris will open the church and welcome you."

In the distance gunshots and sirens could be heard.

A black man emerged from the crowd. "They ain't coming for you, cop. Right now the boys who aren't here are shooting up the Northwest. Anyone who shows will be too late and too few."

A white man came and joined him. "Now, officer, me and mine have no quarrel with you. So why don't you go and leave the reverend and his church to us? And that goes for your little dog too."

This is going to get messy, Tavon thought. *But needs must.* "Me and my dog will stand by the Pastor."

As the crowd surged forward Tavon said, "Talbot." That was Millie's trigger word.

Yorkies are by nature cute little dogs. They are not so cute when they suddenly grow to the size of a pony and start emitting growls that might scare the devil himself. It did scare several members of the crowd, some of whom soiled themselves.

"What in God's name?" Tavon heard Pastor Harris say.

"She once bit a werewolf. It's a long story."

But after some hesitation one of the leaders of the mob shouted out, "It's still just a dog. Shoot it then the two men."

"Shooting just makes her angry," Tavon shouted. "You wouldn't like her when she's angry."

Some left but not enough. Sirens came closer. Beth and the QRT positioned themselves behind the mob and prepared to fire. On the steps of the church, two men and a beast stood ready to defend the House of God. Pastor Harris said a prayer.

And it was answered.

Fire rained down from the sky and encircled the crowd. The ring of flame shrank until the mob could not move without someone getting burned. Between the crowd and the church, an angel landed, in her hand a fiery sword.

"Anyone with guns should drop them now, before the heat of the flames causes them to go off. Then you may leave. But know that this holy place is under His protection. And so you will not forget it ..."

The encircling fire blazed up, singeing those in the crowd with an indelible burn.

"As Cain was marked so are you. All who see you will know what you tried to do. Go now before the fire consumes you."

A gap opened in the burning ring. Most of the crowd fled through it. The few who remained fell to their knees, surrendering and begging forgiveness.

Slowly, the fire abated. When it was gone, Tavon looked at the ones on their knees.

"Your department, Pastor."

Josiah Harris was a believer in miracles. They came with the calling. He had just never expected to see one, much less two in one night. Despite the awe and wonder he was feeling, he had a job to do and so did it.

"Tonight you felt the flames of Hell," he said to the three men and one woman who had remained. "Never forget them. But for now, your sins are forgiven. Go and sin no more."

After the four left the flames made by the fiery sword subsided. As Nika folded her wings, Pastor Harris asked, "Are you an angel?"

"I am," she replied. To Tavon she said, "Bianca sent me."

Tavon nodded. That was all the explanation he needed.

*

At midnight, as Christmas Eve became Christmas day, the

celebration at the headquarters of The BPD Extranormal Investigative Unit was winding down. All the carols had been sung, all the toasts had been made, and all the presents had been given out.

"Are you sure it is okay for me to stay here?" Nika asked.

"Where else will you go? And this is, or was Christmas Eve, a time for all to be welcomed. Welcome to the Freak Show. Stay as long as you like. However ..."

"Yes?"

"Nika, you did not go to Avery Exhibit to see swords and old magazines. You came to meet me. Why?"

"To give you a message. Our mutual adversary is on the edge. Changes are coming, Bianca, ones that will involve you and yours. Prepare yourself."

To Rebehold The Stars

We mounted up, he first and I the second,
Till I beheld through a round aperture
Some of the beauteous things that Heaven doth bear;

Thence we came forth to rebehold the stars.

Dante Alighieri, Inferno, Canto XXXIV

The Grey had gotten bigger. Despite Lucifer's efforts, it was twice as large as it was before he sabotaged Apollonius's recruiting efforts. Still, Hell was infinitely large, and the Grey would have to double its size every damned day for centuries before it became a threat.

Still, the Lord of Hell thought, *I guess I should raise an army to punish his arrogance. There will be centuries of battles, horrible injuries, tortures and mutilation, and in the end—we'll still be in Hell.*

Or I could do—nothing. Just let events play out. And when they do—we'll still be in Hell.

Lucifer looked out over Dys, feeling as he always did the pain and suffering of every damned soul, even those in the Grey, even that of Apollonius.

"At the least," he said aloud, "he should take on the sins of his followers. It's not fair."

This thought amused him, the idea of anything being fair in Hell, other than the fact that everyone in it had earned their place. *I don't care anymore— about anything.*

He wanted to shout this out loud, to scream his newly found apathy at his Creator. He looked up, then out, then inward, and realized it did not matter. *He* was everywhere.

Even here.

This was a new thought, that having created everything, He was a part of everything, even Hell. God was in Hell, or rather, Hell was in Him.

This sudden knowledge shook Morningstar more than anything had since Michael's sword had pierced his soul and sent him spiraling from Heaven.

"You poor bastard," he said, sure that he could be heard, "You feel it too. All of it. You never stopped suffering for our sins, did You?"

Humbled, and finally ashamed, the Lord of Hell fell to his knees.

How long Lucifer knelt there he could not say. But before he could rise he looked up and there she was. Nika's grey wings were unfurled, and there was a smile on her face and a look of satisfaction in her eyes.

"Is there something you wish to say, Morningstar?" she asked.

Lucifer rose to his feet and faced the angel. "Not to you, and not to Him. Take me to Bianca Jones."

*

"That is four of them," he said after he had claimed his latest victim. Another sinner. *Eight more to go. Twelve is the number.* He would make thirteen. Then the Tower of Babylon could be brought down.

Maybe he would prepare the lounge, that den of corruption that used the evil one's image. *That alone is a sin, even if it is a cartoon. They think it clever, and trendy, and possibly a joke to let both sexes use the same bathroom. And those who relieve themselves there, in mixed presence, are themselves sinning and so deserve their fate. Let one disappear where it cannot be hidden. Then it would not be so clever, and not so funny to them. But funny to me,* he thought as he made plans for the lounge then decided to add the nightclub. *Even more appropriate, for that's where these sinners belong.*

*

Bianca Jones and her husband Joe Russo were on the road, taking U.S. Route 50 East, going, as those from Baltimore say, "downy oshun." They were heading for the Hotel Dreadmore in Ocean City, Maryland. Bianca had told Joe of the trip the night before.

"Remember our first trip to Ocean City?" Bianca asked her husband after she gave him the news.

"How could I forget?" Joe answered with a smile. "People were killed, Damon LeVaey was captured, and you and I…" Joe's face turned red.

Bianca was glad that the thought of their first romantic encounter could still cause Joe to blush. She also felt the heat on her cheeks as she went on.

"There was something else, near the end of our stay." Joe looked puzzled. "The hotel, remember? The one the mayor's aides asked us about?"

"I remember now?" Joe said. "The day before we left. We got a call from Karl Shirley, the detective who worked with you to catch LeVaey. He asked us to come to City Hall, said they needed our advice about something."

Bianca got into bed and pulled the covers up to her chin. "We thought it was related to the LeVaey case, or maybe something similar, but instead they wanted my opinion on a stupid horror-themed hotel," Bianca said.

"As I remember," Joe said, getting into bed and under the covers with her, "You said something to the effect that messing with evil in any form was a bad idea."

"A terrible and stupid idea."

"Oh yeah, and that you wanted no part of it."

"I still don't," she said with a weariness that had nothing to do with the lateness of the hour. "But now it seems that there's no choice."

"What do you mean?"

"The damned fools built it. The Hotel Dreadmore opened in April. And just six weeks later, it seems that we're needed."

"Do I have to ask why?"

"The usual reason. Look, I'll explain tomorrow on the drive down. Right now, let's get some sleep. We have a long day tomorrow. Before we leave we have to pack up our clothes and equipment."

Bianca let out a long sigh. Usually, Joe had noticed, when a new case came along Bianca was always a bit excited, regardless of the danger it presented. But now, she just seemed tired.

"Bianca, is something wrong?" If it was, she would tell him. She always had, and he trusted she always would.

Joe waited but no answer came. Soon he heard the steady breathing that told him she was asleep. Turning off the light, he held her close and soon joined her.

"You drive," Bianca said when they finally set out the next day. This was odd. Except in bed, Bianca liked being in control. That she would give over the keys to Joe was another sign that something was worrying her. *She'll tell me when she's ready*, he told himself.

For the first thirty minutes, it was quiet in the car. Then—

"Four people have gone missing from Hotel Dreadmore in the last five weeks," Bianca said.

"Missing, how?"

Bianca shook her head. "No one knows. Henry Pope reported that he and his husband Ryan Fumio had just come in from the beach. Pope went to take a shower, leaving Fumio watching a Law & Order rerun. When Pope got out of the bathroom the TV was still on, Fumio's things were still there, but he was gone."

"Did he take anything?"

"Just the suit he was wearing. No wait, Pope said he found that at the foot of the bed."

"You would think someone in the hotel would have noticed a naked man walking around, unless it's *that kind* of hotel."

"From what the Commissioner told me it's not recommended for children but it's supposed to be a haunted hotel, not the Playboy mansion. The next report was from Timothy Clarke. He said he and his girlfriend Fran Woods went to bed one night and the next morning he was alone. No sign of her since and again, all of Fran's things were still there."

"Where were her nightclothes?"

"According to Clarke, she wasn't wearing any when they finally went to sleep."

"That's two," Joe said as he maneuvered into the E-Z Pass lane of the Chesapeake Bay Bridge Toll Plaza.

"The third one to go missing was Lara Bonner. She was sharing a room with four friends. No one knows quite when she disappeared. 'There was a lot of in and out' one of these friends said, then quickly added that that sounded dirty but wasn't."

"Why add that unless it was?"

"Says the civilian who's spent too much time around cops. But with five people and two beds I thought the same thing. Still, all four reported that nothing was missing except her, not even clothing."

They were on the Bay Bridge now, high over the Chesapeake Bay. Joe noticed Bianca looking out over the water.

"Thinking of Chessie?" he asked.

"Yeah. I worry about her, Joe. Worry that someday someone's going to find proof she's more than a legend. Then people like that Marv Richards will start hunting her."

"But you'll be there to protect her."

"Maybe," Bianca said, then quickly changed the subject. "The last one is Jermaine Barber. He and his fiancé, Denisse Leal, were dressed, ready to make a night of it. Dinner at The Hellfire Lounge, that's the hotel restaurant, and then dancing at the Inferno Nightclub. Before they left, he stepped into the bathroom."

"Let me guess," Joe said. "Leal got tired of waiting for him. Probably asked him something like 'Did you fall in?' then she opened the door and all she found were his clothes.

"Something like that. And that's it, for now. The good news, such as it is, is that most of the routine work has been done—interviews, house and home searches, that sort of thing. The bad news is that nothing's turned up. And as far as we know, there's no connection between any of the victims."

"Or a link hasn't been found," Joe commented. "And let me guess, since there were no signs of foul play, the rooms were released and the victims' personal effects returned to their families or loved ones. So there are no crime scenes and no forensics."

"You got that right. Fortunately, when Karl Shirley heard what was going on and thought of calling us in, he arranged with the families to have "personal items" sent to him by next-day mail. He told them it was for possible DNA matching if anything came up. Also, since I'm doing this on the clock, I get two weeks guaranteed paid leave with comped rooms at the Dreadmore, and you get double your usual consultant fee."

"Nice."

"You would think so."

It was the way that Bianca said this, added to her earlier "Maybe" that caused Joe to pull onto the parking lot of a Burger King, that and he was getting hungry.

"Bianca, what's wrong?"

"I'll tell you after lunch. Let's eat and we'll talk on the way."

It wasn't until they had passed Cambridge and were on Ocean Gateway that Bianca said, "I'm thinking of going off the pill."

"What pill? Oh, *that* pill."

"Yes, Joe, *that* pill."

"Why?"

"I'm tired, Joe. Tired of dealing with the occult and supernatural. Tired of fighting ghosts, and vampires, and all the rest. I want a normal life before it gets too late for me, for us. The way things are now, it's only a matter of time before I face my last monster. If, when I do, then it's too late for us. What do you think?"

"You know what I think. It's what I've wanted for a long time."

"Ever since we said, 'I do.' I know, and I'm sorry it's taken me this long. I think, I think it was seeing that manger."

"Maybe that's why it was there."

"Maybe."

"When."

"Not yet, but soon I think. You'll need time to deal with your books."

"They're not mine, the books in the back of the shop. They'll take care of themselves. But what about Baltimore? Who's going to run the Freak Show?"

Bianca thought back to early Christmas morning. *It's the city that's charmed, Bianca, not you,* Nika had assured her. Maybe that assurance was why the angel was there. If so—

"Like your books, Joe, the city will take care of itself. We can talk about this later, after we find those four missing people."

*

The Hotel Dreadmore was built on a lot where a long-defunct shopping mall had been. When the Ocean City Council finally approved the hotel's construction, all that had been left of the mall was a food store at one end of the L-shaped building and a chain discount store at the other. Now a ten-story structure commanded the property that covered the bayside of Coastal Highway from 94th to 99th street.

The hotel itself was set back from the street, situated in such a way so as to give all who walked or drove by a good view of its carefully designed creepiness. The Dreadmore would not have been out of place in a late-nineteenth century Gothic novel. It was where Victor Frankenstein would have set his laboratory. Dracula would have preferred it over Carfax Abbey. Madame de Ville would have raised her puppies there. It was part Addams, part Bates, and part Overlook—all designed to set the tone for the experience that was the Dreadmore.

A low stone wall bordered the property with wrought-iron gates that creaked appropriately to admit vehicles. As Joe passed through these gates and drove toward the main entrance, Bianca noted free-standing buildings close to the hotel. One was The Hellfire Lounge. Opposite this was The Inferno nightclub. The last, the one closest to the hotel, was Horns and Halos, a combined gift and bookshop.

"What do you think?" Joe asked as they neared the entrance.

Bianca looked around. "Parking lot's almost full."

"Business is good."

"Lots of potential victims. Who knows how many vanishings have not been reported?"

They pulled up and were met by the bell captain, a traditional English butler whose smile revealed long canines. "Names, please."

"Bianca Jones, Joe Russo."

The Bell Captain checked a tablet disguised as a leatherbound ledger. "Ah yes, special guests. Your vehicle will be parked close by." He indicated the rows just beyond the handicap spaces. "Your luggage will be taken to your room." He waved his hand and bellhops that appeared to be ghouls descended on the car and within minutes had their suitcases on a hotel cart. Bianca and Joe quickly grabbed the bags containing their special equipment before the cart could be whisked away.

"I should mention," the vampiric Jeeves said, "that gratuities, although appreciated, are not necessary. The employees of the Hotel Dreadmore are paid very well, those that survive to payday, that is." He said this last with a sinister, well-practiced chuckle. "Now, if you will, check-in is through the doors. Enter freely and of your own will. May you enjoy, and survive, your stay."

The ornate doors opened on a lobby that continued the theme. Mrs. Lovett's Meat Pies and Breakfast Buffet was off to one side and a guest could get their hair styled or cut at Sweeney Todd's Tonsorial Emporium, "Very close shaves our specialty."

The desk clerk was a younger version of either Elvira or Morticia.

She insisted that both Bianca and Joe read and sign the warnings about the haunts, specters, and poltergeists that may or may not be present in the hotel and of the possibility of strange occurrences such as shrieks, screams, maniacal laughter, ghostly appearances, etc.

"There's a note," she said after Bianca and Joe had smilingly signed the waiver. "Mr. Allen said he'd like to meet with you two tomorrow at ten if that would be convenient." Bianca nodded. "And a Karl Shirley left a package for you. It will be in your room." As Bianca thanked her, the desk clerk addressed Joe, who was staring out into the lobby. "Is there something wrong, Mr. Russo?"

"No, it's just that I keep expecting the 'Time Warp' to break out at any minute."

"Tonight at seven. After that, there's a séance in the Drucilla Room followed by a magic show in the Houdini Theater. Have a pleasant stay."

The suite assigned to Bianca and Joe was only a little less macabre than the lobby. In some ways, it was a traditional hotel suite—a living room, a bedroom with a king-sized bed, a bathroom with both a shower and a bath, each large enough for two (or more) people. Their eighth floor view faced the bay. But the decorative motif ran to black and red, the art on the walls was abstract and disturbing, and there was a warning near all the mirrors not to stand in front of them at midnight and say "Bloody Mary" three times.

"Been there, done that, dumped the monster in Hell," Bianca said on reading this caution.

"Have you noticed anything?" Joe asked. "Or rather, not noticed something?"

"Where?"

"Here in the room, or in the hallways, or in the lobby."

"I didn't think you were waiting for Rocky Horror to step out of the elevator. Besides, you hate that movie."

"It was Frank N. Furter and I only hate the ending. No, what I haven't seen are any occult images—pentagrams, runes, anything to do with spells and such."

"So nothing that could accidentally, or deliberately, be causing the disappearances?"

"Nothing obvious," Joe replied, as he looked for and found the switch that disabled the holographic and sound effects for their room.

"Thank you," Bianca said.

"We get enough of that in real life, Bianca. Funny, to the people staying here, horror and monsters are fantasy. To you, me, Beth, and the rest, they're a part of our lives."

For now, Bianca thought but did not say.

Their luggage arrived. After putting it away and making sure that the items in the package from Detective Shirly were intact, Bianca asked, "What do you want to do now? Should we get started or wait to talk with Allen?"

"Let's wait. I think it's best if we do the initial search in one of the rooms where the disappearances occurred."

"Allen's not going to like that. Chances are those rooms are booked. But there are ways of dealing with him. Tomorrow it is. What about this afternoon and tonight?"

"Well," Joe said with a smile, "there's the king-sized bed or the extra-large shower."

"Or," Bianca countered, "there's the king-sized bed now *and* the extra-large shower later tonight, after dinner and an initial recon."

"Good idea," Joe said, taking Bianca's hand and leading her into the bedroom.

*

Dinner at the Hellfire Lounge. The front of the restaurant was emblazoned with a caricature of the Devil, if the Devil were played by Frank Sinatra in a Ratpack heist movie called *Satan's 11*. The same image, apparently the restaurant's logo, appeared on the menu, and on Tee shirts for sale as one left.

"The real 'Nick' would hate this," Bianca said.

"Do you think he's involved? It's not like we're in Baltimore. OC is fair game."

Bianca shook her head. "Not directly, maybe one of his minions. Enough work talk. Here comes the food."

After dinner, Bianca and Joe walked around the grounds. The ground behind the hotel had been cleared to provide a view of Assawoman Bay. Chairs and benches had been placed so that guests could sit and enjoy the view. Closer in a movie screen had been set up and old horror movies were being shown. Joe and Bianca picked one the benches and watched people going up and down the newly installed Baywalk.

"This is nice," Joe said.

"As long as you don't think about why we're here. But let's enjoy tonight. Tomorrow we go back to hunting monsters."

Eventually, they got up and finished walking around the grounds. Horns and Halos was closed but the Inferno was going strong. It was Seventies night and Disco versions of soundtracks from classic horror movies and TV shows could be heard on the parking lot. "The Twilight Zone" theme was being played as Bianca and Joe went back into the hotel.

A long shower, then some TV, then bed. Joe slept deeply. Bianca woke about three but not from dreams. She'd long ago come to grips with the nightmares that came with her job. After several sessions of lucid dreaming, she convinced herself that the nightmares were afraid of her and that kept them at bay.

Besides, she once thought, *I met the real Nightmare. I even have his sword.*

It wasn't dreams that woke Bianca, just a general restlessness that came with sleeping in a strange room. Getting out of bed, she put on a robe, went out on the balcony, and looked out over the bay.

The night was quiet, so quiet that Bianca could hear the screams, wails, and moans—some loud, some faint— that were a part of the hotel's "reality."

The noises caused Bianca to consider how accommodating the Hotel Dreadmore was to murder. A victim could scream their head off crying out for mercy and no one would pay the least bit of attention. Their body wouldn't be found until Housekeeping came to clean the room, and even that could be forestalled by the "Do Not Disturb" sign.

Is that what happened? she silently asked the night. *Did Clarke, Pope, Leal, or one or more of Bonner's friends take advantage of the sound effects? Maybe one, but not all of them. No,* she decided, *this one—this demon, this creature, this monster—is all mine, mine and Joe's. But mostly mine.* As always, she vowed to keep Joe safe.

The night air had become chilling. Bianca went back inside, lost her robe, and cuddled close to the one person in the world she truly loved, the man for whom she'd once given up Heaven.

*

It would take time for him to rebuild his strength, to cast the spell that brought the sinner. At least a week, maybe more. He would use that time to find the next one—one who cohabited in sin, one who mixed races, a man who lay with a man or a woman who lay with a woman, one who in other ways mocked God and His Word.

He had argued against this place. Had agreed with the woman who looked like a child—out of the mouths of babes—when she said that it was a terrible idea. The woman had been a police officer, one who worked for God, and had helped remove a great evil from the city. They should have listened to her, and to him. But they did not. Instead, they listened to the words of Mammon and embraced the sin of Avarice.

He let it go, and as the property was acquired and plans were made, he pretended a change of heart and made his own plans.

He found the books he needed, bought from an estate sale in Pennsylvania. At first, he wondered if he should destroy them rather than use them. They themselves were evil things. He prayed on this and decided if the Devil could quote scripture for his purpose, then surely a good man could use the Fallen One's words against him.

By the time the hotel was ready, so was he.

*

When Bianca awoke she was alone in bed. She wasn't worried, not at first. But when she could not find Joe in the bathroom or the living room she began to worry.

Joe had set protective wards in the suite. It should have been protected. They should have been protected. So where was he? What had happened? Pushing down growing panic, she began to make plans if she couldn't find him. She'd call in the Freak Show and every favor she was owed by The DMA, the London Agency, and the Vatican. Together they'd tear the hotel apart and down to its foundation if need be to find him, then she'd wreak vengeance on those responsible if he was harmed in any way.

Then she looked at the door. The night latch was off. The only way that could happen was if Joe had for some reason let himself out. But why?

A "beep" as a key card unlocked the door. Joe? Or someone else? *It better be Joe*, she thought as she realized her position. She was mostly undressed and nowhere near anything that could be used as a weapon. She was trying to decide if she should go into the bedroom for her robe, the safe for her gun, or her suitcase for her fighting knife when Joe walked in.

He was dressed for Ocean City—cargo shorts and a Dumser's Dairyland tee-shirt. He had a bag over his shoulder. When he saw Bianca in the living room wearing very little he asked, "Are you okay?"

"Yes, it's just, never mind." She went into the bedroom and got her robe. When she came out Joe asked again, "Are you sure you're okay?"

"Yes, just another sign that this job is getting to me." When Joe wisely decided to let it be she asked, "Where were you?"

"I woke up before sunset to set up a protective circle around the hotel. You were sleeping soundly so I decided not to wake you. I guess I should have left a note."

"Yeah," Bianca said idly, her mind on what Joe had said he'd done. "So there's a big circle around the Dreadmore? What did you use, chalk or paint? And won't it be noticed or wash away?"

Putting his bag down, Joe took something from it, then sat on the living room couch. When Bianca joined him he held up two small disks about the size of quarters. The "heads" sides were engraved. The "tails" sides had a small spike protruding from it.

"Those are part of what Tammy was working on, aren't they?" Bianca said. "What does she call it? Forensic sorcery?'"

"Yes, she's combining criminalistics with alchemy. She got the idea when we used that witch's DNA against her and started working on it in earnest when she used wolfbane to separate the two components of the werewolf's DNA. These disks are for creating a protective circle around a large area."

"Like a hotel," Bianca said.

"Or a city if you can generate enough energy. Tammy uses what she calls 'quantum magic.' She inscribed the same runes into each of these disks so they're linked. Placed around a structure, a spell drives them into the ground so they can't be removed, the linkage forms a protective barrier around the building."

"So that's why you were up at sunrise."

"Right. The light banishing the dark adds to the magic. So the Hotel Dreadmore is now protected against magical threats. And if the current one is coming from outside, it can't claim any more victims. And if it's inside the hotel…"

Bianca smiled. "It's trapped inside with us. Good job, Joe. When we get back remind me to tell Tammy that too. Now, let me get dressed and let's have breakfast before we meet with this Richard Allen. Do you want to try Mrs. Lovett's?"

"Why not? I hear they'll serve anyone at all."

*

One moment Lucifer Morningstar was demanding to be taken to Bianca Jones and in the same moment he found himself in a hotel room. He had been in hotel rooms before, but in possessed bodies. For their hearts' desires their owners had bargained away a day or a week of their lives, sometimes even a month or a year, thinking that they would die that much sooner. Unfortunately for them, what they thought was not part of the contract. Instead, their bodies were used by Lucifer or his minions to perform evil on Earth, with their owners' helpless, conscious minds along for the ride.

He remembered the last one. He had used the body of Anthony Patton to deliver a message to Bianca Jones. He had then literally taken the sinner for a ride, leaving him naked in the snow outside an elementary school.

I wonder what happened to him? the Devil thought before he turned to look around the room.

Black and red, my favorite colors, and disturbingly beautiful artwork. The room is small, but adequate to my needs, for now. He had almost completed his turn when he saw himself in the mirror.

There are mirrors in Hell. They are a form of punishment. Some of the damned are locked in a room with them, the silvery surfaces forever reflecting the lives the condemned could have led, and the bad decisions they made that took their souls past the gates of Dys. Others are forever lost in a maze of mirrors whose images forever reflect not their bodies but the corruption of their souls.

Lucifer had looked into a mirror once. It was in Sidon, a century after The Son had been crucified. In that mirror he had seen his body, his beautiful, multi-winged body. But the gold had reflected not his beauty but something ugly, a body bloated with Pride, with the other sins oozing from the pustules that covered it. He had not looked into a mirror since.

But this time it was different. The image that stared back at him was a good-looking middle-aged man dressed in a polo shirt and jeans. His features and complexion were a mix of many races. He was no longer beautiful but ruggedly handsome, his appearance such as to attract various sexes and genders.

There was a bizarre notice next to the mirror, something about not calling on Bloody Mary at midnight. *No need*, he thought, *I'm already here*. On the bureau below the mirror were a key card and a wallet, the latter containing U.S. currency, a credit card, a coupon for ten percent off at someplace called Thrashers, and a Maryland driver's license in the name of Nicholas du Matin.

Cute, Nika, cute.

There was also a binder on the bureau, its front cover reading "Hotel Dreadmore, Ocean City, Maryland."

Where LeVaey failed me. Oh well, it could have been worse. I could be in Baltimore. Now that might have been painful.

Then Lucifer realized something. The Pain was gone, the pain of his separation from Heaven, the pains of the sins of the condemned, the pain of his damned existence. He no longer felt it. For the first time since before he had been Banished, Lucifer Morningstar no longer felt the Pain.

The "Thank You" left his lips before he realized that he and the One who had allowed this respite were not on speaking terms.

Not yet, anyway, he thought and left the room in search of Bianca Jones.

*

Something had changed. The hotel was different. The traps were constrained. He no longer felt the ones he had placed in the restaurant and the nightclub. The ones in the hotel were still there, except for the four that had been used, and one on the eighth floor. That one was— not there, at least it felt like that. Later he would have to check but for now, he had work to do.

*

What is this place? Lucifer-now-Nicholas wondered as he went down to the lobby. There were monsters and creatures everywhere. Not real ones of course, but humans dressed as comic nightmares. There were faux zombies, ghouls, and vampires about, all in service to gaudily-clad guests, some of whom aped the way the employees were dressed. Someone dressed in a gorilla suit walked past him.

I should look for Ms. Jones, he told himself, but the sun was bright and shining through the windows. He went outside. As he did, he felt a frisson as he passed through a protective ward. It should have reacted against his nature, the force of it should have either kept him from leaving or else bounced him across the lobby. But it did neither. It just—tickled.

That convinced him that Bianca Jones was there. Or at least her husband Joe. Nicholas-once-Lucifer respected Bianca. She had proven herself a most worthy adversary who soon just may accomplish that which no one—not popes, saints, or angels—ever had. *Perhaps they never thought to try*, he asked himself. Yes, he respected Bianca, but it was Joe he feared.

Joseph Russo, like his namesake, was a pure soul. So pure that there was no force in Hell that could harm him, not unless it corrupted him first. And there was little chance of that. Joe's love for his wife burned too brightly for that. Had it not uncorrupted the Pit's finest succubus? In addition, Joseph knew a most dangerous word, one that could send him to the Tenth Circle, the one Dante was not told about, the one from which there was no escape or release.

Stepping outside, Nicholas felt the warmth of the sun on his body. He had not felt the sun since, well, ever. His manifestations as himself had been confined to the night and the dark. When he was about during the day, the sun had always been filtered by the skin of whoever he was wearing. He might have driven the body, but it was the body's owner who felt whatever inflicted on it. Whatever pleasure he felt, was allowed to feel, came from the pain and humiliation he caused the owner.

Once outside he paused. There was the sun, there was the salt-scented air, there was the sounds of waves crashing on the nearby beach. He took a moment to enjoy these sensations and more. He was envious of the mortals to whom this had been given then pitied them for taking these gifts for granted.

Still standing just outside and to the left of the lobby door, Nicholas looked around the grounds, appreciating the detail of the theme. He saw the nightclub and smiled at its name. There was the giftshop—Horns and Halos. *I've worn them both, sometimes both at once when I stood on the shoulders of a damned fool who had not yet realized that he was damned.*

He turned and saw the Hellfire Lounge and the caricature of himself. Then, for the first time, Nicholas proved Bianca Jones wrong. On seeing his likeness so portrayed he felt should be angry, but there was something about that "Nick" version of himself, that struck him funny.

Then Satan laughed. He laughed loud and long, so long and loud that passersby stopped and stared before giving him a wide berth. And when he was finished, when he was himself again, from behind him came a voice.

"A very human thing to do."

He turned but there was no one there. Deciding to take a walk and explore this city he had been sent to, he failed to see a winged figure slip back into the lobby.

*

Richard Allen was adamant. "No, absolutely not," he told Bianca when she asked to make the four rooms from which people had disappeared available to her and Joe "for their investigation."

"These rooms are occupied. They have guests in them, paying guests. What am I supposed to do with them?"

"Move them. Upgrade their rooms. Give them all tee-shirts."

Allen lowered his head, rubbed what was left of his thinning grey hair, and sighed as if the weight of the world was on his shoulders. "Miss Jones, I don't think you…"

"It's *Lieutenant* Jones, *Mister* Allen," Bianca said sharply. "It's you who does not understand. Four people, four of your paying guests are missing under unnatural circumstances. I expected you to be more cooperative. However, if you can't, you can't."

At this Allen relaxed, thinking he had won. But he was dealing with Bianca Jones, who had faced down vampires, fought gods and demons, and had twice defeated an evil witch. A hotel manager did not impress her.

"Just tell me this, Mister Allen. How do you plan to accommodate all the journalists?"

"What journalists?" Allen asked, sensing impending doom.

"The ones that will be here at," Bianca made a show of checking the time on her phone then, "It's 10:20 now. When the news media hears that four of your *paying* guests have gone missing, that the OCPD is investigating their disappearances as suspicious, and that the management of the Hotel Dreadmore not only refuses to cooperate but contaminated the possible crime scenes by renting them without notifying the police, their news trucks will be filling your parking lot in time for the four o'clock news."

"You wouldn't."

"No? What do you want to bet that my press release is not scheduled to go out in eighteen, make that seventeen minutes."

Allen paled and again sighed and rubbed his head. Then came salvation.

"Excuse me, Ms., sorry, Lieutenant Jones," said Leo Chase, Allen's assistant. He had been sitting behind his boss mostly unnoticed for the entire meeting. "But how long would it take for the two of you to examine all four rooms."

Bianca looked over at Joe, who, like Chase, had been sitting silently as he watched Bianca be, well, Bianca. At her nod he said,

"Two to three hours, unless there are complications."

"And if there are complications?"

Joe gave Allen a practiced shrug. "Another hour, that is, unless we have to evacuate the hotel." He said this last calmly, which scared Allen more than had Joe uttered dire warnings of impending disaster.

"Not that I think that Mister Russo and Lieutenant Jones will find anything," Chase said in an equally calm voice, "but may I suggest that we comp the family in the room previously occupied by Francine Woods and the couples in the other rooms to the deluxe buffet in the Hellfire Lounge followed by the bay cruise on the OC Penelope Dreadful." He checked the tablet he had on his lap. "None of them have booked the cruise. Allowing ninety minutes for dinner and two hours for the cruise, including the simulated bay monster attack and fireworks display, that should allow plenty of time. And if we do have to evacuate, that would be ten less people we would have to worry about."

Chase said this last with such deadpan delivery that no one was sure if he was joking or not. It didn't matter. Bianca said that this was acceptable, thanked the two men for their cooperation, and left, but not before requesting and receiving a master key card that would give them access to all the controlled areas, including the rooms, in the hotel.

"Well, that went better than we thought," Joe said as he and Bianca left the management suite and emerged into the lobby.

"Yes, it did. We asked for four so we could bargain down to one. Instead, we got the whole package."

"I was thinking, Bianca,"

"Yes?"

"When this is over, we should take that cruise. It sounds like fun. Who knows, maybe Chessie will show up. Or Shelly."

"We could," Bianca agreed, "but Chessie's afraid of loud noises and Shelly doesn't exist, does he?"

"That what Marv Richards said on *Challenge of the Unknown* and we both know he wouldn't lie."

The two laughed and set out to play tourist for a few hours before it was time for a late lunch then preparing for the night's activities.

As they left, neither Bianca nor Joe took notice of the man sitting in the lobby reading the *Experience Ocean City* tourist guide. Sensing her presence, Nicholas had come down to the lobby with the hope of speaking with her. But on seeing her…

She's working, he realized, *that explains the protective circle. I wonder if they're trying to keep something in or out. I'll approach Ms. Jones when they're done. In the meantime I'll keep an eye on her in case she should need my help.* He then turned his attention to the guide. *This Ocean Gallery sounds interesting, its chaos appeals to me. And maybe I'll try a funnel cake, whatever that is.*

*

Bianca opened the door to the room from where Ryan Fumio had disappeared. Like the other three rooms, this one had the disordered neatness of people on vacation.

"Try not to disturb anything," she said for the fourth time that night. Like every smart husband, Joe did not point this out but went to work.

Wearing gloves, Joe reached into his bag, removed a toothbrush taken from Fumio's home bathroom. He drew a magicked circle on a table near the window and placed the toothbrush inside. Similar items were in the other rooms—Jermaine Barber's unwashed shirt, Lara Bonner's hairbrush, Fran Woods's ring. All were within their own circles that were identical to that which Joe had just drawn.

"Are you sure this will work?"

"Yes," Joe assured Bianca, even as he thought, *At least I hope it will. It should. If not, we have time to try something else.*

"Quantum magic again. The circles are linked by design and intent. That links the items within. Well, here goes."

Joe appeared to be a strange sort of sorcerer—no robes, no hat, no wand, not for this kind of magic. Instead, with Bianca as his guardian and protector, he stood before the table in his M.R. Ducks tee and a pair of cargo shorts and stared at the toothbrush, using his mind to sense its nature, its connection with Ryan Fumio. Through it, he felt the man. Born in Japan, brought to San Francisco at seven, moved to Baltimore at thirteen. There was bullying in his teens, some because he was the new kid, some because he was Asian, mostly because of his sexual preference, which he stopped hiding when he was seventeen and in love for the first time. He made it through thanks to his parents, understanding teachers, and the boyfriend who was stronger than he was and whom he finally married. Now Ryan Fumio was gone and Joe had to find him.

From the toothbrush to the ring, Fran Woods's ring. Her life contained some trauma, some tragedy, but mostly joy and laughter. Timothy Clarke was her third serious boyfriend, the second one with whom she'd been intimate, the first she'd gone away with. Now she too was gone.

From the ring to the shirt. Jermaine Barber had grown up poor and troubled on Baltimore's west side. He'd had his problems with the dealers and the police but didn't let either break him. What anger he had he turned to energy. He apprenticed as a carpenter, took night classes and got a BA in economics and became a master carpenter with his own business. He met Denise Leal in night school. They became friends, then friends with benefits. Things grew from there. He was almost as surprised as she was when he proposed to her at the end of the Jolly Roger Pier their first night down the ocean. He disappeared on the third night.

From the shirt to the hairbrush. Lara Bonner and her friends had come to Ocean City for a wild time. The rule in the room was "anything goes" except pics and videos. She'd done things in that room she never thought she would, thinking she'd never do them again. She may have been right.

Joe was now sitting on the bed, the four people, the four rooms linked. The rooms were cold. There was no magic, no otherworld power in any of them. As for the people—

"Where are you?" Joe asked them collectively. No answer. He did not feel either their bodies or their spirits. He asked again, this time exerting his will. Still no answer. Something, or some thing, pushed back, resisting his efforts and denying the question. It was less a threat and more of a wall or a barrier, an impersonal force that blocked his efforts, much like the circle he'd drawn around the Dreadmore or the ward he'd placed in his and Bianca's room.

Joe knew how to deal with wards. Barriers can be made to yield and walls could be crumbled. But first…

Occupied buildings are much like living things, their room their organs, their hallways their veins and arteries, their managers and staff their brains and nervous systems, and the people within them their souls.

Keeping this thought in mind, Joe demanded of the hotel, "Where are they?" Again, silence. Again, the barrier, but a weakened one. Possibly a different approach. He calmed his mind and realized that he, too, was part of the body of the hotel. He slowed his thoughts, felt the rhythm of the building, and joined it.

Suddenly he was everywhere. In a sense, he *was* the Hotel Dreadmore. He felt the thrum of its power plant and the rush of its waters. He knew the rooms, and the offices, and the open spaces. There were a few dark rooms and areas. And in this everywhere, Joe felt that which was Fumio, Woods, Bonner, and Barber. Like him, they were part of the hotel. Unlike him, their collective spirit was dispersed throughout. Of their bodies there was no trace.

Joe pulled back, tried another approach, a different direction. He considered the hotel as a whole, its aura rather than its body or spirit. He saw its bright and dark spots. He studied energy patterns, then he saw it. The room he was in, the rooms linked to it, his and Bianca's suite—their auras were slightly different, somewhat duller, chandeliers with one bulb out. *Yes, of course, that's how I would have done it.*

Then he felt—something, some thing present. Actually, it was two things. Neither was the missing people. One was simply an amused presence. The other was different, it seemed malevolent, and it was searching for him.

Joe was many things but he was not a fighter, not on the physical or nonphysical planes. He knew his limitations. With that part of his mind that was always linked to his one, true love he shouted out, "Bianca."

He heard Bianca cry out "Joe." He felt himself being shaken out of his trance.

"How long was I out?" he asked.

"Not long, five minutes maybe."

"Funny, seemed longer."

Later, Bianca told him that he had walked back to their suite under his own power. He did not remember doing so. Nor did he remember collapsing on their bed in exhaustion while Bianca retrieved the talismans and erased the magic circles.

He awoke the next morning, the rising sun in his face. There was something about the morning sun that triggered a memory of the previous night but as soon as he thought this it was gone. He would have tried to recover it but Bianca enveloped him in a hug and, kissing his cheek, said, "Good morning."

"Bianca, I have to tell you …"

"It can wait. Dress, shower, shave, and whatever. Then it's breakfast—pancakes, bacon, orange juice, chocolate milk. I think there are also Berger Cookies and I'm not going to miss them. Later, we'll hit the beach and we can talk there."

*

Dressed for the beach—Joe in trunks and a tee, Bianca in a coverup and shaded by a wide hat—they hit the sand. Taking advantage of the beach chairs the Dreadmore had on hand for its guests, they sat there watching the ocean and enjoying the sounds of the waves and the gulls. It was peaceful there, and for a time Bianca was able to put aside thoughts of everything else in her life. *Nice to get away*, she thought. *It would be nicer still if I wasn't on the job. Maybe soon I won't be. Wrap this up, spend a few more days, then, well, we'll see.*

Thoughts of work drifted in, Bianca worried about her crew and her city. *How can I leave them? Who will take over? Who will protect it?* It would be hard, she knew, but if her heart and mind weren't in it…

"Ready to talk?"

Joe's question broke into her thoughts. "Yes, what happened?" He told her what he had experienced. "So the rooms are all traps, except for our suite and the four we dealt with last night. Can we deactivate them?"

"Whatever set them knew I was there. I felt it coming towards me. That's when I called you. I could go back in, maybe take out one or two, but that would alert whatever is behind this."

"What if you collapsed the protective circle, drew in into a point then let it out again?"

Joe thought about this. "It might work, but it might destroy the spirits of the four victims and harm anyone in the hotel who's sensitive to that kind of magic."

"So that's no good. What about the victims? Are they still alive?"

"I think they are. But whether as individuals or as a collective I don't know. It could be that they're now a part of the hotel."

"Allen would like that. He'd have real ghosts. It's some kind of ritual, isn't it, Joe. Whoever is behind this is collecting souls and when they get enough, something truly bad will happen. They may even use the souls to bring down the hotel. But how many is enough?"

"Could be any number. Five, six, seven, nine, twelve, even thirteen—all have magical properties."

"So it stops at four. And it stops tonight," Bianca said in a determined tone.

Joe knew what that tone meant. "But Bianca…" he wanted to say then try to talk her out of whatever she was planning. But he knew he couldn't. She was a warrior and tonight she was going into battle against Evil. As she always did. On the ride east, she'd given him hope that it would soon end, that she'd give up the life she, they were living. Now, seeing the look on her face, he was afraid that she'd continue to fight the never-ending battle until one day she faced her last monster. Joe only hoped that he'd be there as well, to fight and fall alongside her.

"It would help if we knew who was behind it," Joe said. "And what they did with the bodies."

"I think I know that. I'll have to call Shirley to make sure of a few things."

"Getting a warrant?" Joe asked, knowing the answer.

"I don't need no stinking warrant. This is not going to end up in court."

*

Not too far from where Bianca and Joe were, Nicholas du Matin sat sunning himself. He could see them but he had made sure that they could not see him. To his right, a family had set up—husband, wife, their two children, her father. That latter seemed to enjoy complaining, first that the beach chairs on hand were reserved for the "weirdos staying at that creepy hotel." Next, it was the seagulls, forever hovering in hopes of snatching a treat. Finally, it was the heat—the sand was too hot, the breeze was too hot, the sun was too hot.

My friend, Nicholas said to himself, *you do not know what "too hot" really is.* He took a peek into the old man's soul and was surprised to find himself relieved to learn that the old man probably never would.

Nicholas shifted his attention back to Joe and Bianca. The air had changed around them. Bianca was about to do something brave and dangerous. He wasn't worried. Bianca could handle anything. She had handled him, hadn't she? She'd handled Apollonius. *But just the same,* he decided, *I better make sure.*

*

The information from Detective Shirley confirmed what Bianca suspected. It didn't matter. She would not be confronting her suspect, not on this plane anyway.

*

Who was that? What is happening? He had been certain that the ones who had been brought in would find nothing, that no one could find anything, but the man had almost taken over the hotel, *his* hotel. Yes, his blocks had held. No, the four had not been found. Yes, he had chased him away. But it was a strain. It had cost him the power he needed to capture the fifth one. Maybe he should end it now, not stop it, end it. Would four be enough? No, he had planned for twelve. But plans change. Maybe he could do it with five. Invert the pentagram, call on the power of the Goat. Would that not damn him? No, he was doing this for the good. Using the Goat for good was only right. Fight fire with fire, fight evil with evil for the greater good. There was no sin in that, was there?

It had to be that night. It would exhaust his power but he could do it. Do it just after sunset then finish things at midnight. There would not be the devastation for which he'd hope, the entire hotel would not collapse and kill all the sinners within, but maybe he'd do enough damage and kill enough people to shut things down and show everyone the evil they had invited into the city.

*

Bianca had learned the technique of lucid dreaming out of necessity. Early on in the career that had chosen her, she had had to enter the Dream Plane to confront a monster, an incubus that was invading the dreams of young girls, corrupting them, and leading them into darkness. She succeeded but at a cost. For a while, she had had a monster inside her and one of the girls was ultimately lost.

What she wore in these dreams was what she had on when she went to sleep. That night she dressed for battle—tactical long-sleeved shirt and cargo pants, body armor, combat boots. On her duty belt she wore her service pistol on the right and the sword Tromluí on her left. The sword, really a long knife, had used up its magic when she fought Apollonius but that didn't matter. A knife always worked.

Before she lay down, Bianca handed Joe a pistol loaded with explosive cartridges blessed at the Vatican.

"I hate this part, this possibility," he said.

"Remember, if anything that comes through the door take it down. And if something that isn't me wakes up in my body, do what needs to be done. The real me will be past caring."

With the man she loved watching over her, Bianca lay down and closed her eyes. Steadying her breathing, she mentally recited the mantra that would take her beyond sleep and into dream.

She found herself standing in front of a large mansion. Slowly, the front door opened. When she stepped inside there was a stairway. She climbed it and found herself in a long hallway.

Bianca knew she was dreaming. She reminded herself that dream or not, what she might face was very real, and that dead was dead, no matter where or how you died.

A long hallway, ten rooms on either side and one at the end. The room at the end was empty. A monster had lived once there. She had used it to kill the incubus. Then she took it inside her only to later leave it at the gates of Hell.

Slowly, she walked the hall. Behind one door she heard the sounds of a woman comforting a child. They had been there a long time and if the child ever forgave the woman and the woman the child they might move on. Behind another door, a couple made noisy and passionate love. Behind a third was a young boy, afraid of what nightmare might come out of his closet, the door of which, if opened that night, would lead to a long hallway.

None of these was her door. That was the sixth one on her right. It looked like the door to her suite at the Hotel Dreadmore. In many ways it was. She opened the door and went in.

There was Joe, sitting at her bedside. His worry for her was a dull orange, and his love bright green and blue. He was watching her, guarding her as she slept.

First things first, Bianca thought. Joe had told her that most of the rooms were traps, that there was something in them designed to snare both body and soul and then to separate them. At her insistence and over his objections, Joe had removed the wards that protected their suite. Bianca looked around and easily found the spell. It was woven into the disturbingly abstract art that was in every room of the suite, including the bathroom. Bianca felt its latent power, ready and waiting to be triggered.

Suddenly two pictures flared red, allowing Bianca to see the tracings of the spells within. She observed they were different. *One for the body, one for the soul*, she thought as she realized that the spells had been invoked to claim another victim.

Bianca checked on Joe. He did not seem at risk. Neither did she feel any pull of magic. *Someone else then. Only one thing to do.*

She pulled Tromluí from its scabbard, transferred it to her left hand. With her right she drew her pistol. She fired at the painting furthest from her while stabbing the one closest with her knife. *Quantum magic,* she thought, and hoped she was right.

The gunshot echoed in the dream room but otherwise all was quiet. The paintings flared again and Bianca thought she'd failed. But then they went dark. As they did so there was a scream of pain followed by the cry of a soul in anguish. Behind it was a different voice, one she almost recognized. "Damn that hurt," it said, "but I've had much worse."

Ignoring the second voice, Bianca followed the first. She left the room and entered what was now the hallway outside the suite. *It's not smart to take dream elevators,* she told herself, *Take the stairs. A door here and at the bottom. Make sure to stay in the hotel.*

Seventh floor, sixth floor, so on to the lobby.

The dream lobby was dark. There was the shade of the bored desk clerk who was dressed as Eddie Munster. Shadows of bored guests who could not sleep read in lobby chairs. In the doorway of Sweeny Todd's the dream selves of a couple kissed. It was easy for Bianca to see that though they were married it was not to each other.

None of the shades took notice of her, nor of the anguished moans coming from the management suite.

Another door, behind which was a hallway. Bianca counted. There were 21 offices, more than in real life. The Dream Plane paying tricks. If she wasn't careful she could end up anywhere.

The names on the pebbled glass of the offices did not make sense and changed every few seconds. Bianca ignored them and went by her memory of her meeting with Richard Allen. His was the last office of five. To her left were those of the financial manager and quality assurance officer. Guest Services was at the front right. That left the Assistant Manager's office, the one with the open door, the one from which the whimpering was coming.

Bianca walked into that office and found the soul of Leo Chase writhing in agony on the floor. She wondered if his mortal self was also suffering, or if they were now parted. *Someone should have told Chase that bad things happen when a spell goes wrong. Well, he knows it now.*

There was no mercy in Bianca's voice as she said, "I thought it might be you, Chase."

Through his pain he asked, "H-how?"

"You used Fran Woods's full name, which not even she does. You knew that we wouldn't find anything in those room, and you knew why. Plus your social history shows vehement opposition to the building of this hotel followed by a sudden change of heart. But none of that matters. We would have found you anyway."

Bianca leaned down to him, her knife drawn and pointing to a delicate part of him. "Listen closely, Chase. I have some questions which you better answer."

Despite his pain, there was defiance in his eyes as he asked, "W-hy s-should I?"

Bianca pressed the tip of the knife against his delicate part. "We're on the Dream Plane now, Chase, and trust me when I tell you that the demons in Hell would weep in pity for the things I can do to your soul." Seeing the truth in Bianca's eyes Chase trembled in fear. "And right now you have but one chance to avoid joining those demons. One shot at redemption. What did you do with the bodies?"

Chase was not worried about his redemption. He was sure that he had done the right thing, that his actions were justified and that should this woman kill him, he would be welcomed into Heaven. But the pain he was experiencing was excruciating and he was convinced that this woman could and would make it worse and so he told her.

"Phys-physical Plant, Mechanical Room. Under t-tarps." One of the dark places Joe had "seen" the night before.

"Why did you keep them?"

"Need-needed them to com-combine with souls. Reunion would cause destruction."

So it was possible to reunite the bodies and souls. She'd just have to figure out how without blowing the place up. She thought maybe she had an idea. But there was one last question but it was more to herself than to Chase.

"Just what am I going to do with you?"

"Maybe I can help you with that, Ms. Jones."

Bianca turned and there in the doorway stood a man, a man she remembered seeing around the hotel a few times. He was tall, dark, and good-looking, his features a mix of Europe, Asia, and sub-Saharan Africa by way of the Middle East. But the Dream Plane shows one's true self, and so this image was overlaid by one Bianca knew that all too well.

"Morningstar. What are you doing here? Are you behind this?"

There was a name Joe had taught her. She had never uttered it, had never needed to. But she was ready to do it then and send the one in front of her to the torment of the Tenth Circle.

Nicholas realized this and before Bianca could speak the word he said, "Miss Jones, wait. I swear by all that we both hold holy that I mean no harm. Please, let me help."

All that we both hold holy? Please? Bianca looked deep into the eyes of the Adversary expecting to see the Abyss. All she found was the truth.

"Help how, Morningstar?"

"The spell that was cast has been broken. Let me deal with this," he looked down at Chase, "creature. You have until sunrise to save his victims."

"Save them how?"

He gave her a very familiar smile. "You're Bianca Jones. You'll figure it out. If you haven't already. And please, call me 'Nicholas.'"

*

After Bianca left, Nicholas looked down at the suffering soul at his feet. "I suppose if I can inflict pain I should be able to relieve it." This was as much a prayer as a comment but he found when he touched the soul of Leo Chase the man's writhing stopped. "Mmm, I wonder how much longer I'll be able to do that?"

Reaching down, he pulled on Chase's arm. "Get up, you damned fool."

When Chase did the shadow of his mortal self remained. He looked down at it. "What about…" Chase asked.

"Never mind that. You won't be needing it anymore."

"Who are you?"

Nicholas smiled as he replied, "You'll have to guess my name." Then he dragged Chase to the lobby door. On opening it, they passed through and were in Nicholas's room.

"Miss Jones is not the only one who can use dream doors," he remarked. Grabbing Chase by the shoulders, he looked him in the eye.

"Tell me, Mr. Chase, why you were playing with the forces of Damnation?"

"It was—the Lord's work. The evil of this place, the sinners who use it, must be destroyed. I used evil to destroy evil."

"I see, ends and means and all that. I think I taught humanity that idea in Uruk about 6500 years ago." Nicholas turned Chase to the mirror. "Here, see what your good intentions have led to."

Leo Chase looked in the mirror. At first, he saw himself and what he thought was the righteousness in his soul. Then that was replaced with presumption, the hubris that led him to try to usurp the Divine's Right to judge and punish. Then he saw the families, lovers, and friends of those gone missing and felt their pain and agony over the loss of their loved ones. The view shifted forward and Chase experienced the effects of what would have happened had his plan succeeded. The innocents who would have died or been injured. The pain of their families, lovers, and friends. The lawsuits that would have broken and destroyed the lives of all those involved with the hotel. More deaths—from injuries, illness, and suicide, some of the latter damned by their despair.

The sight broke the soul of Leo Chase when he realized the enormity of it all. He collapsed on the floor crying out, "Oh God, what have I done. I'm sorry!"

The sight of the man lying on the floor of his hotel room reminded Nicholas of being on his knees at the top of the tallest tower of Dys.

"I hope you are. If so, you won't suffer long, if at all."

As he said this, Nicholas pushed the soul of Leo Chase through the mirror, sending him to Judgment.

*

Bianca forced herself awake. Before Joe could react she called out the safe word to let him know it was really her.

"Bianca, how did it g…"

"No time, Joe," she said, stripping off her body armor. She thought about leaving her pistol and sword behind, decided against it. "Grab your magic bag and the victims' personal effects and let's go. And take some of those large beach towels. Hurry, we don't have much time. Make sure you take the master key card."

Joe got himself together and followed Bianca out of the room and down the stairs. "Elevators get stuck, Joe," she explained. "Stairs are like knives, they always work."

As they ran down Joe asked, "Was it Chase?"

"Yeah."

"What happened to him? Where is he?"

"Morningstar has him. Don't ask. It's confusing but I think he's on our side on this one."

"Probably mad at that restaurant logo."

Down the stairs, past the do the lobby, down to the basement.

Bianca looked around. In the center was the elevator mechanism. To her right was a large fenced-in area containing seasonal outdoor equipment. There were cinderblock rooms with signs reading Water and Sewage, Electrical, Mechanical.

"That one." Bianca ran over to it. The door had a real lock, not a card reader. "Dammit."

She had drawn Tromluí in order to pry the door open when Joe said, "Let me." He placed the master key card against the door and it opened.

"How?"

"The master is meant to open all the doors in the hotel. After Allen gave it to us, I made sure it would."

A quick kiss. "That's why I love you," she said. Then, "Look for tarps."

The room was not that big. Bianca and Joe found the tarps in a far corner. Under them were the bodies of the missing people, each in a clear plastic vacuum sealing bag.

"Always wondered when someone would think of that," the cop in Bianca observed. Then to Joe, "Are they alive?"

"Let me see. They were alive when their spirits were separated from their bodies. That means they didn't die then. There's some kind of preservation spell on these bags. So I would have to say there's a chance."

Bianca and Joe looked at each other. When their eyes met, a silent message passed between them, one that said, "A chance is all we need."

"Joe, you get ready. I'll get these four out of their bags. And hurry, we only have until sunrise."

"Who says?"

"Morningst… oh."

"The Lord of Hell might know about sin and damnation but he doesn't know my kind of magic. Now, let's take a breath and do this right. They need to be eased back into their bodies, not forced. Don't take them out of the bags, Bianca, just unzip them. The preservation spell will help protect them."

Bianca unzipped and opened the bags and was relieved that there was no odor of decay or signs of decomposition. Joe took the victims' effects—Barber's shirt, Bonner's hairbrush, Woods's ring, Fumio's toothbrush—and placed them on their abdomens.

Joe was then ready to begin the reunification ritual using sympathetic magic.

"Why the worried look?" Bianca asked.

"Because I'm not sure this will work. As I said, when I encountered them last night I wasn't sure if they were still individual spirits or if they've formed into a collective."

"Individuals," Bianca said with certainty. "Remember, Chase was planning to reunite them. Just make sure you don't put the souls into the wrong bodies."

"That would be a mess, or a bad remake of *Freaky Friday*."

Joe began. He linked the personal items to the bodies, then used the combination to find the spirits. He sent his summons floor by floor, seeking them out, calling them in.

At first, there was no reaction. Then, minor signs—the fluttering of eyelids, the twitching of fingers and toes, shallow breathing, at least with three of them. Lara Bonner's body still lacked any sign of life.

Moans were heard as air filled lungs and blood flowed again through limbs.

Bianca took the beach towels and covered the bodies. She looked over at Lara Bonner who was still inert. "I'm worried about her."

"Don't be," came a voice from behind. Bianca and Joe turned to see a spectral form hovering about an inch above the floor.

Bianca and Joe looked from the ghost to the body of Lara Bonner. They were the same, except that clothes had formed around the ghost.

"Can't float around naked, can I? As I said, don't worry about me. The last couple of weeks I've been floating around the hotel having fun. My 'life' wasn't all that much, guess that's why I came on this trip, looking for something. Well, being 'dead' I found it and I think I'd like to stay a ghost. After all, I'm in the right place for it."

"Are you sure?" Joe asked. A ghost had once worked for the Freak Show. It went badly.

"Yes, I'm sure."

"Well, we'll work some way for you to get in touch with us should you change your mind," Joe said.

"No, we won't," corrected Bianca. "This is a one-time offer, Lara. Take it or leave it."

Lara Bonner thought about it. "Then I'll leave it." With that, she was gone.

"What was that all about?" Joe wanted to know. He'd never known Bianca to abandon an innocent soul.

"It was about our discussion on the way here. I don't want to make any commitments we can't keep. But don't worry. Remember Kevin Meares? He's that ghost hunter the city called in to check out our HQ when it was still disappearing and reappearing. I'll get in touch with him and contract him to look in on Lara from time to time."

"Sounds like a good idea."

By then the other three were waking up. There was some confusion but, like Lara Bonner, their spirits had been alert and ghosting through the hotel. Joe helped them out of the bags. With no cell signal in the basement, Bianca used a hotel service phone to call the front desk.

"Front desk," the voice on the phone seemed unusually alert for the early morning hour.

"This is Lieutenant Jones. Wake Allen up and tell him we'll need some rooms and clothing for two men and a woman."

"Mr. Allen is awake, Lieutenant. He's with Detective Shirley right now. The cleaning crew found Leo Chase dead in his office. One of them said that it looked like he'd been scared to death."

"Have Shirley brought to the phone." He did. "Karl, Bianca. Joe and I found them … Three are alive, one is, well, that's a story … Yeah, Chase was behind it. I'll tell you all about it. Late breakfast at the Dough Roller is on you. Meanwhile, send medics, patrol, and your crime scene people to the basement."

*

The usual business police surrounding the sudden death of Leo Chase, the return of three missing people, and the mysterious circumstances surrounding the death of a fourth took most of the day. In addition to the routine paperwork, certain facts had to be obscured, reinterpreted, or omitted. Chase was blamed for the kidnappings. In furtherance of this, it was arranged to have his body and that of Lara Bonner transported to the Medical Examiner's Office in Baltimore so that Dominic Jones could perform the autopsies and provide believable causes of deaths. Karl Shirley was, of course, given the complete story, including the choice made by Lara Bonner.

"So the Dreadmore is well and truly haunted now?" When Bianca assured the detective that it was he reply was, "I'll have to tell Richard Allen."

"Do you have to?" Joe asked.

"Of course. How else is the young lady going to get paid? After all, she's now part of the entertainment staff."

It was evening by the time Bianca and Joe returned to the Hotel Dreadmore. As she had expected, the being she knew as Lucifer Morningstar was sitting at a table in the lobby. When she saw him she said, "Joe, go up to our suite."

"Is that…?"

"Yes."

"I think I should stay."

"No, this business, whatever it is, is between him and me."

"And maybe her."

Joe indicated a figure standing near the front desk. It was Nika. Her grey wings with their flame-blackened tips were on full display. Of course, in a place like the Dreadmore no one took notice except for some children who came up to hold her hand and rub her feathers. The angel suffered this while keeping watch on Morningstar.

Instead of going up to the suite, Joe walked over to Nika.

"What's going on?"

"Something wondrous, Joseph. The fulfillment of two destinies. The end of an age. Watch closely for we will never see the like of this again."

Bianca went over and to the table and without waiting to be invited sat across from Nicholas.

"What did you do with Leo Chase?"

"Let's just say that he's on the paved road to Redemption. Speaking of which, Ms. Jones, we have to talk."

"About what, Morningstar?"

"As I said last night, call me Nicholas, for that is now my name. Nicholas du Matin." He took a breath. This was the hardest thing he ever had to do, and that included convincing much of the world that he did not exist.

"Miss Jones, Bianca, I am sorry."

There was excitement in Heaven, and panic in Hell.

"Sorry for what—Nicholas?"

"For everything. Let me do this properly, according to the Rite." For the first time ever, the Devil made the sign of the Cross and said, "Bless me, Bianca Jones, for I have sinned. I have sinned both by action and inaction. I have committed horrible deeds and seduced others into doing so as well. In my Pride and out of Envy I rebelled against my lawful Lord and Creator. For these sins, the sins of my entire existence, and the sins committed by all those who followed me, I am truly sorry."

Bianca Jones had thought herself beyond surprise, beyond shock. That day she discovered that she had been wrong. She sat there quietly for a few minutes until her unconscious mind told her conscious one that yes, she had just heard the Devil's confession and yes, it was a true and sincere one. She found herself asking,

"Anything else?"

Nicholas smiled. "Yes, I am sorry I made fun of your height." To his surprise, Bianca returned the smile. Looking up, she saw Joe and Nika watching and waved them over. With them standing behind her, she dared to say,

"Nicholas du Matin, formerly Lucifer Morningstar, in the presence of witnesses from Heaven and Earth I ask,

"Do you renounce Hell?"

"I do."

"And all its works?"

"I do."

"And all its false promises?"

"I do."

"Then I absolve you of your sins in the Name of the Father, the Son, and the Spirit. Go and sin no more."

Then, because it was her right and duty to do, she gave him his penance, which he had to agree was right, just, and appropriate.

And there was great rejoicing in Heaven at the return of the Prodigal, and a war of succession began in Hell.

INTO THE DARKNESS

At first, it was just a simple patch of black on the sidewalk behind the school at Riverside and Warren Avenues. About a foot around, no one took notice of it. If they had, they would have thought it just a shadow. No matter that there was nothing there that could have cast one.

Evening came. The sun was slow to set as if it were reluctant to give up on this nice summer day. The shadows now present were long against the west side of the school. A few teens were there, hidden by an alcove created by an extended outdoor entryway. There they smoked tobacco and weed, drank from bottles and cans taken from home or bought by older brothers, and passed phones back and forth to share videos. Closer to the doorway two couples made out. Nothing serious, just kissing and feeling.

Then this guy named Brooks, whose father was an Orioles fan and who had a brother named Cal and a sister named Palmer, saw something that his mind told him shouldn't be there. It was a shadow on a wall opposite the other shadows. This didn't bother him, after all, light plays tricks. But this shadow was moving, gently swaying back and forth. Brooks put this down to the weed. *Good stuff,* he thought. He started moving in rhythm with what he was seeing, calling up a tune in his head to go with the movement.

"You guys seeing this?" he asked. Except for one of the couples near the door, the rest joined him, and yes, they saw it too. Someone found soft beats on their phone and soon they were all moving with the shadow and hoping that the sun would stay fixed for just a little longer.

Then the shadow stopped swaying. A girl named Alyce screamed as it doubled in size. There were shining eyes, sharp teeth, and long claws. Was it going for them? No one wanted to wait to see. Brooks and his friend Trey pulled the couple from the doorway and they all booked out of there.

It was a story worth telling. Most of the people they told it to thought it was the weed. Some asked where they had scored it. Or it was the weed and the beer and maybe the sun. The story spread through the Hill and down to Riverside and over to Sharp Leadenhall. By then it was a monster who had gone after this guy named Freddie whom no one knew and who wasn't even there.

But there were a few who remembered a time years ago when it was said a monster had haunted the streets and alleys of Federal Hill. Several women had died in what the police called cult slayings. At least, that was the story the cops put out.

Maybe it was just the dope. When you're high and drunk, cracks in the wall can look like anything. Someone thinks they see something and then everyone sees it. And a monster makes for a better story than being stupid, stoned, and scared over nothing.

Whatever it was, it was just a story, a new urban legend in the making. Baltimore was filled with them, like Black Aggie, that disappearing house, and the creatures that are supposed to haunt Leakin Park.

*

It was next seen inside the Cross Street Market. This time it was a silhouette of a man, arms down and flat against the west wall. Most people thought it was some kind of artwork. The Baltimore Cultural Council was always commissioning strange and different works of art. Like the time it hired a nationally known avant-gardist to set up an exhibit in Patterson Park. No one quite knew what all the flags were for or why the faux bushes were placed just so. Not until the Channel 11 news chopper flew over the finished piece and revealed its true nature. Some called it profound and others obscene. Whatever it was, most agreed that it was anatomically correct. During the week it was up, air traffic over the park increased to the point that the FAA had to shut things down.

However the silhouette got on the wall, it was there when the Cross Street Market opened. Few people paid it much attention, not until the crepe guy noticed that the shadow man was now a woman, or a man in a skirt.

"When did it change?" someone wondered aloud.

"Was the left arm always up?" asked another.

Over the next few hours, the figure changed shape and size, always when no one was looking. Sometimes there was a skirt, sometimes not. Once there was a hat. And were the projections that briefly appeared on the side of its head horns or just big ears?

A search was made for projectors. None were found. The Baltimore Cultural Council was called. A spokesperson denied that it was one of their projects but since the Patterson Park incident they always did. People took pictures and were surprised when all that showed up on their phones was a bare wall. A few tried standing in front of the figure trying to block whatever it was that was casting it. They never found the right angle.

The Cross Street Marker around noon was a place of vendors and buyers, none of whom had time to pay much attention to a shadow on the wall. But after the lunch hour there was always someone with an eye on it. A curious neighbor who had heard of it. A friend who had been sent a text or read a tweet. So there were a few witnesses when the shadow smiled.

It was a big, toothy grin, the white of which broke up the darkness of the figure. The teeth were sharp and pointed. At the cry of "Look at that," more than a few began to watch it.

"Don't get too close," someone joked. "It might bite."

The small group of watchers laughed. A young woman moved close and stuck out a finger. Then the silhouette opened its red, glowing eyes.

The woman quickly pulled her finger away. There was a scream. The watchers stepped back. Then whatever it was disappeared.

Later, when interviewed on the evening news, the woman who baked and sold cupcakes decorated with the buyer's choice of team logos (Steelers, Yankees, and Patriots excluded) stated that "The Thing" (as she called it) had stepped away from the wall, turned sidewise and was gone. No one believed her, no one except a retired nurse who had once seen what looked like a space alien in her alley.

*

Bianca Jones learned of the Federal Hill Shadow when she and Joe returned from Ocean City. Reporting to Commissioner Williams, she told him that the disappearances there had been solved. "Three alive, one not, the person responsible is dead as well."

The Commissioner did not press her for details. He hardly ever did, preferring not to know about the darkness she fought on behalf of the city. All he asked was, "This Leo Chase, how did he…"

"The official cause of death was a heart attack. Unofficially, the evil he was doing backfired and fatally bit him on the ass. The Hotel is now protected against most supernatural threats but is on the Department of Mystic Affairs' watchlist. For now, there's an agent in place."

"Good job." The Commissioner seemed pleased. Bianca decided not to tell him that the "agent" was the reformed Lucifer Morningstar, late ruler of Hell, or about her role in his redemption. If he chose to assume the "agent" was from the DMA that was on him.

"Is that all, Sir?"

"No, Bianca, it's not. Mayor Brandon has been talking to the governor and the state's county executives."

"About?" Bianca did not think she was going to like the answer.

"About expanding The Extranormal Investigative Unit to a state-wide agency." When he saw the scowl on Bianca's face, Williams added, "It's just an acknowledgment of what the Freak Show is doing anyway."

Bianca did not like her unit's nickname but had grown used to it. She let that go and said, "With respect, Sir, right now you and I have control over the unit's activities. That would end if the State took over. Our governor is a very political animal, the kind that would send the team after Chessie or to take out the snallygasters in Frederick County if he thought it would get him votes."

"I've been assured that you'd still be overall command."

Should I tell him I'm thinking of leaving? Bianca wondered. *No, he doesn't need to know. Not yet, anyway.*

"Sir, my responsibility is and always will be Baltimore. I will not leave her unprotected. If this goes through, it will be without me."

Williams knew from experience not to push Bianca on this. After all, without her, there was no Freak Show. Better to keep things as they were and lend the team out as needed. That way, both he and the mayor racked up the favors.

At Bianca's "Anything else, Sir?" Williams said,

"Yes, since you've been gone there have been incidents in Federal Hill." He told her about what happened outside the school and in the Cross Street Market. "And there have been numerous sightings over the last week. Some are pranksters and vandals spray painting and stenciling shadows on walls, and graffiti reading 'Who knows what evil?' and the like. Supposedly the Battery West Boys have changed their name to the FHS."

"Federal Hill Shadows?"

Williams nodded. "Exactly. But along with the nonsense, including some kind of cease and desist order from Conde Nast, are some legitimate sightings. Moving shadows that shouldn't be there, shadows with teeth, eyes, and claws. The newest report came in yesterday. A patch of blackness in an alley off Harvey Street. Two witnesses said it was man-sized and in the middle of the alley."

"Did either of the witnesses enter the patch?"

"Would you?" Williams asked, then remembered to whom he was speaking. "Well, you would. No, they didn't. One got close but backed off when the air grew cold. Both tried to take pictures but, like at the Cross Street Market, nothing showed on their phones."

"Can we get copies of those pics?" Bianca asked.

"Already done, along with some of those taken at the market." He handed her a thumb drive.

"Commissioner, has anyone been hurt?"

"There have been rumors but no reports and nothing's been confirmed. Besides, how can a shadow hurt you?"

You'd be surprised, Bianca said to herself.

*

Bianca and Joe met the rest of her investigative unit at the house that was their headquarters. Gifts from Ocean City were given out—Fishers Popcorn, Fudge and Salt Water Taffy from Dolle's, tee shirts from their hotel. On the front of the latter was an artist's rendition of the hotel. On the back was printed, "Welcome to the Hotel Dreadmore. Hope you survive your stay."

"Looks like a fun place," Tavon Greggs said. "Do they welcome pets?"

"Millie they will," Joe assured him. "Not only is she a registered K9, but she fits right in."

"Plus there's a generous Freak Show discount," Bianca said. "A 'thank you' for clearing up their problem." She told her crew what had happened, again leaving out any mention of her encounter with the

Morningstar. "Tammy, good job with the protective disks. I don't think Joe and I could have gotten the job done without your quantum magic." At the criminalist's "Thank you," Bianca added, "Just keep working on that forensic sorcery of yours. I have a feeling the unit's going to be relying on it more and more. Speaking of which, I have some photos I need you to examine and maybe enhance."

"The Federal Hill Shadow?" Tammy asked.

"Yes, how did you know?"

"What else could it be? Beth called Williams when we first heard about it to see if we were needed. He said that nothing had been reported and he was waiting for you."

A phone rang to the *Hill Street Blues* theme. It was Detective Bethany Steele's ring tone. She answered it, said, "Uh-huh, uh-huh," a few times then asked the caller, "So why do they need Homicide?" A pause then, "Okay, I see." She hung up.

"Shots fired in a house in Federal Hill."

"Anyone hit?" Tavon asked. Beth shook her head. "Then why… never mind. It's that shadow, isn't it?"

This time Beth nodded and looked at Bianca. "Call it, Boss."

"Beth, you and me. Tammy, we'll need you to work the scene. If you have a magic camera bring it. Tavon, you got anything?"

The Quick Response lieutenant smiled. "Been working on a few things since that shade hit the Hill."

"Get them ready. Joe, drive to Fell's Point and see what your books tell you."

*

The BWB drug gang, now the FHS, had a house on Battery Avenue just off of E. West Street. Everyone knew about it. The BPD knew, but the BWB had never given the department any probable cause to raid it. The neighbors knew, but since the policy of the gang was not to deal where they lived, and they had made it clear that the area around Battery and West was off-limits, the locals hoods and rival gangs refrained from causing any trouble there.

There were four of them in the Battery Avenue house that day— Kevin (Herman) Munster, Kizzy Jefferson, Doug (Doogie) Lambert, and Andre Waller, aka Brick. Munster was the gang's chief enforcer.

The large red-haired man belied the stereotypes of his Irish ancestry. He did not drink ("Don't like the stuff") and didn't fight ("No need if you're smart"). Instead, he was much like a shadow himself. His targets never saw him coming and when he left there was no trace of him. Doogie and Brick were the gang's money men. They kept track of what went out and what came in. They did not work together. Instead, they did their jobs separately, adding and subtracting the same sets of figures. If their results showed more than minor discrepancies, one or both of them would be getting a visit from Munster.

To the FHS, Kizzy Jefferson was both mother hen and mother superior. With a bachelor's in business from Towson University and a law degree from the University of Baltimore, Kizzy ran the gang like a business that, in every way that mattered, was seemingly legal.

The guns were a mistake, even Kizzy later admitted that. Even though their presence in her home was perfectly legal, they should not have been there. It is the purpose of guns to be fired and the nature of people who have guns to fire them. So when the shadow started dancing in her bedroom, Kizzy's current fancy man (as she called him) took out the gun that was kept in the nightstand drawer. When red eyes and teeth appeared, he put a few slugs in the wall.

The shadow didn't mind. It just kept smiling as Kizzy made sure that all personal use product was flushed and all computers and cloud devices were shut down. The shadow faded just as the police knock was heard on the door.

Exigent circumstances gave the police the right to search for possible gunshot victims. The holes in the wall and the nine on the dresser made up probable cause for a warrant.

To save time, Kizzy waived the warrant and allowed a consent search. She expected detectives and the drug police. What she did not expect was a small, slender woman whose pale skin had somehow resisted two weeks of Ocean City sunlight.

Kizzy knew about Bianca Jones. She knew what Jones did and admired her for it. But Kizzy did not fear her. She dealt in drugs. She did not deal in monsters.

They met in the living room.

"Ms. Jefferson."

"Detective Jones."

"It's lieutenant, but detective will do. It's what I am. Tell me about the shadow."

Kizzy told Bianca what had happened. She even told her what she and her man had been doing just before they saw the shadow.

"It may have been there a while," Kizzy remarked. "I wasn't in the right position to notice."

"I understand," Bianca said. "Ms. Jefferson, We're going to recover the pistol found in your bedroom, as well as any firearms, cartridges, and ammunition components we find in the house. The bullets in the bedroom wall will be removed with as much care as possible. The weapons will be test-fired. If they come up clean they will be returned to you. If they match any open cases, well, that's a conversation for another time."

Kizzy Jefferson wasn't worried. She knew the guns were clean. To her and her crew, guns were like burner phones, use them then lose them. But when she considered that the guns' profiles would be entered in the BPD and federal databases, she said,

"Keep them, Lieutenant, they're no more use to me."

Bianca nodded. The two women understood each other. "Ms. Jefferson, do you have any idea why this … thing … appeared in your house?" At Kizzy's shrug Bianca went on. "I think it's because you took its name."

"Shadows don't have names."

"This one was given a name, a name your—group took for itself. That might have made it mad. In addition, your man shot at it."

Another shrug. "Can't hurt a shadow."

"Maybe yes, maybe no. I think that sooner or later I'm going to have to try. Consider, Ms. Jefferson, what would you do if someone let loose on you? You don't have to answer. We both know."

Bianca gave Kizzy time to think. "This house is no longer safe. I think you should take what you need from it and move out, maybe to one of your safe houses, maybe the apartment on Byrd Street or the house off Fort. And change your name again." Bianca gave Kizzy a smile that had no humor in it. "Just remember, The Freak Show's been taken."

Kizzy was not surprised that the police knew about her other houses. They were the police, it was their job to know. Just as it was her job to have houses they did not know about. "I will consider your advice, Lieutenant."

"Don't take too long. This shadow thing hasn't hurt anyone—yet. But you're the only one that it might be mad at."

Kizzy Jefferson moved her people out the next day. Two nights later, when there was no moon in the sky, the streetlights mysteriously went out. When the sun rose in the morning, there was a vacant lot where the Battery Avenue house had been.

*

"Think it will be back?" Beth asked when the team met on the day of the house's disappearance. She made a point of looking around the conference room. The building where the Freak Show was located had once had a habit of coming and going.

"Let's hope not," Bianca said.

Tavon held up a copy of the late edition of the Sun. "Paper seems to think so. There's an article that goes into the long history of our place. This may explain why the media is camped out front. Maybe I should take Millie outside and show them what she can do."

Everyone but Bianca laughed. "I doubt if that would help."

"Bianca?"

"Yes, Tammy?"

"There's also an article about a series of rapes and murders in Federal Hill several years ago. It says that the Department closed it out by saying it was cult-related. But that's all—no convictions, no arrests, no explanation." Tammy left her question unasked.

Bianca answered it anyway. "Shub-Niggurath, a creature out of nightmare that haunted Federal Hill. It was using women to breed offspring that could exist completely on this plane. It was the first real monster I ever faced. I went after it with no idea of what I was doing or what I was facing. I was lucky. I got it before it got me. That's how Joe and I met. He broke almost as many rules as I did in helping me destroy the creature. After that, well, do a job once and it's yours. And so here we are."

"Do you think this Shub-whatever is back?"

"No, Beth, because no one's dead—yet. But last night it took a vacant house. I don't want to wait for it to start taking people. Joe, what have you found out?"

"There are things called 'shadow people.' Examples are the Hat

Man or the Hooded Monk. But ours doesn't quite fit."

"How can they be stopped?"

"No one knows. Tavon and I are working on it."

"Work harder. Tammy?"

"Nothing from the Battery Avenue scene. Photos were normal. No IBIS firearms matches on any of the bullets, cartridge cases, or guns recovered. No AFIS hits on the recovered latent prints."

"What about the photos taken of the shadow thing that don't show it?"

Tammy lit up with a smile of success. "I placed one of our laptops in a magicked circle, then copied the photos to it. I had to try a few different methods but here's what I came up with."

Tammy passed around prints she had made. In each one, the shadow thing was clearly visible but it was red, not black. "Heat signature?" Tavon asked.

"I think so. Don't ask me how I conjured infrared but I did."

Bianca's "Another good job" was almost lost under Beth's "Infernal?"

Tammy nodded her thanks to Bianca then replied to Beth. "Not in this city. Something supernatural but what it is I don't know."

"Maybe that Christmas angel who saved my butt can help? Whatever happened to her?"

Bianca knew but wasn't telling. She gave Tavon a non-committal shrug. "Flew away I guess."

There were more random shadow sightings—some genuine, others faked or imagined—over the next few days. Media interest grew with every report. Commissioner Williams called every day, at first asking for progress reports then demanding progress, especially when the name "Freak Show" appeared in the Sun and was picked up by the TV stations. Experts like Marv Richards and Kevin Meares were approached but both of them wisely declined to comment.

*

Exactly one week after the house on Battery Avenue disappeared, a sphere of seemingly solid shadow was seen hovering a foot over the lot where the house had been. By the time officers arrived the sphere had settled and had begun to grow.

Bianca had warned Commissioner Williams that something of this nature might occur, either on Battery Avenue or elsewhere in Federal Hill, and so there was a response plan. Two square blocks centering on the sphere were evacuated. The airspace over the sphere was restricted. It was announced that unauthorized drones would be shot down.

News choppers arrived and hovered on the edge of the restricted space, hoping to broadcast the scene live and late breaking. They soon left in disappointment when it became clear that, due to the nature of still growing shadow being, all they were sending to their studios were images of a vacant lot.

Tavon's Quick Response team arrived and surrounded the now ten-foot-tall shadow. On his order, his officers discharged weapons that fired high-intensity light that covered the spectrum from ultra-violet to infrared. The creature only absorbed the light, growing larger as it did.

"QRT to base," Tavon transmitted. "Negative on the light guns."

Bianca and the rest of her team had taken over the Maryland Science Center as their command center. She, Joe, Beth, and Tammy sat in the cafeteria, the windows of which overlooked the Inner Harbor. They were very much aware that they were being watched by Mayor Brandon, Commissioner Williams, and representatives of the governor, several churches, and The Federal Hill Community Organization. All these people were coto banish this menace once and for all.

"So much for the easy way," Bianca said when she heard Tavon's broadcast. From the looks on the faces of the surrounding crowd, Williams had heard it as well and had conveyed the message to the others. "Joe, tell me that you and Tammy have a Plan B."

Joe was not smiling when he said, "We do thanks to Doctor Hegazy, the mummy Amenmose, and Egypt's Bureau of Occult Affairs. There is a spell, a very potent one, that calls on the power of Aten-Ra, the Egyptian sun god. He was a strong god to begin with and grew in power when Akhenaten allowed him to briefly supplant all the other gods."

"Good, let's use it."

Joe shook his head. "It's a banishment spell, but it cannot be used against darkness. It must be used *within* the darkness. And when it is unleashed, well, think of it as being at the center of a massive explosion."

"I'll do it," Tammy said. "I let you all down with Apollonius. This will make up for it."

"No," Joe said firmly. "I spent most of two days mastering this spell.

There's no time to teach it to you. In addition," Joe paused, looked directly at Bianca, "It requires the life force of two people to enact it."

Before either Beth or Tammy could volunteer, Bianca said, "You and me, then. As it was so let it be. Beth, in the middle drawer of my desk there's an envelope. It will tell you what you need to know. There's another one for Williams."

"And Tammy," Joe added, "when you get back to the house you'll find there's a new room in the basement. It's locked but will open for you. It's full of books. May they guide you as well as they guided me."

For a long moment, no one said anything. Then Joe asked Bianca, "Would you like to take a walk?"

Bianca nodded. "It's a good day for it. Who knows, maybe I'll finally get a tan."

As the two stood up so did Beth and Tammy. "Joe, Bianca," Beth said, "it has been an honor."

"The honor," Bianca replied, "was ours." Then she and Joe left through the cafeteria doors and began walking toward Battery Avenue. Beth and Tammy watched until the two were out of sight. When they were, Beth looked down and saw that Bianca had left the sword Tromluí on the table.

*

Tavon was waiting for Bianca and Joe when they arrived at Battery and West. Beth must have called him because at their approach he stood to attention and snapped them a salute. As much as he wanted to, he did not offer to take her place. He was, at heart, a soldier and he understood duty and sacrifice.

By now the creature was two stories tall and had taken on form and substance. Its red eyes were glowing, its teeth were parted in a menacing smile, and its claws were extended. Bianca and Joe paused at the corner to look up at it.

"The last monster," she said.

"The last monster," he echoed. "I love you, Bianca."

"And I love you, Joe."

Hand in hand they walked into the darkness.

For a moment nothing happened. Then there was an explosion of light that was felt rather than heard. Those watching were temporarily blinded as their shadows were burned into the walls behind them.

When they could see again the shadow being was gone, never to return.

No trace of Bianca Jones or Joe Russo was ever found.

CODA

Memorial services for Bianca Jones and Joe Russo were held a week after their deaths. A well-attended mass of remembrance was said at the church in which they'd been married. Following Bishop Anton Lawrence's "Go in peace to love and serve the Lord" and the playing of "The Parting Glass" on the Uilleann pipes as the recessional song, there was a luncheon at the 10-44, a cop bar in Baltimore's Southern District.

Later that day, wreaths were laid on the vacant lot where the two had faced their last monster. Already, the memory and awareness of the creature they had faced and the sacrifice they had made were fading from public awareness, for that was the nature of magic. Soon, only those who had been directly involved with the creature or who had worked with, known, or loved Joe and Bianca would remember what they had done for the city.

The following day, members of the Extranormal Investigative Unit gathered in the front hallway as a memorial plaque to Joe and Bianca's service and memory was dedicated by Commissioner Williams and blessed by Bishop Lawrence. Following a toast and a moment of silence the commissioner said, "I would like you all to meet here again tomorrow to discuss the future of this unit." At the worried look on their faces, he quickly added, "Don't worry, the Freak Show will go on. The letter Bianca left me insisted on it."

After Williams and Bishop Lawrence left, the squad held their own service—drinking, eating, and occasionally weeping as they told stories of Bianca and Joe long into the night.

Outside the house where the wake was taking place, the former Lord of Hell and his self-appointed guardian angel stood watching.

"Are you ready for tomorrow?" Nika asked.

"I have to be," came the reply. "It was the penance she laid on me. 'Nicholas du Matin,' she told me, 'in reparations for your many sins I charge you to guard and protect Baltimore City as I did. Keep it safe from the dark things that would destroy it.' And so I shall. But Nika, before you leave me, tell me one thing. What you did, the way you did it, was that necessary?"

Her answer satisfied him after which she spread her wings and flew off into the night.

The next day, Inspector Nicholas du Matin was introduced to the members of the Freak Show as the new commander of The Extranormal Investigative Unit.

"The department doesn't have an inspector rank," Tavon observed.

"It does now. It was Bianca's idea," Commissioner Williams explained. "In her letter to me in which she recommended Nicholas she explained that it would keep people wondering where he fit into the chain of command and give him more latitude."

"Where do you fit in, Inspector?" Beth asked.

"Wherever I want, Detective," Nicholas said with a disarming smile. "And please, all of you, call me Nick. And let me just say that I know that Bianca is, quite literally, the reason I am standing before you today. I will never be able to replace her, but I swear to you that I will protect our city in a way that will make her proud. Now then, any questions or comments?"

"Just one." Beth stepped forward and handed her new commander a fighting knife. "Its name is Tromluí. It was Bianca's. It's yours now. There's a space for it on the wall in Bianca's…your office."

As Nicholas took the knife, its history flowed into him and he realized that it had twice been used to kill Apollonius, the would-be messiah and now a contender for the throne of Hell.

This will prove useful, he thought. To Beth and the rest he said, "Thank you. Now then, take the rest of the day off. Tomorrow, it's back to work."

That night, as she was about to get into bed, Beth Steele gave one more thought to all that had happened and said one more goodbye to her friends. Then her detective's mind began to work.

"What was it Nick said?" she asked her cat. "Bianca *is* the reason. A way that *will* make her proud." She thought of the letter Bianca had left her, the last line of which was "Trust him." Trust who? It had to be Nick. How did she know?

There was only one conclusion. "Well, I'll be damned," she said to the cat then wished her friends well.

*

When the angel Nika flew away from Nicholas, she hovered out of sight for a while, watching him, watching the house, and praying that all would work out as planned. So far it had. She thought back to that night, "That Night" as it would forever be remembered, when the Morningstar repented of his sins thanks to a mortal woman. Joe Russo was in his suite, asleep in his bed. The newly forgiven Nicholas was likewise in his room, marveling at his new status and wondering about his penance. Nika and Bianca were behind the hotel, sitting on beach chairs, watching the Bay and enjoying the night.

"You have done a great thing, Bianca. How may Heaven reward you?"

"His repentance was its own reward. Yet..."

"Yet?"

"I would like a normal life. Well, one more normal than the one I have now. I want Joe and me to have a family and grow old together. I want the fairy tale ending, the happily ever after."

"It's possible," the angel assured her, then told her how and what it would cost.

"That's a lot of pain for a lot of people," Bianca pointed out.

"It's the only way to keep you safe. And it is pain they would still feel, sooner or later."

"Okay. When?"

"You and Joe will know when the moment comes. Until then let's just relax, forget, and enjoy the night."

Bianca did forget and did not remember until she and Joe were facing the shadow being.

Bianca and Joe had paused to look up at it.

"The last monster," she said.

"The last monster," he echoed. "I love you, Bianca."

"And I love you too, Joe."

Hand in hand they walked into the darkness.

And as they entered the darkness Nika was waiting for them, and Bianca remembered, and Joe knew and agreed. There was a flash of light and they were gone.

*

Henderson is a small city in northeastern Ohio. It's on Lake Erie, just across the border from Pennsylvania. Morgan Shaw is a detective for the Henderson PD, working in the violent crimes unit. She is a bit taller than she once was and has a better shape but she is still the same woman she was when she fought monsters in Baltimore. Her husband Jason is a stay-at-home dad, taking care of their daughters while running an online used book business. Like his wife, he once had a different life. Late at night, when their girls are asleep, they sometimes talk about the life they led in years past. All things considered, they were happy then. And all things considered, they are happier now, for never again will they have to fight monsters.

But not so their daughters, but that's a story for another time.

BIOGRAPHY

JOHN L. FRENCH is a retired crime scene supervisor with forty years' experience. He has seen more than his share of murders, shootings, and serious assaults. As a break from the realities of his job, he started writing science fiction, pulp, horror, fantasy, and, of course, crime fiction.

John's first story "Past Sins" was published in Hardboiled Magazine and was cited as one of the best Hardboiled stories of 1993. More crime fiction followed, appearing in Alfred Hitchcock's Mystery Magazine, the Fading Shadows magazines and in collections by Barnes and Noble. Association with writers like James Chambers and the late, great C.J. Henderson led him to try horror fiction and to a still growing fascination with zombies and other undead things. His first horror story "The Right Solution" appeared in Marietta Publishing's Lin Carter's Anton Zarnak. Other horror stories followed in anthologies such as The Dead Walk and Dark Furies, both published by Die Monster Die books. It was in Dark Furies that his character Bianca Jones made her literary debut in "21 Doors," a story based on an old Baltimore legend and a creepy game his daughter used to play with her friends.

John's first book was The Devil of Harbor City, a novel done in the old pulp style. Past Sins and Here There Be Monsters followed. John was also consulting editor for Chelsea House's Criminal Investigation series. His other books include The Assassins' Ball (written with Patrick Thomas), Souls on Fire, The Nightmare Strikes, Monsters Among Us, The Last Redhead, the Magic of Simon Tombs, The Santa Heist (written with Patrick Thomas), When the Moon Shines, and Mortal Sins. John is the editor of To Hell in a Fast Car, Mermaids 13, C. J. Henderson's Challenge of the Unknown, Camelot 13 (with Patrick Thomas), With Great Power ... (with Greg Schauer) and Devilish and Devine (with Danielle Ackley-McPhail).

You can find John on Facebook or you can email him at jfrenchfam@aol.com.

Welcome to the Freakshow!
Monsters Among Us
a Bianca Jones collection

PAST SINS

Bad Cop...
No Donut

THE GREY MONK
SOULS ON FIRE
JOHN L. FRENCH

L.
CH

THE NIGHT MARE STRIKE
"THE NIGHTMARE
JOHN L. FRENC

Welcome to Baltimore!
Here There Be MONSTERS
a Bianca Jones collection
JOHN L. FRENCH

IT'S A CRIME
TO MISS THESE
GREAT STORIES!
from author
John L. French
WWW.PADWOLF.COM

You can't get better than 13!

APOCALYPSE 13
DEFCON

Camelot 13

LUCK 13
EDITED BY EDWARD J. McFAR
John L. French and Patrick Thomas

AGENTS OF THE ABYSS

Sometimes it takes a monster to keep the Abyss at bay.

DOWN THESE MEANS STREETS
of Magic & Monsters walk the

MYSTIC INVESTIGATORS

THE STARSCAPE PROJECT

As his quest begins, an artificial intelligence life form enters the galaxy and launches a series of covert attacks against the Empire. The Teconeans assume that the Federation is responsible, and galactic peace is about to unravel. As Stryker chases his nemesis into Teconean space, he finds himself thrown into the middle of the battle. Knowing that Earth will be the aliens' next target, Stryker must decide whether to let them destroy the Empire, or to join forces with his Teconean enemies against the invaders. The key to the mysterious aliens lies buried on the moon of Kennedy Prime, and it's up to Stryker to solve the puzzle before war begins. The fate of the galaxy is at stake.

ZONE OF THE TENTH DGREE

1912, an alien ship crash lands in the Atlantic Ocean, setting up a secret colony that remains undetected for centuries, allowing them to manipulate some of the most important events in human history -- from the sinking of the Titanic to the Bermuda triangle to global warming. Now, the technology of the 26th century has uncovered the aliens' distress beacon, and it's a race against time as the Navy tries to stop a terrorist armed with a nuclear weapon from destroying the colony and triggering an all-out war as the mother-ship approaches

Now available from
PADWOLF PUBLISHING

The Collected Advice Columns Of DEAR CTHULHU
AVE Dark DAY
PATRICK THOMAS

The Collected Advice Columns Of DEAR CTHULHU
GOOD ADVICE for BAD PEOPLE
PATRICK THOMAS

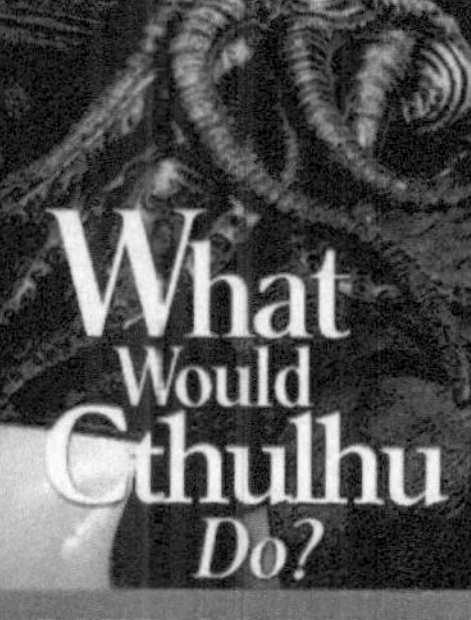

CTHULHU KNOWS BEST
The Collected Advice Columns Of DEAR CTHULHU
PATRICK THOMAS

The Collected Advice Columns Of DEAR CTHULHU
What Would Cthulhu Do?
PATRICK THOMAS

The Collected Advice Columns of DEAR CTHULHU
CTHULHU HAPPENS
PATRICK THOMAS

The Collected Advice Columns of DEAR CTHULHU
CTHULHU Explains It All
1. Humans are pathetic
2. Cthulhu Knows Best
3. Ask What Would Cthulhu Do?
4. Obey Cthulhu
5. Buy This book!
PATRICK THOMAS

DEAR CTHULHU
The advice column to END all advice columns

WWW.DEARCTHULHU.COM
WWW.PADWOLF.COM